# 404

## By Mabert Mazyck

One Printers Way
Altona, MB R0G 0B0
Canada

www.friesenpress.com

**Copyright © 2024 by Mabert Mazyck**
First Edition — 2024

All rights reserved.

No part of this publication may be reproduced in any form, or by any means, electronic or mechanical, including photocopying, recording, or any information browsing, storage, or retrieval system, without permission in writing from FriesenPress.

ISBN
978-1-03-830586-2 (Hardcover)
978-1-03-830585-5 (Paperback)
978-1-03-830587-9 (eBook)

1. FICTION, ROMANCE, CONTEMPORARY

Distributed to the trade by The Ingram Book Company

For T.N, for loving and supporting me while allowing me to spread my wings to pursue my dreams.

*My love,*

*For the winds that swept our faces, and the string that bound us together, I can never forget the warmth of your touch, the love in your voice, and the sparkle in your eyes. I long to be in your arms, to kiss your hand, your cheeks, your lips, and your body. One day when time permits, I will appear with all of myself, solely existing to be with you and to love only you. You are the centre of my love, my heart, and my soul. Two souls that have kindled a fiery connection have more power than any trouble or burden could ever have. I hope that you know that I think of you fondly and with longing every moment, every day.*

*Forget me not,*

*Yours truly.*

# Chapter 1

"Coffee?"

Yvonne peered over to her side. Luther stood next to her desk, hands placed on his hips in those perfectly tailored pants. His lanyard and tag swung from his neck, grazing his button collared shirt in a metronomic way.

"...alright," she responded, caving into the tantalising idea of tonka bean and caramel coffee. She swivelled back to focus on her work at hand, now that she had the much needed coffee. Yvonne checked the time and sighed. How was it only 10:00 a.m.?

"So I accept cash or e-transfer," Luther began. Yvonne shot him a glare.

"I paid last time. Don't think I'm that daft." Her eyes were menacing, especially with the curvature and color of them—dark, mosaic brown and fox-like shaping, with lashes that drooped ever so slightly, giving a sultry look.

"Hahaha, thought I got you there." He paced backwards to retrieve the coffee. Yvonne groaned, stretching her arms and rolling her neck before getting back to work. Eyes plastered to the screen, she efficiently reviewed the reports and details like no other. Never had she been the type to dilly-dally, nor had she ever failed in what she put her mind to. One remark people made frequently though was that she faltered in the aspect of sociability. Everyday, she wore a respectable plain outfit. It rotated between pleated dress pants and a silk blouse or a pencil skirt with back seamed stockings, a white dress shirt and some sort of cardigan or blazer. Shoes? Oh she never missed. Elegance and class was her game. Red bottom stilettos or clean loafers were her usuals. Once in a while, she might bust out those unique, rare ones, but not often as they were hard to obtain. Her hair was always excellently kept up, never down. Bun, sleek ponytail, or claw clips—nothing else. Not only was she too primmed and dressed, but her aura was stoic and almost intimidating. Many people found it hard to approach her and rather admired her from afar or didn't pay her any mind at all.

Luther was one of the few who approached her. He had difficulty making connections with Yvonne, but had successfully made constant conversation through their mutual interest in coffee.

Within minutes, Luther returned with her iced tonka bean caramel coffee, precipitation dripping down the cup and running over his middle finger.

"M'lady, your coffee has arrived."

"Thanks," she said in a monotone voice. She grabbed it from him and swirled it, not bothering to look away from the screen. "Straw?"

Luther tensed and patted down his pockets. "Gaw dam. I'll be right back, you wait here."

"No, it's fine. I think I might have a stray one somewhere in my drawers. Thanks for grabbing the coffee." Yvonne rummaged through her second drawer, pushing aside the miscellaneous debris and packets of quick snacks. She paused and sighed, looked up at him, and shook her head. "You know what, save the turtles."

"We don't use plastic straws anymore…they're paper," he remarked.

Yvonne sighed, dismissing Luther from her work space.

Luther rolled his eyes before walking off. She gingerly sipped the edge of the cup after removing the lid, not paying much attention to his departure.

Yvonne never thought much of Luther besides that he was an eager male wanting to make connections with almost every walking pair of smooth legs. His black hair was always trimmed appropriately, never too short but never too long, and was lightly brushed back, allowing his fringe to curve down and sweep his forehead. His eyebrows framed his dark molasses eyes symmetrically, the bottom bit always a bit cheeky looking, flirtatious. Slim to average build, he tried taking care of his appearance physically as well but never really talked about it. He always wore the classic office attire: black dress pants, belt, and a white buttoned dress shirt with just two of the buttons from the top undone. His square toed loafers made Yvonne tolerate him a bit more. Good taste, good style, good impression.

Their work was never boring; cyber security was much needed and many financial institutes and businesses used their type of company as support. Yvonne enjoyed the clerical work of perfect reports, financial analysis, and other ends and odds. Luther worked in the investigating department. Although it wasn't like being an officer or official interrogator, it had some similar aspects. Luther was a good talker; amazing in fact. As aloof as he played himself to be, he could crack down and critically think on a dime. Nothing was too interesting these days, just regular security protocols and reporting. Luther didn't mind, though. He enjoyed making big bucks without over extending his skills.

"The Piliath case?" Luther scoffed, then boasted, "Easy. Piece of cake."

A couple of women were crowded around his desk, taking in their eye-candy. One of them asked, "How did you know, though?"

"It was a typical hacker wannabe student. They simply went into the administrative office computer, located the passcode for the director's laptop, and inserted the hacking USB to derive the information they needed to take out automatic transfers from everyone's accounts to their own trap account." He crossed his legs on top of his desk, newly shined loafers clunking onto it.

"You're so amazing, Luther," one girl chimed in, touching his shoulder and giggling. The other girl grimaced and attempted to grab his attention as well.

"After all that hard work, don't you think you deserve a celebration of some sort?" She leaned in further, resting her manicured hands on his forearm.

"Eh, not much to celebrate. Usual type of situation anyway." He brushed them off and got up, adjusting his shirt and pants. Although Luther enjoyed the attention from the girls, he was a little bit irritated that he could never get Yvonne's attention like that.

"Yes, that's right. I sent the report just now. Let me know when you've received it." Yvonne hung on the line as she waited for her attendant's approval.

"All good, thanks for all your work!" They cheered before hanging up. She gave herself a pat on the back, happy she completed the report earlier than anticipated. She started gathering all her things and glanced at her watch; it was nearly 7:00 p.m.. Food was the only thing on her mind now. She made sure to lock up the office as she was the last one to leave her department. Being a creature of habit, she made her way to ' Warui Ramen,' her go-to ramen stop.

"Irashaimase!" Hyouko exclaimed with a smirk and a wave as soon as Yvonne stepped into the restaurant. She sat down near the bar area and placed her bag on the floor.

"Same as usual?" Hyouko asked, setting down a glass of water. He knew she was sensitive to caffeine, and at this hour, there was no way she would fall asleep if she had tea.

"You know me so well," she said with an eager nod. Surveying the restaurant, she noticed Haruka wasn't working.

"Is Haruka off today?"

"Yeah, some sort of family junction, you know, she's very family orientated."

"Well isn't it normal to go to a family dinner of sorts when it's called for?"

He shrugged and wandered off to assist other customers. Hyouko was an expert at customer service skills and had a brilliant sense of what people desired. She didn't know how, but he did.

"One tonkatsu ramen with extra green onion!" The lavish smell of pork broth enveloped Yvonne's nose, causing her to drool just a bit off the side of her lip.

"They made an extra spicy version... Jun-san went crazy last weekend and made one super spicy. If you can finish it, I'll buy you sake."

Yvonne's ears perked up. A challenge, not to mention sake. She looked at the time.

"Maybe next visit. It's a bit late tonight. Besides, I don't think I can finish two ramen."

Hyouko crossed his arms and leaned in. "I can finish your ramen and you get the extra spicy one," he proposed, already trying to take the bowl from Yvonne.

Yvonne slightly blushed. "Ah, no, my germs are all over it."

"Don't matter to me. Yvonne is clean, I think," he joked. "Seriously, the ramen packs some heat."

Tempted, Yvonne agreed and Hyouko ran off with her partly eaten ramen.

Yvonne decided to check her phone while she waited for the spicy ramen, though she was never keen on keeping in contact with people via online platforms. Instead, she much preferred text messaging or emails or the occasional phone call. A ping came through and Yvonne looked at her phone; it was Luther.

*Luther: 7:43P.M What are you up to?*

Yvonne debated on responding, but left him on read since she was unsure of what he wanted. Honestly, she couldn't care less about Luther.

"Are you ready to conquer the spicy ramen?!" Hyouko spun around and placed the ramen in front of her, the spice already burning her nostrils.

*Oh shit,* she thought.

Hyouko must've read her mind, as he snickered and sat across from her with the bowl of her partly eaten ramen. Yvonne was slightly taken aback.

"You're off?" she asked as she poked around the ramen, chilli pieces and blotches of red oil spinning around the crevices of each noodle.

"You betcha," he said, slurping up the luke-warm noodles. It was mushy but he didn't complain. "What are you waiting for? Come on, dig in!"

Yvonne reluctantly took a bite, the noodles saturating her tongue with red oils and engraving its essence into every pore. It took her a moment to realise how spicy it was. There was no flavour but spiciness. She couldn't comprehend anything else but the capsaicin.

"Holy—" Choking, she yearned for some water. Hyouko laughed and passed her a glass.

"You know water doesn't actually help? It makes it worse," he said before retrieving some milk. "This will help a bit better."

Yvonne eagerly grabbed the milk and drank it all.

"How is anyone supposed to eat this?" She stuck her tongue out, throbbing and red from just one taste. "Unbelievable."

"I guess no free sake for you, Yvonne-san," he said, reaching for her bowl of noodles and swapping it back with her prior one.

"Is that even sanitary…?" she remarked, looking at it with a slight disgust.

"Hey! I am a very clean individual. If you don't want it, I'll have it." He began slurping up the spicy noodles, driblets of spicy broth spraying every which way.

"Oh f—" he began before curdling into himself a bit. He leaned back into his seat, beads of sweat forming on his face.

"Exactly." Yvonne shook her head in disappointment. "Who's a weakling now?"

"I never called you a weakling. I just didn't think Jun-san would make it *that* spicy." He shook his head and began slurping up mouthfuls at a time, almost forcing himself to finish it.

"Please don't puke," she said, putting her hands in front of her like a barricade. Yvonne was a bit hungry still, so she put aside her qualms about germs and continued to eat the ramen.

"GAAAH DONE," he exclaimed, wapping the empty bowl down onto the table. "Now," he burped, "you owe *me* a sake," he triumphantly claimed.

"Hey, hey, *hey.* That wasn't part of the deal."

"It is now," he teased.

Comfort was the essence and goal of Yvonne's apartment. She had a pleasant apartment, not too extravagant but a little bit more expensive than average. As she should, of course; she worked hard for her money and was allowed to enjoy herself. The walls were covered in dark, oak-brown installments, accompanied by decor that matched the theme. Though it was mostly shades of grey and black, she indulged in the burgundy wine red pops of color that were littered around. She especially loved the antique clock that hung above the red brick fireplace that not only had a fascinatingly intricate design, but the color was so rich and enticing. Definitely couldn't find one of those anymore.

*Luther: 10:52P.M Hey are you ignoring me?*

She shuddered. What does he want? Though slightly annoyed, she responded. After all, she had to see him tomorrow at work anyway.

*Yvonne: 10:53P.M Was there something you needed?*

She stared at the screen, waiting for his response.

*Luther: 10:53P.M Well, I was gonna ask if you wanted to go grab drinks but I bet you're one of those people that won't stay up past 12.*

*Yvonne: 10:55P.M Well you guessed right. Goodnight.*

*Luther: 10:55P.M Wait wait wait come on humour me lets be rebels nd enjoy some drinks on a work night.*

She typed *I don't know* but then paused, thinking of how she'd just finished that report. She deleted what she'd typed and wrote a new text.

*Yvonne: 10:57P.M Ok, only if you're buying.*

*Luther: 10:57P.M Really?! Ok yes let's meet at Barrison's Lounge. I'll be there in 10.*

*Yvonne: 10:58P.M It'll take me about 15. I'm walking. See you then.*

She let out a slight exhale and went to change into a warmer cardigan and kept her skirt and undershirt on. After sliding into her favourite loafers, she headed back out.

"Is it just me or has tonight been pain-stakingly long." Yvonne sipped on the blue curacao concoction as Luther watched her every movement in a type of awe.

"What?" he said, coming out of the trance.

"I feel like I've been seeing way too many people and having way too many interactions today."

"Should I feel bad about that?" he asked, calling for the bartender with a simple gesture.

"Not sure."

"Hey, can I get another one for the lady here, and a rum on the rocks for myself? Thank you."

The bartender nodded and smiled, as if to give Luther some encouragement.

"Well I won't feel bad. I'll make your time worthwhile." His eyes glinted in the dark ambience. Was the alcohol getting to her? She blushed ever so slightly and took another sip. The liquor had an astringent smell; however, the blue curacao balanced it out with a refreshing yet alluring taste, entertaining every sense of smell, taste, and feel. It was Luther—he was known to be trouble, and quite frankly, Yvonne wasn't the type to mess around with playboys or man-boys. She didn't want the stress and heartache of one of those scenarios.

"Don't be like that," she mumbled into her cup.

"What?" He leaned in. "It's a lil' hard to hear in here cuz, you know, music and all."

She could smell the rum off his breath. It was hot and bold, sending shivers into her head and down her spine. She leaned back a bit, trying to be nonchalant about it, but he caught on and retreated.

"Sorry, I didn't mean to make you uncomfortable." He brushed his hand against his face a little, as if to self-soothe his embarrassment.

"Are you shy?" Yvonne asked, carefully eying Luther's reaction. She was a little taken aback from his reaction and found it a bit cute. It had to be the alcohol.

Luther felt a little warm seeing her attractive face. It was already hard enough not to stare at her at work, but now he was seeing her in a more vulnerable situation. Her cheeks illuminated a rosy color and her eyes were slightly glossy, sparkling in the lighting. Her lips were full and lathered in a shine, though he wasn't sure if it was from lipgloss or a reminiscence of the drink she was having. He coughed to try to regain his composure.

"Not shy. I just don't intend to make you uncomfortable. Ever." He was so serious. He stared directly into her eyes to show his intent. She was flustered and faced the bar, sipping on her drink some more.

"Whoa, slow down there," he said, almost reaching for her glass, but stopped.

"Ah, don't worry. I can take it." That was a lie. She knew she couldn't handle alcohol all that well, but she wanted to fib so he wouldn't see how ruffled she was. On second thought, she stopped drinking as soon as she hit the bottom. "No, you're right. We have work tomorrow."

"Yvonne's so responsible," he said, half humorously. "Do you need a ride home?"

Yvonne hadn't thought of that yet. She nodded awkwardly. A cab was too expensive and she definitely didn't feel safe walking back by herself.

"Let's head out then." Luther placed a few bills on the bar and waved at the bartender. He collected his leather jacket off the bar stool and swung it over his shoulder. He gestured towards Yvonne, offering a hand to help her off the ottoman.

"It's okay..." she said, dangling her legs off to the side and inching toward the floor. She wobbled a bit and went off balance, Luther coming in to help support her.

"Learn to accept help." He held her upper back, but didn't put his body too close to hers. Her hands grasped his firm forearm as she regained her composure.

"I think maybe I drank too much." Her eyes averted his, too bashful to peer into his view.

His car was parked around the block; it was crazy how busy it was on a Wednesday night. Didn't people have work the next day? Luther opened the passenger side door and assisted Yvonne inside.

"Thank you." Yvonne glanced at Luther. He had a slight smirk on his face, his fringe hanging down onto his forehead, eyes shimmering in the night light.

"Don't mention it."

His hands confidently held the steering wheel as he reversed out the parking spot, his jawline clearly visible to Yvonne. She couldn't help but stare. Her eyes travelled down to observe his outfit, so tidy and sleek. He really knew how to dress himself.

"Yes?" he questioned. He must've felt her gawking eyes on him.

"Nothing," she promptly responded. "Thinking about the report." She whisked her hair out of her face with a brisk motion.

"Nice car." She glanced around the interior; the car had red leather seats, clean, modern appliances, and definitely had the same aura as him.

He laughed and peered over. He knew Yvonne was just commenting and didn't really mean to have any engaging conversation. She still seemed buzzed as her eyes flickered here and there. Before she knew it, they had arrived at her apartment complex.

"Thank you, Luther." Yvonne gave a small smile before retrieving her purse.

Luther gazed into her eyes. "Don't leave yet."

Yvonne's breathing shortened. Was she panicked or extremely intrigued by those words? Luther got out of the car and opened her door.

"A lady as fine as you should never open her own door."

Modestly, she exited the car and did a little bow as a thank you. He watched her ascend the stairs. She paused, looked back from the door, waved, and headed in. Luther breathed a deep breath out and looked up at the sky.

"Here." The cup rattled, dripping a bit of water from the melting ice. A few eyes watched the interaction. They couldn't believe it was Yvonne who had approached Luther for once.

"What's this?" Luther rolled his chair out, accepting the drink.

"Take it as a token of gratitude. It's iced coffee, nothing special." Yvonne turned around and headed back to her desk.

"Is it oat milk?" he hollered, but Yvonne didn't turn back. When Yvonne arrived at her desk, there was a letter waiting for her. She looked at it suspiciously, as it said *confidential* and had her last name written on it. She surveyed the office, but nothing was out of place and her three other coworkers were still at their desks as well, unbothered.

"Hey, did someone leave this at my desk?" Yvonne asked Cherise, a clerical worker who did more basic work. She was in charge of preliminary reports and details.

"I'm not sure. Sorry, Yvonne." Cherise shrugged and looked curiously at the letter. "Looks like real heavy cardstock. Must be important."

Yvonne sat at her desk and carefully opened the letter. Nothing was peculiar at first, besides the confidential warning and the fact she hadn't been expecting any mail, but the first couple words sent her brain into overdrive.

> *Do not disclose to anyone else.*
>
> *This task is assigned to you, Yvonne Kalman, as a confidant in this case.*
>
> *There is a cyber-security issue at Tamocus Inc. They require the utmost secrecy and confidentiality in this matter. Please assure they will be provided only with the best work, confidentiality, and are disclosed only to the parties involved. You will only work on this case by paper trail. Nothing cyber. Do not type (typewriter excluded), or use anything electronic based application to complete this case. Please consult the people listed below as needed.*
>
> *You will be provided with any and all needs for this by the case manager. Any time you buy things out of your own pocket that adheres to this, please formally submit the receipt to the case manager.*
>
> *Please meet with the case manager at 2:00 p.m. today at the address listed.*
>
> *Please shred and dispose of this letter once read.*
>
> *Ms. Foxx*
>
> *Headquarters Management*
>
> *888-555-8956*

Yvonne took a few shallow breaths. This was certified and sent by her company for sure. She was extremely nervous and hadn't dealt with a case this sensitive. The mentioned address for the case manager was attached. A list of people and their contacts were listed on cardstock paper, folded neatly in another envelope. She made sure to fasten both the envelope and the address tightly to her person. She shredded the letter carefully and scattered it within the heaps of shredded paper. She flashed a look at her watch. It was only 9:30 a.m. Today was going to be a long one.

The address led to a somewhat secluded area. The walls were run-down and definitely needed a renovation. To make it less suspicious, the rendezvous point was semi-public; there were others within the vicinity, but nothing extraordinary. The floorboards were comically creaky and had obvious water damage. From the outside, one wouldn't even consider coming around for a nice cup of tea, nevermind a meet-up. Most who wandered in were elderly people seeking some melancholy tone, and often took smoking as an activity to do. Smoke was the most prominent smell encasing the entire area, alongside the common breeze and musk from the public. It didn't matter that they weren't allowed to smoke inside, as the fumes seeped in through every crack and draughty window. Once Yvonne entered the vicinity, she felt a few eyes on her, watching her, wondering why she would be there. Yvonne spotted the person she was supposed to meet. A woman was in the far back of the building, whom Yvonne could only assume was Kersa, sitting on a cold stone bench. A chipped marble table sat in front of her, hosting the cup of coffee, a cigarette tray next to it. Yvonne found it a little disgusting, especially since smoking was one of her least favourite things mankind had made.

"Kersa?" Yvonne cautiously sat down across from her. Kersa did a one up at Yvonne, took another puff of her cigarette, and tapped the butt onto the tray. She held it between her pointer and thumb, never breaking contact with Yvonne's eyes.

"Yes, that's right. You must be Ms. Kalman."

Yvonne's ears reddened a bit. She was never really addressed by her last name and didn't prefer it.

"Yes. Sorry I'm a minute late. It was rather hard to find this place...not listed on the maps and all." She straightened her posture but couldn't help but to feel overwhelmingly nauseous. Maybe the smog was getting to her.

"Don't let it happen again," Kersa sternly warned. "This is serious, ya know."

"Understood," she complied, quivering.

"Here's what's gonna happen." Kersa drew out a portfolio from beside her and placed it on the table. "You need to review these details and have everything covered and engraved into your brain by next month." She tapped the buckle with her pointer finger. It was seriously stained by tobacco.

"Everything? Do I need to have a general understanding or an extremely detailed understanding?" Yvonne panicked, thinking about how stressful this would be. She hadn't had to memorise something of this calibre since her college days.

"You need to be able to understand what people are talking about when they are talking about it. You need to remember and know the code words and read between the lines. Don't forget how critical this report is. I'm not expecting you to memorise every variable in expenses and losses, but at least have an idea." Kersa seemed to have doubts about Yvonne's capabilities. Afterall, Yvonne looked like the typical office worker, dressed professionally with fancy kicks. "You might seem intimidating to your regular coworkers, but I see right through you." Kersa gave her a piercing look, eyes daggering like a predator. Shivers ran down Yvonne's spine. She's never felt so fearful over a simple conversation. She wasn't sure what she was getting into.

"I got it. I'll make sure to do my very best." Yvonne tried to brush off her distress and responded in a cool tone.

"Very best won't cut it. You know how much you're being compensated for this job, so act like it. Be the money." Kersa tossed a burner phone onto the table along with her direct mailing address. Yvonne quickly collected the items and tucked them away.

"I understand." She did remember seeing the compensation paper and thinking it must've been an error. But at this point, she didn't think it was anymore.

"Do not contact me unless it is case related, and do NOT address me as Kersa when we converse. Call me Sophia." Sophia did not suit her at all. Yvonne tried to suppress a smirk but Kersa saw it.

"Don't laugh." Debris fell off the cigarette between her lips, staining her trousers. "Now sign this NDA."

It wasn't long before Yvonne whipped out the portfolio in her own space to review the papers. There was an immense amount of information she needed to retain and understand. Though she'd taken cases with high confidentiality marks, she'd never taken one to this extent, and with this much stuff. Headquarters allowed Yvonne to work from home most days for this case, as it was too sensitive to risk the chance that others would see. The portfolio was secured quite well, requiring a passcode and a manual key. All information was recorded manually by paper, dated, signed, and clipped immaculately. She recognized a couple of the names from the contact forms on the information and reports included. It became obvious that everyone used a code name or their last name, but never their first. She also had no indication of what their real identity was, nor what they looked like. J.J. Cruz had a messy style that could be picked out from a mile away. Their writing was hard to read and their tone in the way they wrote was almost arrogant. Yvonne wasn't surprised. J.J. Cruz sounded like quite the character, and was the lead investigator, detailing every interaction and any suspicions. They focused on one person so far, a suspect they code named *St. Sylke*. St. Sylke seemed to be rather stone walling J.J. even after trying to connect over a few weeks. *A few weeks?!* Yvonne thought.

She pondered as to why she was involved so late. It quickly became known that the case was evolving slowly and she wasn't needed till now. A revelation had been made only three days ago: a lump sum of $45,000 was extracted on Monday night at 11:43 p.m. Mackie, the connections/hacker confidant, reported this finding in one of the papers. Apparently they were monitoring the data from Tamocus Inc when a breach was flagged. It was highly coded and Mackie could only uncover the amount and time that the transaction was made. A typewriter was used to report the findings, and she could tell Mackie was beyond frustrated that they couldn't uncover more. Yvonne looked at all the reports and transactions that were printed off for her. She found many discrepancies just by flipping through the pages. She already had some plans in her head, as well as ways to strengthen their security. This was going to be difficult.

> *'St. Sylke doesn't like when i approach them. Stand offish. Tuesday morning still doing regular routine. Nothing of the ordinary.J.J. Cruz'*

J.J needed a re-up on grammar and punctuation.

> *'Sylke has a bunch of keys but its hard to get them off the person. Cannot locate exact place of residence- highly paranoid individual.*
>
> *J.J. Cruz'*

Yvonne furrowed her brow. She knew this was going to be a doozy. Mindful, she took this seriously. The harder it was to get a clear suspect, the less of a chance they had to resolve the case in a timely manner.

# Chapter 2

*Tap, tap, tap.*

A sundry of cardamom, licorice, and musk winded throughout the bungalow while rain pitter-pattered outside. One would think it was meditative, but it was not. It was an eerie disarray of melodies as the aromatics danced away in the night. There wasn't much light, just a dusty shadow of one. Luminescents of yellow and vibrating electricity hummed through the ceiling, hiding in the cracks of neglected wallpaper. Vintage? No. Unloved, unkept, and dead. The rustic brick flooring was laid in a distressed manner, craters leaving a gap with no proper conditioning, just cement and dirt. The bungalow hosted a mysterious individual with no ration or heart, just contempt.

Yvonne quivered as the chill set in her bones. Why did it have to rain last night? It had been about six days since she received the portfolio, which she kept under her bed at all times and never let out of her sight. Luther had inquired about her absence from work a couple times, and even texted her by the second day. Yvonne simply informed him that she was busy with a case and had to handle it elsewhere. Although that wasn't typical, Luther understood. He'd been sending pictures of coffee since then, as if to reel her back into the office.

*Luther: 12:04 p.m. Lookie here. (1 Attachment)*

It was her signature tonka bean with caramel sauce latte. She winced, envious of him. It had been a while since she's had her favourite drink. The case had occupied her mind night and day, so she hadn't had the chance to step out and actually enjoy life. It gave her great anxiety to leave the case at home without her watching eye. Over the past three days, she's received and sent a few letters between the authorised contacts.

*Luther: 12:15 p.m. Come on, talk to me I'm bored at work lolz.*

Yvonne grinned, thinking of what an idiot he was.

*Yvonne: 12:16 p.m. Should I report this to your supervisor?*

*Luther: 12:17 p.m. Whoa hang on there don't be a party pooper.*

*Luther: 12:21 p.m. So what's been keeping m'lady so caught up that she can't come into office?*

*Yvonne: 12:22 p.m. Don't call me m'lady, that's weird.*

*Yvonne: 12:23 p.m. It's just a harder case that's all. I have a lot of cases going on.*

*Luther: 12:24 p.m. Let me help! You know I'm good at what I do.*

Yvonne put her phone down. She knew she couldn't let anyone assist her in her work; that was never her style anyway.

*Yvonne: 12:30 p.m. No thanks. You should go back to your work.*

*Luther: 12:31 p.m. Thought I lost you there lololol. Alright fine, but only if you get out of your hermit shell and come out tonight with me.*

*Yvonne: 12:33 p.m. Yeah maybe, I should get out the house, even if it's with you.*

*Luther: 12:33 p.m. Ouch, but I'll take it. I'll pick you up at 8.*

She smirked and looked over to her bed. Anxiety pierced her, but she really needed a break. Thinking back to some cliche methods, she flipped her bed over, cut a big enough slit through the bottom, and stuffed the portfolio in before setting the mattress back down. No one would know there was something under there, especially with the heaps of pillows and clothes thrown across her bed. Yvonne came to realise how dishevelled she had become over the past few days. She wore a merino sweatshirt and bloomers, which was vandalised with food stains and wrinkles. She claimed it aired out her lady parts quite nicely, though of course only disclosed to her plush animal that resided with her. Disturbingly, her hair hasn't been washed in a while, too. Every strand was coated in scalp oil and had a musty smell that wafted everywhere she went. It would be detrimental if someone from work saw her this unkempt.

After a nice shower, Yvonne felt back to her normal state and excitedly changed into luxury clothing. Not the luxury you may think, but luxury in terms of material and cut. It was out of this world, and everything was tailored perfectly to each curve and dip on her body. The material slid and wrapped her up in comfort like a second skin. She applied makeup diligently and finished it off with a dark maroon lip tint. After spritzing herself with her signature scent of fresh rose and extravagant white musk with a variety of other notes, she felt complete. Red bottom stilettos slid on perfectly to the groove of her arch, caressing her heel and toes.

Luther was excited to see Yvonne. He had missed her quite a bit since she'd been working remotely. He carried a small bag of chocolate covered caramels that were infused with espresso. It seemed to be something she'd like, so he instantly got it without thinking. He admittedly felt a little frazzled; doing something so small somehow felt so intimate. He checked the rear-view mirror, making sure he looked presentable. His outfit wasn't anything out of the ordinary, just his usual work attire with a bit of flare; flare being a nicer watch and snakeskin oxfords. His hands grazed his collar, assuring it wasn't crooked. 7:53 p.m. It was almost time.

Yvonne stared out the window from her apartment, watching Luther wait for her out front. Riddled with butterflies, she began to check everything in her apartment and took one last look at herself in the mirror before departing.

"What's this?" she asked curiously, cupping the little baggie of confections that were delicately wrapped in cellophane and had an elegant bow at the top.

"I thought you'd like it," Luther responded, beginning to regret getting it due to embarrassment. "If you don't want it, just tell me. Don't feel forced to take it."

Yvonne hugged it closer to herself. She thoroughly missed the taste of sweets, especially ones infused with coffee.

"No, thank you Luther." She felt hesitant to accept his gift since she wanted to keep her guard up around him, but he was swooning her so well. She gently traced the bow along its path before her finger scrumpled the cellophane.

Luther coughed before gesturing towards her. There it was again, that glint in his eye.

"Then, shall we head on?"

# Chapter 3

She didn't want it to seem like a date, but it really did. The atmosphere and theme of the restaurant felt way too fancy to be a casual hangout. They sat in the waiting area on the leather love seats. Yvonne felt a bit uneasy, and it clearly showed on her face.

"Are you okay? Did you want to go back home?" Luther asked, noticing her body language as she tightly gripped her cardigan to her body in an attempt to make herself smaller. He couldn't help but feel like an idiot. Was he doing too much?

"Yvonne?"

Yvonne whipped around to see Hyouko and Haruka at the entrance of the restaurant. Were they on a date?! Luther grimaced as he saw Hyouko, as he was conventionally attractive. He had jet black hair that had grown out long enough to make into a bun. His eyes were captivating with a mischievous tone, yet somehow warm and comforting, not to mention the elegantly placed beauty mark on his eyelid. His build was slightly muscular and nicely toned. Luther could gather this just by seeing his forearms that were adorned with irezumi. He had dimples that practically mocked Luther, complimenting his perfectly proportioned lips and teeth that had uniquely sharp canines.

"Hyouko! Haruka!" Yvonne exclaimed, going in to greet the two. "Are you on a date?"

Haruka bursted out laughing.

"Are you crazy! Hyouko and I are just out here to grab a bite to eat with another friend of ours," she replied, slapping Yvonne's shoulder playfully.

Hyouko laughed along with Haruka and then locked eyes with Yvonne.

"So, you haven't come by to eat for a while," Hyouko joked with a wink.

"I'm Luther," Luther interjected.

There was an awkward pause between the group.

"Ah, oh, nice to meet you!" Hyouko replied, offering a hand to Luther. Luther shook his hand firmly. Yvonne and Haruka glanced at each other.

"My name is Haruka. Nice to meet you too, Luther!" She shook both the men's hands in a strange three-way shake.

Yvonne snickered amidst the tension. Haruka was always so pleasant and funny to be around.

"So, what brings you here, Yvonne, Luther?" Hyouko asked as he released the handshake.

"Oh, Luther proposed we grab a bite to eat. I've been cooped up in a pile of work," Yvonne replied, stealing a look at Luther, though Luther still looked at Hyouko.

"Wow! Sounds great. This place is really good, I recommend the black cod saikyou. It has a lavish marinade you can't miss!" Haruka said.

Luther haphazardly responded with an, "Oh, sounds great."

"Anyway, I think we should get to our table. Oh! DANIEL!" Haruka exclaimed as she rushed towards Daniel as if she wanted to get away from the thick air. Daniel was a lanky fellow. He had blond hair that grew past his ears. The wispy ends of his fringe acted like rays of sun above his smoky grey eyes. His lashes were voluminous, sprawling every which way and adding to the theme from his fringe. He wore a grey waffle shirt with chino tailored pants in the same monochrome attire. His shoes were definitely casual—grey slip on boat shoes in a suede material. There were spots of stains on it but he didn't seem to mind. There was a distinctual beauty mark right below his left eye and one below his right bottom lip. It was sensual and rather hard to look away from. It was as if he was casted right out of a fantasy novel. Admittedly, Yvonne thought he was dashing and couldn't look away. Luther took note of this and became even more sour.

"I think our table is ready," he remarked, snapping her out of her shameless staring session.

"Oh, yes, for sure." Yvonne clumsily followed Luther to their table.

The mood was stale for the rest of the dinner. They ate in a semi-silent cloud. Luther was still conflicted, which Yvonne picked up on. She was slightly agitated due to his attitude. He had no right to be upset about anything; she was clearly uncomfortable with his possessiveness. Yvonne was very emotionally perceptive and knew what he was feeling by the way he acted.

"I think we should wrap up soon," she said, breaking the silence. She waved for the waiter.

"Uh, no, I mean—" Luther wiped his mouth and tried to reel Yvonne's interest back in. "Sorry, I'm not sure what came over me."

"Luther, to be quite frank, I'm uncomfortable with the possessiveness and attitude you have towards me. We are not a thing and it's kind of scary to see you like this when we are merely acquaintances."

Those words shot through Luther's head, making him feel dizzy and like a child. She was right though, but Luther was too egoistic to apologise properly.

"Pfft, you're joking," he began. Yvonne obtained two boxes from the waiter and started packing her remains. "Sorry, I mean, work has been rough. Especially with you gone from the office." He desperately tried to reason with her.

"That's no excuse. I am no one's property and I don't stand for that type of treatment. Hyouko is a good friend of mine," Yvonne snapped.

Luther hesitated before responding, but Yvonne was on a roll.

"I'm done for now. Good night." She sternly placed her portion of the tab on the table and left. Luther knew better than to follow her out, and instead sat in a puddle of his own shame.

"Luther, you fuckin' idiot," he said to himself, averting his gaze from bystanders.

It was a brisk night out, but that didn't stop Yvonne from storming out in her delicate outfit. After a couple minutes, she slowed down and took in the night sky. She sighed, trying to calm her pounding head. She hated men that objectified women, even in this microaggressive way. She had suspicions that Luther may have taken an interest towards her, and she hadn't minded, but this was too far. Checking her watch, she took note to be more cautious. It was just after 10:00 p.m., and nightlife in the city was something to be wary of.

"Hey."

Yvonne spun around, tense and alert. She let her guard down when she saw it was Hyouko.

"Oh, it's you." Yvonne made her way toward him, strutting elegantly in her heels.

"You okay?" he asked, his eyes softening and masking his usual roguish behaviour. Yvonne murmured a 'yeah' but Hyouko knew she was fibbing. "Do you need anything, Yvonne-san?"

They started walking towards a bench at the nearby park to sit at. There was just a moment of silence before Yvonne responded again.

"I think life can be too stressful at times," she began, locking eyes with him. "Work and all."

He chuckled and crossed his legs, raising his arms to put them behind his head.

"Tell me 'bout it."

"Hahaha, what? Did a customer lash out at you again?" Yvonne teased.

"You know it! Everyday, all day." He groaned as he reminisced about the memory. "Hey, you still owe me a sake. Don't think I forgot about that."

Yvonne tsked him. "I don't remember agreeing on that part of the bet." She gave him a daring look. "But you know what, it's been a hell of a day, so let's get some drinks."

His ears perked up and he excitedly got up. "Oh hell yeah!"

Yvonne pondered for a moment. She wanted to head home to check on the portfolio but didn't want to make the situation too intimate. She had faith in Hyouko and it had been a few months since she first met him, so she thought to give it a go.

"How 'bout we go to my place? I need to check up on some stuff back home."

Hyouko was startled but smirked. "Why not. Let's go get some drinks!"

It was humorous how differently they were dressed. Yvonne looked very elegant and fancy while Hyouko seemed like a rebellious Japanese man, especially with his updo. The bag rustled as the various bottles of sake and alcoholic beverages clanked inside as they hurried into her apartment complex. Yvonne's feet were killing her, especially with the amount of time she spent on her heels. Though they were classy and stunning, they definitely did not always feel that way.

"They must hurt, huh?" Hyouko pointed at Yvonne's feet. While trying to stay steady, Yvonne held the bag of beverages and balanced on her left leg to bring up her right heel.

"Well why don't you try 'em?" she said with a challenging look. She smiled, removed her heels, and passed them to him.

"You're joking… I don't want your foot scent near me!" he exclaimed, backing into the hall's wall.

"Whoa now, be careful!" Yvonne practically leaped in concern toward him, gently grabbing his bicep, which admittedly gave her butterflies. His arm was so strong and chiselled she had to refrain from making an inappropriate face. They both laughed and Yvonne was relieved it wasn't awkward. Hyouko truly was good at making her comfortable and understanding peoples' needs. Suddenly, he flexed his arms and his muscles became even firmer, which startled Yvonne into a blush as she flared her arms up in a frenzy.

"You like that, huh?" he teased, flexing more muscle and posing as though he was doing a photoshoot for Centerfold.

"Stop it, I'll die…" Yvonne cried in embarrassment. She hid her face with her one empty hand and trudged along towards her door. She hurriedly unlocked her door and opened it, letting Hyouko enter. He just continued to snicker and winked.

"So this is Yvonne's pad." He surveyed the apartment excitedly and looked back at her "So sensual… Yvonne don't *50 shades of Grey* me."

She turned bright red and almost dropped the bag.

"I WOULD NEVER," she yelled in desperation. She wasn't very good with physical touch and this teasing was far too much for her.

"Hahaha just joking, but seriously this color theme is very alluring. Is this the inside of Yvonne's true personality?" he gasped with saucer eyes. Yvonne rolled her eyes and set the bag down on the table, beginning to unpack the drinks and grabbing two glass cups.

"Get over here and start drinking. I wanna drink till I can't remember this night." The sake filled both cups deliciously, allowing Yvonne to get wafts of the saturatingly sweet rice scent. They clinked their cups together and glugged it down. It gave a warm, fuzzy feeling in her stomach, and she poured some more into their cups.

"So who was that Daniel guy?" Yvonne asked, eyeing Hyouko from the rim of her cup.

He licked the sake off his lips before responding.

"Oh, Daniel? He's a new friend of ours. Haruka-san met him at a party and he seemed like a fun guy; we started seeing him every so often." He looked at Yvonne curiously. "Hm…is Yvonne-san interested in the angel-like Daniel-san?" he flippantly said, raising his cup to his lips and slowly brushing them against the rim. Yvonne's core tightened and she looked away.

"What? Is it not normal to ask about a new friend?" She brushed her hair behind her ear, displaying a compelling aura of submission and elusiveness. Hyouko cleared his throat, finding it hard to look away from Yvonne in this state. The sake was not helping his case at all. His face was also flushed, eyes gleaming and pupils dilated. His hair was tousled in a messy but sexy way as his body positioned in a dominant demeanour.

"No, you can." He drank the last droplet of sake before reaching for more. His strong arm extended towards the bottle next to Yvonne. The dress she wore was too provocative, and his eyes lingered at the cleavage that was unveiled ever-so-slightly due to her arm pushing her breast up as she rested her body weight on it. "Fuck," he whispered under his breath, facing downwards so Yvonne wouldn't catch onto his honesty. He grasped the bottle and cracked it open.

"Did you say something?" Yvonne asked, cocking her head to the side as her hair fell delicately, some strands hanging onto her shoulder. She gestured for a refill and smiled.

"No, nothing." Hyouko diligently refilled her cup and gazed into her eyes. Her heart skipped a beat and every part of her body shivered yet felt overwhelmingly warm.

"So, is Luther your boyfriend?" The question completely shot down the tension in an instant. Yvonne furrowed her brows and sighed.

"Absolutely not. He asked to grab a bite since I haven't been in the office for a week." Yvonne gulped down another cup of sake. "Don't get the wrong idea. He and I are not a thing."

Suddenly, Yvonne felt Hyouko's breath and she stared into his eyes. She was uncontrollably red and opened her mouth to speak, before Hyouko cupped her face. This shut her up immediately.

"Then, Yvonne, may I?"

Her eyes widened. He didn't add the suffix at the end. Such a small piece of language removed made it that much more intimate. She was unable to respond, and wasn't sure what to really say or do. She'd never had a boyfriend or much intimacy since her first year of college. Hyouko's eyes slowly traced her face, down her chest, and back up. His ears were red, too, small particles of perspiration decorating his face. Warm tingling sensations travelled between the two as his face inched closer to her parted lips. He brushed his lips softly on hers, only a thin space of warm boozy air between them. Yvonne's body gave out and her hips rested on the floor. Hyouko's body grew closer to hers, and Yvonne became flustered but frozen, unsure what to do or what to expect.

"Do you trust me?" Hyouko whispered lowly into her ear. It tickled and had her hair standing up, back arching. His bun had become slightly undone and part of his front hairs grazed her face.

"W-what do you mean?" stuttered Yvonne, shyly trying to hide her face. He moved her hand away from her face.

"You know what I mean," Hyouko said, kissing her hand while gazing into her eyes. His eyes intensely connected with hers.

"I do," Yvonne said in a wavering voice. "But what do you expect from this?" She was scared of getting hurt and didn't know Hyouko's true intentions. To be fair, she barely knew him beyond being a ramen shop waiter she saw every week or so. Overall, he'd been an extremely kind, fun, and interesting guy, but she never expected him to be interested in her.

"I like Yvonne," he said, slowly rubbing his thumb against her cheek, feeling the overbearing warmth radiating from her face.

"I don't want to get hurt," she said, trembling. Hyouko stopped and slowly helped Yvonne sit back up.

"I don't want to hurt you," he responded, looking away and observing the clock above the fireplace. There was a brief pause where the only sound was the ticking of the clock. Yvonne didn't know what Hyouko was thinking. She wouldn't mind dating Hyouko, but he seemed to be a little bit flirty in general; she wouldn't be able to handle that much longer towards other women. Although his job wasn't ideal, it wasn't a big issue for her since she could sustain herself. Hyouko rubbed his face and hair in frustration before looking back to Yvonne.

"You'll see. I will be here for you. I won't hurt you." His face became profound, indicating his earnestness.

"Yvonne, may you go out with me this Tuesday on a date?"

Yvonne nodded timidly. She wanted to give him a chance, and wanted to experience love properly. He brightly smiled before grabbing her hand again and placing a gentle kiss on it.

"You'll never be sad or afraid with me."

# Chapter 4

*St. Sylke has been rigid. Boring. Trying to get closer to them is difficult.*

*J.J. Cruz*

Yvonne intently read the new mail that was delivered to her apartment. She carefully placed it into the portfolio and began digging into the new database Kersa had sent. It was an extensive folder of names and information that she had requested.

This case was going far slower than she expected. It didn't help that most information and communications had to be done without electronics. Even sending that text message to Kersa was barely allowed, as it could give away too much. Amongst everything, Luther had tried contacting her after that night. She blatantly ignored it since she didn't have any reason to reply or humour his advances. Yvonne was the loyal type and kept Hyouko's persuasion in mind. It got her giddy at times but then anxious at another. It wasn't like she had time to flirt around or even had that mentality in the first place. After that night of sake and conversation, they exchanged phone numbers and Yvonne bid him a goodnight, waving to him from her balcony window. He returned her farewell with a wink and blew her a kiss. Yvonne snapped out of it and reminded herself to focus and be more mature. Love was a fickle thing. She knew that, which was why she wasn't so keen on getting into a relationship in general. As she skimmed the documents in her hand, she tried to find a pattern or consistency. Anything odd would've been ideal, but nothing popped up yet. She recognized that there were six people who prominently handled the affairs of the company: the Executive Director, Administrator, Secretary, Vice Executive, Accounting Manager, and Reception. Their names came up quite frequently, which wasn't a surprise. There were tons of employees under this company and it was hard to pinpoint who would have breached their security. Of course, the accounting manager was the first one people pinpointed when it came to anything involving money. But what they didn't know was that it wasn't always them, but rather some angry subordinate under them that overthrew their power and created a ruse so complex it was almost impossible to figure out. Yvonne carefully read the names of the cyber team and accounting teams. It would be hard for just one of the accounting members to infiltrate the security system and seamlessly extract a large sum of money without tripping a wire or two. Yvonne wondered if J.J. Cruz had an idea of this potential situation.

*J.J.,*

*is it just St. Sylke you've pinpointed? Any other suspects? It's unlikely it's only one person pulling this off, especially in such an incredibly stealthy way.*

*Kalman*

Yvonne copied four off the printer and sent them to each of the members involved in the case: J.J. Cruz, Mackie, Kersa, and Vos. She hurriedly ran to her designated drop off point. It was inconspicuous, a typical mailing post manned by an older fellow. Yvonne had to triple check that this was indeed the right place, looking around at the landmarks Kersa had mentioned. The man just watched her plainly. Yvonne stepped up to him and awkwardly spoke. She gave the code word 'Thorn Bush.' and the man nodded. He accepted the letters with names written on each envelope and disappeared into the back. Yvonne waited a couple minutes for the elderly fellow to come back but eventually realised that he probably wasn't. Once that was done, she reviewed the files again and again. All employees seemed pretty normal, some missing days here and there, and quite a few that had just been hired. She gathered that the company must've expanded exponentially, thus the influx of hires. She noted in her booklet that measures should be taken carefully when hiring new people. It was a security thing, and more often than not, employers didn't do background checks. She wondered if there was a human resources team. There was, but she found it was too small for the ratio of people. Boosting the numbers in HR and having credible employees was beneficial. She pondered if maybe the suspect might be someone outside of the company, which wasn't unlikely, but rather impossible to determine. That was a job for J.J.

Yvonne wrote down how much the company had lost due to the suspect: a grappling sum of $85,000 so far. At this rate, they couldn't go much longer if there was a consistent flow leaving their pockets. Yvonne curiously searched up what Tamocus Inc actually was as a company and soon discovered why they could have potentially spared that money. Tamocus was lucky they'd had great success with selling various eccentric supplements that were said to give various effects and were highly potent. It sounded a little bit sketchy, especially because it wasn't necessarily moderated or accepted in pharmaceutical institutions. Since it was arbitrary in the way it went through different individuals, many bought into the hype to see what it was all about. Secret formula, they said, as though it was the antidote to life or even the secret sauce of successful fast food joints. There was a catalogue of supplements they provided for a pretty penny. Most popular was '*Honey Silk*,' which had more raving reviews than poor; notable comments were about the feel of the supplement engorging their taste buds, slipping down their throat in a warm, tingly sensation, and warming their stomachs before sending a shiver into their brain and making them go fuzzy. Some comments were straight out of a horror book, explicitly describing their experience of hell after taking it. There was obviously some sort of controlled substance in them, but clearly wasn't dangerous if the FDA hadn't gotten to them.

*No thanks, I'll stick to my booze,* Yvonne thought, closing off the search tab and peering out her window.

It was 3:00 p.m. on a clear fall day. Yvonne felt the urge to go out and explore the city in her oxfords and casual fall wear—stockings, along with a light brown cashmere sweater that was beautifully designed to hug the right curves and loosen elegantly on the rest. She paired it with a grey accordion skirt and a dainty pearl necklace that modestly rested between her collar bones. She swung a vintage leather bag onto her shoulder that held her phone and wallet.

The fall breeze licked Yvonne's face, giving off a subtle fragrance of rain. The trees bared their leaves as they flew away and onto everything they could touch. Vibrant colors of orange, yellow, red, and brown could be seen in a masquerade of visual eroticism. It was backed by the brown-bricked buildings, faint chimney smoke, and a clock tower clock many people came to take touristy photos of. That was one thing Yvonne loved about where she lived—it made her feel so comfy with how old fashioned and historic some places stayed. There were specialty and commodity shops nearby, as well as independent grocers. If one were to walk another ten minutes or so, they would hit the main streets of bustling commuters, shops, and more. Yvonne spotted a new coffee shop that had popped up on the back corner of the street. She breathlessly sped to the entrance that bore decorative yarrow embossed in metal along the door. The cafe had a saudade feel to it, and there were notes of coffee bean, lavender, and a spritz of bourbon in the air. The coffee tables were rustic, a thick slab of oak wood hoisted by an abstract footing with black spray paint. The chairs shared the same theme, only having a seat with no backing. Artisanal, as some may call it. They served a variety of caffeinated beverages, as well as in-house pastries that looked ever so delectable. The barista smiled warmly, patiently waiting for Yvonne to approach the register to order. It was exhilarating for her to view all the new drinks and bakery items. She didn't know what to choose!

"Did you have any questions about our items?" the barista asked, taking notice of Yvonne's squirrel-like behaviour.

"What would you recommend?" she asked eagerly. The barista looked over the items and then back at Yvonne.

"I think I've got just the right beverage for you. Sit tight."

Yvonne waited patiently, watching as the barista smoothly blended and mixed the drink for her. After they vigorously shook it in an abundance of ice, they effortlessly poured it into a plastic cup and handed it to her.

"Try it out, it's our house special iced espresso," the barista said. "By the way, the name's Blake."

"Hi Blake, thank you! My name's Yvonne." She smiled and accepted the drink, carefully sipping to aerate the flavours into her mouth. It was outstanding. Not only was the beverage frothy and silky, but the taste of chicory and white chocolate was consoling. The profile of the drink matched perfectly with the season outside and really emanated how the cafe was.

"Wow." Yvonne was speechless. Something so otherwise ordinary came together and blended harmoniously. "Just wow."

"Haha, glad you like it. I created this drink, so it totally gives me a boost in ego." Blake stuck their nose in the air to show how snooty they felt. Yvonne giggled and felt an immense admiration for them.

Then, she felt her phone vibrate in her purse. Yvonne swiftly checked it and saw it was Luther again, sending a picture of his daily coffee with a side message of '*hey you ok?*' She felt obligated to reply after stone walling him long enough.

*Yvonne: 3:25 p.m. Yes, thanks for asking.*

*Luther: 3:25 p.m. No problem, I'm here for you.*

She left it at that.

"Oooh, your boyfriend?" Blake asked, jokingly examining her phone.

"As if," Yvonne tartly vocalised as she stuffed the phone back into her bag. Another buzz came through.

"Oh for Pete's sake."

*Hyouko: 3:26 p.m. Hey hey hey! ~ hope you're doing well. Thinking of you.*

Yvonne's sour face quickly disappeared, turning into a gushing display.

"*That* must be your boyfriend," they laughed, washing the utensils they used.

"No, I mean, not really. We are just trying to go out on a couple dates. Nothing official yet," Yvonne explained, brushing her hair out of her face and quickly typing a response.

*Yvonne: 3:27 p.m. Yes! I am doing well Hyouko, I hope you are too.*

She wasn't good with words, nor was she confident in anything romantic-like. She waited for him to respond, but after a minute, she put her phone away.

"Thank you, Blake, for introducing me to this amazing drink. I'll come often. Till next time." Yvonne waved at the kind barista, in which they returned the farewell.

*Yvonne: 4:00 p.m. Hyouko, I bet it's busy at work huh? Don't forget to take a break.*

There wasn't a response at all, and it didn't seem like he even read it. She assumed it must be crazy busy. Who wouldn't want a hot bowl of ramen during the fall? Yvonne returned to her apartment complex. A tall woman stood in the front entrance of the lobby, staring up. She wore a hat, trench coat, and black slacks, and her long, blonde hair blew in the wind. Yvonne stood a few feet away, observing the woman. She only stared at the building and did nothing more. She looked left and right a couple times before spotting Yvonne behind her. She made intense eye contact, then walked away in her meticulous heels. Jet black stilettos with bows on the back. Yvonne appreciated the style and felt impulsive, wanting to buy a pair for herself. When she passed the mailbox area, she noticed a few letters addressed to her. She abruptly picked them up and headed to her unit. Today was a busy day, with more mail than usual. Quickly glancing at the ones in her hand, she could tell that two were pertinent to the case, one was a bill, and the other was unknown with nothing but her unit on it. Yvonne curiously opened the unknown one. It was rather cryptic.

### 7286250108 Weeping Widow

An eerie feeling set into her skin. The note was ominous and had no indication as to what it meant or what it even referred to. She tried examining the paper, envelope, and message. The envelope was a standard white envelope, nothing special or different. The paper was letter grade and the message only occupied the middle part. No signature, and typed instead of handwritten. Maybe Vos sent it and forgot to address the letter and put their signature on it? Afterall, Yvonne hadn't heard anything from Vos since being on the case and had no idea what style they had. Yvonne's phone buzzed, interrupting her train of thought.

"Hello?" Yvonne answered the call without checking the caller ID.

"Hey, miss me?"

Yvonne's face warmed.

"Hyouko... how was your day?" Yvonne said, quickly putting away her mail before plopping onto her bed like a giddy teenager.

"Missing you a lot, is all," he groaned. There was a rustling sound in the back which cleared up almost just as quick. "Listen, I don't have too much time right now, but I promise I'll make Tuesday the best date you'll ever have."

Disappointed, Yvonne mustered up a *'sounds great, text me when you can'* before he hung up, but not after he gave a kiss over the phone. This was something she had to get used to. Even though she wasn't the type to swoon over relationships and clinginess, she was finding herself more and more drawn to him, and with space apart, her heart only grew fonder. To distract herself, she went back to viewing the rest of the mail.

> *St. Sylke has been peculiarly apprehensive when asked simple questions. Trying to back off so they don't completely shut me out.*

> *Hemlock is asking me questions a little bit intrusively. Seems to be everywhere I am 'coincidentally.' Could be a potential suspect as well. Guarding.*

> *J.J. Cruz*

It was worrisome that the suspects weren't giving anything to build off of. So far, it had just been suspicion and a mouse chase. Although it wasn't in her position to do much in regards to investigating, she couldn't help but feel anxious and impatient with it all.

> *Another sum of money was extracted last night. A small amount, but they encrypted a mocking bunch of numerals.*

> *Sum: $1,000*

> *Mackie*

It was a meagre amount compared to the ones they'd pulled off before, but it was solely to mock them. Mackie seemed the type to take things personally, so Yvonne couldn't imagine how Mackie reacted when they saw the pattern of binary codes. Conscientiously, Yvonne wrote up a small report and some comprehensive thoughts on all that had happened so far, hoping to come up with the best patch system for them.

Meanwhile, in a dimly lit bar, Luther eyed the woman he was with, giving no heed to the words she'd just spoken. "Don't be idiotic," he said. "I don't think it's a good idea."

The woman looked him straight in the eyes. "I just told you. Get it done," she warned.

Luther scornfully tsked, readjusting himself out of annoyance. Luther only happened to come across the lady while he was visiting a friend there. It was unfortunate they had to meet in such a public space. Her eyes were gaunt and narrow despite the small glimmers of eyeshadow that flitted around her lids. Her lips were lavished with a dark, blood-red shade and were adorned with a silver lip ring. She was rather small, but her energy was fierce and one not to bargain with. Long, black hair covered the woman's head, falling down her shoulders and stopping just past her bosom. The shadows casted on Luther's face somberly sent a message to the woman once more.

"I'm done with that. Don't talk to me so familiarly." He slapped a bill on the table and proceeded to exit the bar.

The woman harshly warned Luther. "Remember the deal. You're the one that got yourself into this mess. No one else."

# Chapter 5

Yvonne didn't think Tuesday would come so quickly; she was ill prepared and hastily got herself together, hoping to seem presentable. Hyouko had confirmed over text to meet at 7:00 p.m. for a date. She wasn't sure what type of date, but that made it all the more exciting. Usually, she would be confident in herself and what she chose to wear, but this time, she went through her closet like a maniac. Eventually she settled with a flowy light brown halter dress that stopped right above her knees. For her outerwear, she carefully tied a wrap cashmere sweater in case it got cold out. She tastefully paired it with two-toned oak brown and linen slingback stiletto pumps. Her hair was held together with a tortoise shell claw clip which brought everything together.

Yvonne nearly jumped when she heard the knock on the door. She quickly went to open it. Hyouko's eyes widened at the sight of her.

"Yvonne…wow…seeing you like this almost makes me not want to take you out and instead have you all to myself here."

Yvonne immediately turned crimson and she timidly looked down, not sure how to respond.

"You look handsome yourself," she said, though she didn't get the chance to take in what he was wearing since she was avoiding eye-contact at all costs. Hyouko found it humorous how she could come off flat while looking so embarrassed. He slyly brushed her cheek, which made her flinch back, but he finally got her to look into his eyes.

"Let's head out, huh?" His hand reached for hers, and she gently accepted.

Hyouko wanted to impress Yvonne, so he brought her to a wine-tasting at a fancy establishment. Yvonne *was* impressed, but found it odd that Hyouko would choose this as a first date. It had red carpets, the walls were decorated with antiquities, and a chandelier hung in the middle of the room from a high ceiling, casting brilliant spots of shine despite the lighting being fairly dim. A soft jazzy tune played throughout, and the seating arrangements were elegant. The place was aged for sure, but like the wine, it was well bodied. Wine and sake were quite different despite their similarity with preservation and fermentation. Yvonne could tell that Hyouko found some of the wines distasteful, though he tried to hide it the best he could. He went the whole yard, dressing in refined black cotton-blend slacks, fitted white dress shirt, and a leather belt fastened appropriately to his waist. His hair was gelled slightly to give a more sophisticated look, and he even wore a watch. Yvonne was taking it all in, finding it erotic and definitely sexy. He donned a pair of smooth black oxfords, giving him an extra point for delectable taste.

"Is it that good?" Hyouko asked, his face insinuating something more than friendly. He held the wine glass carefully and took in the notes of the Merlot.

"Wait, what." Yvonne snapped out of her lustful study and blinked a few times.

"The wine, is it that good? You were zoning out." Hyouko continued sipping the Merlot, but then paused and set it down. He did not enjoy it.

Yvonne giggled to herself before responding. "Hahaha, no, just thinking about things. How was work? You seem to be really busy."

"Gahh just trouble, trouble, trouble," he lamented. "Don't worry Yvonne, I wouldn't ever bring my work stress home." Hyouko winked and poured a new wine to taste. Chardonnay.

"You know, you're traditionally supposed to taste wine from lightest to heaviest," Yvonne remarked. "And what stress? Stress from customers complaining their broth isn't hot enough?" She laughed at her own joke, venturing into the Chardonnay.

"Hey, you'd be surprised. And whaaatt…I had no clue. I'm not sure if that would make that much of a difference to me though. Nothing beats sake or a good ol' mint julep."

Yvonne nearly spat her wine out.

"Mint julep? You?" She pointed at him and covered her mouth, flabbergasted.

Mint juleps were generally enjoyed by beginner alcoholics, or women. For someone so bold and fun, it was hard to believe Hyouko's top drinks included a mint julep.

Hyouko clasped her pointer finger and held it tightly.

"Hey, what's wrong with having a little fun?" he said seductively.

He was full of flirt, and she wasn't used to it yet. His hand was so firm and warm, comforting. All of these small efficacious sports of affection caused a little bit of uneasiness for Yvonne, as she wasn't sure if he was only flirty to her, or flirty to all.

"What's wrong?" Hyouko noticed. He gently placed her hand on the table, still holding on as if it were a flower.

"Are you like this to everyone?" Yvonne questioned, crinkling her eyebrow the slightest.

"Is everyone Yvonne?" he replied. He resisted the urge to make *Yvonne* sound like *Yveryonne* as a joke, since this seemed important to her.

Yvonne examined his expression carefully. He did seem earnest while still having a playful aspect to him, which put her more at ease.

"But anyway, what do you think of the Chardonnay?" Yvonne tried to divert the tension a little and nodded toward his glass.

"I told you I wouldn't make you sad with me," he said strongly before slowly letting go of her hand to take a sip of the Chardonnay. "If a lime and sand made a liquid baby, this would be it." He smacked his lips to soak in the notes a bit more. "I imagine myself in an antique shop, licking every crevice of a dust engulfed curtain tie back in a fancy get up. I would pretend I'm so high class for enjoying this ancient tasting beverage and snobbily look down on anyone that thinks it's detestable."

Yvonne snorted and belted out laughing, thinking of Hyouko on his hands and knees licking some antique's fermented dust in an animalistic way.

"Stop that, I can't control my laughter!" The corner of her eyes started tearing up from the pain of laughter in her abdomen. Hyouko enjoyed making her laugh, and stared in awe of her beauty. It wasn't like Yvonne had a bad experience with her past relationship in college. In fact, it was pretty normal and things had just become too difficult between the two. It was a mutual dissolution and Yvonne felt they had started to veer away from her and towards other women. Yvonne was too busy studying anyway and wanted a stable, lucrative career. She was a go-getter and very bright; no man could take that away from her. Since it had been so long since she'd been open to relationships, she just wanted to protect her sanity, as most would. Suddenly, there was a tap on Hyouko's shoulder. It was a beautiful lady, maybe in her thirties, long legs, and short curly hair. She wore a tight fitted black silk dress that bloomed at the end, along with classic stilettos. Her collar bones were prominent and stuck out like daggers, complimenting a sensitive pearl necklace. Hyouko looked back to see who it was. His face went solemn, and Yvonne watched carefully and curiously. The lady didn't say anything, merely gestured to speak with him at the other side of the establishment.

"Yvonne, sorry, may I excuse myself for a moment?" He hastily got up, furrowing his brows as his fringe unravelled a bit.

"Oh, yeah of course, I'll wait right here." Yvonne wouldn't say no, how could she? She didn't know what the situation was, who the mysterious woman was, or what Hyouko was thinking.

Patiently, she poured a new tasting of Cabernet while following the two with her eyes. The Cabernet was dominant, full-bodied, and dark. Like a whistling, winding wood, the taste left a bitter earthy tone in her mouth. They seemed to be intensely conversing; did something happen? Although Yvonne was curious, she didn't want to be one of those people who stuck their nose in everything. A hint of black currant simmered in her mouth after the initial notes and slowly melted into another. It almost stung her sinuses as she swallowed the rest of the liquid like a pungent red sea down her throat. Truthfully Yvonne didn't prefer bolder wines and enjoyed the lighter, fruitier ones. Like how she enjoyed a nice, comforting latte rather than black coffee. She did appreciate the gist and idea of them both, but her taste buds couldn't get used to the dauntless aftertaste that lingered. Hyouko shook his head violently, angrily, as the woman continued to speak. Yvonne so badly wanted to know what it's about.

When Hyouko returned, Yvonne tried to pry a little. "So, who was that woman?" It was awkward to be in that situation and not get any information as to what had just happened. After sipping on the Cabernet, and Hyouko's hilarious reaction to the bold wine, they left the vicinity and went to stroll around the park nearby.

"Hmmm, work stuff I guess," Hyouko said jokingly.

"Don't play with me." Yvonne nudged his shoulder lightly. His arms were solid like an oak tree.

"Haha, don't worry Yvonne. It's just some family stuff." He slowly reached to embrace her hand. His fingers intertwined with hers, and soon, his warmth filled her palm. She beamed chastely and gripped his hand tighter.

"You looked angry," Yvonne pointed out, stealing a glance at him. He chagrined and stared at the vast starry sky.

"Well, she just said something that wasn't to my liking, is all." He grinned at Yvonne and pinched her cheek. "Don't be so cute or I'll have to eat you."

Yvonne became flustered, as she easily was. She knew he was avoiding the interaction as a whole, so she left it at that.

"Why do you like me?" Yvonne questioned earnestly.

Hyouko was caught off guard and scoffed. "What brought that on?" He stopped and turned to face her. "Did something happen?"

Yvonne wanted someone who would love her as a whole being, and not due to elementary reasons.

"Just tell me, why do you like me? Why me?"

Hyouko scratched the back of his head and closed his eyes for a moment.

"I think Yvonne is very bright. You're beautiful, and your personality emanates the same. Everytime I see you, before and now, I am happy. You make me calm yet sentimental. The way you interact with people, your hard working characteristics, your mysterious attitude, and your honesty. Yvonne, your eyes show me everything."

Hyouko stepped closer to Yvonne, carefully holding the back of her head. Her heart pounded and her breath quickened, shallow and soft.

"I want to know more of you," he said, coming even closer and taking in all of her facial features. "I want to see everything."

Yvonne stood still, shivering from the amount of emotions and nerves taking over her body. Hyouko slowly came closer to her lips, which were stained with the red pigment of the Cabernet.

"May I kiss you, Yvonne?"

Yvonne stiffly nodded, her eyes glossy as the starry night sky reflected off her pupils. It made Hyouko excited. He refrained from kissing too strongly, and instead softly caressed her lips with his own, holding it for a few seconds before continuing to kiss every part of her lips. Yvonne quickly warmed as heat spread to every part of her body. Her abdomen ached and her knees started to buckle. Hyouko held her close to his own body, and Yvonne sniffed the scents coming off of him. It was intoxicating.

Hyouko pulled away and stared at Yvonne's messy expression. Locks of her hair had come undone from the clip that was holding it together. Some framed her face, and others loosely blew in the soft wind.

"You look so beautiful," he whispered. The words tickled her ears, and blushed pigment seeped into her skin like watercolour. Yvonne wanted more, but she couldn't be greedy. She didn't want Hyouko to see how undone he made her, and she wanted to develop their potential relationship slowly. Hyouko could feel that boundary, and knew to stop there.

"You tell me when you're ready for more," he said quietly, holding her tightly as his biceps pillowed her body and the sound of his heart beat against her ear. He smelled pleasant. It was a gentle floral and white musk scent, mixed with the natural smell of his skin. Yvonne closed her eyes and lavished in the comfort of his embrace.

"Thank you, Hyouko."

# Chapter 6

"Look who's back in office!"

Yvonne spun around to face Luther, who was a little nervous to see her for the first time since that night. Yvonne had to return to the office sometimes so that her coworkers and others who might be looking into the case wouldn't get suspicious.

"Well, how can she get anything done here when there's an incessant bug around at all times?" Cherise chimed in, giving an understanding look to Yvonne. Yvonne gave a thankful look to Cherise before responding to Luther.

"I told you my work is very busy right now, and they require me to be working remotely and in the office. Hybrid mix."

Luther rolled his eyes.

"Anyway, coffee?" It was odd that Luther was trying to act normal after that night. Maybe he was trying to cover it all up and act like nothing happened.

"Alright." Yvonne reached for her wallet. "It's my turn to pay anyway." Luther stopped Yvonne.

"You know it's my turn. I owe you." He looked at her knowingly.

"No, forget about that. It's all good." Yvonne didn't want to give Luther the opportunity to redeem himself, especially when she wasn't interested. Luther backed off, knowing Yvonne wasn't going to settle with his proposition. Cherise watched this go on and tried her best not to seem like a peeping tom.

"I'll be back, same as usual?"

Luther nodded.

"Cherise, did you want anything?"

Cherise perked up. "Oh! I mean, I would like some coffee. Get me whatever you recommend, just not too sweet!"

It was startling to hear from Kersa again, since she hadn't since the beginning of Yvonne being on the case. Yvonne had just settled into her desk before Kersa rang her cell. Yvonne stopped for a moment, wondering why she might be calling. After all, they weren't allowed to contact in this way unless it was urgent.

"Please step away from your desk and find a place with privacy," Kersa instructed sternly.

Yvonne merely gave a confirmation before heading out as inconspicuous as she could.

"I'm away from there now." Her heart beat rapidly as she tried to infer what she might say next.

"The portfolio, where is it?" Kersa's words sliced through the line.

Cold sweat broke out over her skin and she carefully recounted her steps before leaving her apartment.

"It's safe in my apartment, why?" Yvonne replied swiftly, replaying her steps in her mind over and over. Portfolio, under the bed, under the bed, in the makeshift hide, in the makeshift hide, portfolio.

"Did you lock your doors?" Kersa sounded rushed, ominous. Yvonne tried remembering if she locked her doors. She always did, but for some reason, she couldn't recall this time.

"I'm sure I did. Why? What's happening?" Her palms were starting to get clammy and her breath shortened.

"I got a tip that someone has been trying to retrieve our team's portfolio. Has there been anyone you've been seeing, anyone suspicious? Anyone around your apartment as of late?"

Yvonne only thought of Hyouko, Luther, and the mysterious woman that one day.

"I've only had one person in my apartment, and two people around. One was a lady that looked a little bit suspicious but I don't know for sure if she's even related to anything. The other one is a coworker," Yvonne reported, trying not to make her quivering noticeable.

"What lady? Did you get a chance to see their face?"

Yvonne vividly remembered the lady's outfit and style and could give a general description of her face.

"Long blonde hair, wearing all black; hat, trench coat, slacks, stilettos with bows on the back. Her eyes were blue-ish grey, slim top lip, plumpier bottom, high cheek-bones, and pale skin." Yvonne was a little amazed at herself with how she could recite that so fluidly. "Anything else? Did you speak with her or anything?" Kersa pressed.

"No." Yvonne held her tongue, wanting to ask more questions but didn't think it was a good time.

"Be very careful Kalman. Don't lose sight of that portfolio." Then she hung up. Yvonne was unable to ask anything else. A little panicked, she couldn't help but feel anxiety once again over the portfolio. Had she been too absent-minded with Hyouko's feelings? She restlessly continued on with her day in the office until it was 5:00 p.m.. Then she left immediately, not spending a second of time more in the building.

There it was again, that fragrant smell of cardamom and licorice.

"Any updates?" The debris of cigarettes dropped down, littering itself on the barren floor.

"Not much, slow." A shuffling could be heard, but only momentarily.

A puff of smoke billowed and dispersed, leaving only a reminisce of tobacco to breathe in. It was dreary; even the furniture seemed to weep in existence. Like a bruise, there was a panging feel that bled in this whole, unsettling being. Was it just a joke? Or was it something more nefarious?

"Deliver them this." A wrinkled letter fell to the floor, sorely ridden with water stains.

"Alright, Endymion."

It was a relief for Yvonne to be home. The first thing she did was check underneath her mattress for the portfolio. There it was, stuffed in the same spot she'd left it. It was a pain that the springs were starting to fall out of their casing. They jagged out as if to threaten Yvonne everytime she removed or placed the portfolio. The folio was starting to inflate with information and papers. It created a bulge underneath her hip whenever she slept. It was a sleek, black portfolio. Pre-loved, but reliable. She could tell, since there were various scratches on it that she definitely didn't create. It was of flexible material, containing dividers and pockets for various uses. Yvonne did enjoy the aspect of tangible documentation and filing. It reminded her of when she was in school, spending countless hours studying and organising her work.

*Knock knock.*

Yvonne jumped. Who could it be? How did they gain access to her building without a key? Was it maybe her neighbour? She sprinted from her bed to the front door, peeking through the peephole.

"Yvonne it's me!"

Through the fisheye lens, she saw Hyouko standing there, waiting to be let in. She unclasped the lock and opened the door.

"You scared me, how'd you get in?" she asked as he sprung inside her apartment with a bunch of mail.

"Oh, someone that lives in this building let me in." He handed her the pile. "Here, I saw these laying out by your mailbox."

She grabbed them quickly, startling Hyouko. He jumped back a little bit in surprise.

"Whoa now, don't worry. I won't look at your porn invoices," he joked.

"Thanks, and haha, very funny." Yvonne placed the bunch of letters in one of the drawers in her common area. She was a bit tense, especially when she wasn't expecting anyone.

*The portfolio.*

Yvonne jumped up and ran towards her bed area where the documents and portfolio was scattered on the floor. She kicked it under her bed but it was too late.

"What's that?" Hyouko asked, seeing the papers gain some air time as she flounced around and kicked them, attempting to hide it all.

"Just work stuff." She tried to brush it off and tried to push Hyouko towards the couch and divert his attention elsewhere.

Hyouko followed along with her and sat on the couch in front of the fireplace. She nervously sat beside him.

"So what do I owe this surprise?" Yvonne held his hand tightly. It wasn't out of affection, but rather to control and prevent him from venturing more.

Hyouko was silent for a moment.

"I thought to ask you to have some food with me today, but maybe it's not a good day," he said, looking anywhere but at Yvonne. Yvonne felt a panging guilt. She didn't mean to hurt his feelings, but she couldn't compromise the case.

"What do you do for work, again? I don't think I ever asked." Hyouko seemed so serious. Was he concerned about Yvonne hiding something in their courting?

"Oh, right. I just do reports and analysis for a big company. Nothing special." She laughed, trying to ease the tension.

"What company?"

Yvonne had to think for a moment. Was it okay to let him know what company? It was normal for people to exchange professions, but it was a bit harder when she was dealing with something confidential.

"Uh the…" She tried to get a look at Hyouko's eyes. He seemed pestered but she wasn't sure why. "I work for a corporation that deals with some sensitive things. I am not sure if I can tell you at this time, but maybe later?" Hyouko had a pained face. It hurt her seeing his usually happy face so strained.

"Hey, what's wrong?" Yvonne nudged him.

"Alright..." he finally responded. He didn't follow up on that, and they sat in silence for what felt like an excruciating eternity.

"How does comfort food sound to you?" Hyouko suddenly asked, facing Yvonne and gently placed his hand on top of hers.

"Sounds lovely. What comfort food?"

He pondered for a moment and then grinned cheekily. "Have you ever had a smorgasbord?"

Yvonne blinked a few times.

"A what?" It sounded familiar to her but she couldn't one hundred percent say yes to what it was.

"A smorgasbord is one of my comfort meals. It's what memories are made of," Hyouko explained, as if he was in one of his memories. "I remember loving smorgasbord , especially as a child."

Yvonne didn't need to hear anymore.

"Yes! Let's have a smorgasbord." She was enthusiastic due to the way he was reminiscing his memories.

They walked into the city as the sun set along the horizon, kissing the Earth's skin with a milky, saturated orange and black ombre. Fall had begun to get chilly, so Yvonne donned a heavy cotton trench coat in a soft grey tint. She didn't have time to do her hair up, and quite honestly forgot to. Hyouko stared at her long locks of sleek hair. It wasn't usual for her to have her hair so relaxed and her attire so casual. The only thing that was classic was the coat. She didn't even think to change out of her indoor clothes, wearing only a cotton tee and sweatpants. Yvonne's mind was too preoccupied and stirring with thoughts. Hyouko enjoyed seeing her in a more intimate way, the clothes not too structured, her hair loosely blowing in the wind, and her eyes deep in thought. The sun kissed her face with a gentle glow as though she was in a renaissance painting. It

404

was cinematic the way the leaves blew past her face and slid onto the floor. The tones were perfect for a romantic to propose or do some great gesture.

"Have you thought of what you wanted to eat?" Hyouko broke the silence, wanting to hear her voice and garner her attention.

"Oh, sorry, right," Yvonne replied, coming back to reality. "How do burgers sound? This type of weather calls for something fatty and comforting. I'm not sure how we could do a smorgasbord, besides, it'll be simpler and more accessible to just get food in just one shop."

Hyouko beamed in excitement.

"You're totally right, but I think we can grab a couple snacks along the way- our own make-shift smorgasbord!"

There was a moment of melancholy again. It wasn't a sad moment at all, but rather a moment of touching souls and comfort that Yvonne was desperately trying to grasp onto in fear of it leaving again.

Luckily, there was a burger joint nearby that had been serving burgers for as long as she could remember. It wasn't often that she indulged in a burger, only because it was something to be enjoyed socially, not alone. The place was a little run down with grease stains running up and down the tile walls. As soon as they got near, they could smell the oozing juices that spilled from the patties. Homemade patties were stacked to be displayed before they were cooked. A team of three cooks and one cashier worked tirelessly to provide the juicy bundles of food that would be ravished by loyal customers. It was clear that their profits weren't put towards decorating or renovating the place, but rather to keep up with costs of ingredients and employment. That's how people knew their food was good and not just a sham.

"What are you going to get?" Hyouko's stomach began to rumble. He'd tried hiding his hunger as best as he could up to that point.

Yvonne felt a little bad for making him this hungry.

"Leave it to me. My treat," she said, hurriedly placing her order in for the both of them.

It was irresistible. They had to take a few bites and walk to get them through to the next stop. Yvonne agreed with Hyouko that they needed to get some snacks and drinks before making it back to her place. A local convenience store was on the way back and they quickly bought some gummies and chocolates along with two beverages. This time, they decided not to have alcoholic drinks and stay sober.

"Don't tell me you like chocolate covered raisins," Yvonne gawked as Hyouko placed the little box onto the counter.

"Hey, don't judge me! They have a bad rep but taste so good, like childhood!" he defended his choice of bonbons and handed some cash to the register. Yvonne chose chocolate covered wafers and sour gummies.

"Why do you like them?" Yvonne asked as they exited the store. Hyouko opened the box and rattled some out onto his hand. He picked one up and slowly pressed it into her mouth. His thumb rested on her lips and she accepted the covered delicacy. His thumb was warm yet somewhat tough. He retracted his hand and watched her chew into the treat while popping a few into his own mouth. Yvonne didn't really like the taste of raisins mixed with chocolate but still gave it a chance as the raisin slowly mushed in her mouth along with the cacao taste. Gritty, yet sweet.

"Now imagine," Hyouko said, closing his eyes, "your mom brings a box of these home. She works hard for her money but can only afford this box once a month. It costs only a couple dollars, but for a mother that barely makes ends meet, it meant a lot." Yvonne listened carefully. It began to resonate with her as Hyouko continued. "The kid she brings this box to always beams and cheers with joy whenever they hear the rattle of the box behind the mother's back. It was the only sweet thing they would get every so often after days and weeks of bland food. Significantly different from what they'd eat on the daily, the raisin would mash into the chocolate, creating a symphony of jubilation in their mouth." Hyouko made eye contact with Yvonne. "That's why I love these little chocolate covered raisins."

Yvonne stayed silent for a moment to absorb all of the imagery and feel.

"May I have one more?" she asked sheepishly.

Hyouko's eyes twinkled as he reached into the bag to retrieve the goods.

It only took a few more minutes before they reached her apartment again. As they got inside, Yvonne couldn't refrain from going in for a kiss. Hyouko was surprised but accepted this initiation. She nervously smashed her lips into his. His smile could be felt under her kiss, and he took over and went in deeper. He dropped all the bags to the floor and held her body tightly against his, one hand on her waist and the other holding her head. He kissed passionately. The tempo started slowly but gradually increased as he became more and more excited. Yvonne could feel how much bigger his body was compared to hers. His arms were thick and muscular, and his face loomed over hers as his body covered her whole silhouette like a wall. Yvonne's knees buckled, but that didn't stop him from caressing her lips. He held the weight of her body effortlessly, while she became more and more undone. She gasped for air as he momentarily released the kiss to take in her expression. Hyouko could barely control himself seeing her hair in a mess, her face flushed, eyes watering, and her clothing so plush and dishevelled. Yvonne's expression cried for more. More, more, more of what? Yvonne wasn't even sure what more she wanted. It would seem haphazard if a more intimate action were to start. She didn't want Hyouko to think she was easy with men, but she desperately wanted to feel more.

"You're being too honest," Hyouko said in a low voice. It vibrated in her ear, causing warmth to grow in her body. "But not now."

Yvonne was a little surprised yet disappointed and relieved—a plethora of emotions. She awkwardly nodded while fixing her hair.

Hyouko caressed her face and gave a pained smile which Yvonne couldn't decode.

"Let's dig in, shall we?" he said in a normal voice, unpacking the burgers and fries onto the coffee table. It was alarming how nonchalant he was after that heated moment. Yvonne stumbled towards the smorgasbord and sat across from him in a trance.

"Yvonne!"

A yell could be heard from the outside. Yvonne and Hyouko exchanged confused looks. The voice yelled out her name once more and Yvonne instantly recognised it. It was Luther. Yvonne scrambled to her feet and opened her balcony to see Luther standing on the cobblestone pathway, staring up at her. He waved and bore a smile, a single rose in his hand. It was delicately wrapped in cellophane, bright red pigment encapsulated in every petal. Yvonne's heart jumped to her throat.

"Who is it?" Hyouko asked, walking towards the balcony to peer over the edge. As soon as he saw who it was, he grimaced. Luther gave a disheartened look. Yvonne could barely see his expression but his body language slowly became defensive and unmotivated. The air seemed to steal Yvonne's breath as she struggled to form words.

"Hey, Luther, right? What brings you here?" Hyouko hollered back firmly. His arm wrapped around Yvonne's waist, bringing her closer.

Luther winced as if he was hit by a rock. The rose hung upside down, hitting his knee, rose petals falling off the stem.

"Luther, did you need something?" Yvonne managed to ask, feeling stiff and uncomfortable with the whole situation. Hyouko examined Yvonne's distraught expression.

"I need to talk to you," Luther said, scowling at Hyouko.

Yvonne looked up at Hyouko as if to ask for permission. Hyouko let go of her waist and shrugged.

"Just stay here for a minute, okay?" Yvonne said, quickly leaving her apartment to speak with Luther.

"What are you doing here?" Yvonne was frantic and embarrassed. She hated the tense situation and it seemed like a habit Luther was putting her into.

"Don't be with him. Be with me," Luther blurted, going in to grab her shoulders. Yvonne dodged his grasp and he retracted.

"What are you doing?" Yvonne gasped. She held her arms tight to her body in a defensive manner.

"He's not right for you, I am," Luther desperately pleaded. It was unbecoming of him to see him in this way. If anyone had said Luther acted this way, no one would've believed it. Something about Yvonne drove Luther crazy and it pained him to see her swept away by someone else.

"He's a waiter, for God's sake, Yvonne," he argued, becoming more confident in his case. "He can't support your needs and wants. How do you know he'll be there in a time of need?"

Yvonne gave him a warning look.

"Don't over step here, Luther. I don't know what made you think it's okay for you to barge into my private life and tell me what I need and want, but you better straighten up." Yvonne didn't take shit from any man. She absolutely hated being minimised and treated like some incapable woman. Luther looked up towards the balcony again, where Hyouko stared down. Luther felt inferior to him and it irritated him further.

"I would do anything for you, Yvonne. Anything." His gaze fell to the ground as if he knew he wasn't going to win this fight. "I'll be waiting for you." He handed her the rose, in which she declined, pushing it back towards him.

"Go home, Luther," Yvonne sternly worded, concerned about how their work relationship would be after this. She was exasperated and squeezed her eyes with her fingers.

"I know I'm meant to be with you," he conveyed, before turning around and leaving with his head hung low.

Yvonne couldn't comprehend why Luther was so keen on being with her. It wasn't even like they shared many memories or saw each other outside of work. She felt almost disturbed thinking about the time they went to get drinks and she was nearly swooned by his actions and words. Yvonne shook her head and got herself together before heading back up to Hyouko.

"I should probably get going; late night," Hyouko said softly, holding Yvonne's hand.

"Wait, I'm sorry." She didn't want to lose Hyouko and didn't want him to think anything bad about her.

Hyouko shook his head and smiled.

"Don't worry, I know." He carefully raised her hand to his lips and planted a loving kiss on it.

Yvonne felt disheartened but couldn't be needy and cry for more time with him.

"When will I see you again?" Yvonne asked.

Hyouko burst into a small laugh.

"Eager, are we?" he teased and lightly pinched her cheek. "Don't worry, I can't stay away from you for too long." His eyes were filled with a concoction of yearning and sadness, something Yvonne couldn't help but feel guilty for. It must've been the fact that Luther was threatening Hyouko's interest.

She wasn't satisfied by that answer but let him go off into the night. Yvonne watched him get swallowed into the dark as he walked further and further away into the distance.

The burgers laid messily on the coffee table, half finished.

# Chapter 7

*St. Sylke has been absent from their usual routine.*

*J.J. Cruz*

*Hemlock and St. Sylke have been conversing a lot. Are they in cahoots?*

*J.J. Cruz*

*St. Sylke has mentioned they are leaving for vacation. I have investigated and noted that they are staying within the city. They are telling coworkers otherwise. Will tag along with them.*

*Hemlock has notably been acting suspicious. They ask lots of personal questions about me and St. Sylke. St. Sylke has brought a new filing cabinet with a lock in place. If I can get those keys, I may be able to pick the lock and see what's inside.*

*J.J. Cruz*

Yvonne studied the new information that had come in the past couple of days. Things had begun to pick up. Mackie reported of more funds being extracted, as well as little 'pranks' and mementos left in the system. The sum of how much had been taken rose from

$85,000 to $138,000 very quickly. It was alarming and Kersa had started pressing them harder to get the case cracked. Yvonne was losing track of time as each report came through. Revising the plans and searching through databases made her head spin, giving her anxiety. It was clear at this point that St. Sylke seemed to be the main suspect and the only one that had stood out. J.J. hadn't disclosed what position St. Sylke was in the company, so Yvonne stopped looking at the employees, as it made no difference. When the time was right, she'd be notified and could close off that tie. All Yvonne could do at this point was add extra authentication steps, as well as having a constantly secure network and employees. In theory, it was simple, but this case was somehow eluding them all. Training all employees was one thing, but having everyone abide was another. Phishing and spyware were common leak holes that allowed data breaches to occur. Again, a huge part of this happening was the sudden influx of success and employees being hired. In the end, the company probably lost more money than they had gained from their success. If they were more careful and logical, a massive continuing loss like this could've been prevented. Companies were often targeted based on their success, system, and vulnerability. The most common targets that Yvonne had seen were those that hired many elderly people that refused to go through internet training and protocols, and those that didn't fund their cyber security team appropriately. Yvonne couldn't imagine the amount of stress and responsibility J.J. had. Being the sole investigator in this case, as well as the main source of progress, would be incredibly demanding.

*Luther: 9:45 a.m. Hey, want to go grab a coffee?*

It was tiresome that Luther was still being persistent. Yvonne knew he had ulterior motives and that it wasn't just a friendly coffee.

*Yvonne: 9:45 a.m. I thought you'd catch on. Please don't be so persistent.*

404

Although Hyouko and Yvonne hadn't established the nature of their relationship yet, it was clear that Yvonne wanted to stay exclusive to Hyouko. It sunk in that she never knew what Hyouko was thinking. Did he want the same? Or did he think this was still casual? As much as she wanted to ask him right then and there, she resisted. Yvonne hated feeling like she was at the mercy of another person, but really wanted to know exactly what he thought.

*Yvonne: 9:47 a.m. Hyouko, are you busy? Did you want to meet tonight?*

Hyouko had been silent for the past couple days, only sending a brief hello, good morning, or good night. Yvonne gave the benefit of the doubt that he was busy and preoccupied with life. It was a valid assumption, and not one she could be mad about, especially when she was busy with work as well. It was a shame that Luther and Yvonne's relationship had gotten so complicated. Yvonne sorely needed a coffee.

Yvonne felt alive wearing such fashionable clothing. She'd grown tired of wearing sweatpants and tees and threw on a knitted baby blue pencil skirt with a small slit up the back seam, a cream bustier top in luxurious cashmere, complimented with a grey wool cardigan that went just above the knees. Her favourite part of the outfit were the shoes. She wore cream kitten pumps with a tie back accent. It looked stunning and the colours meshed together perfectly. It truly made her day. Even though it was the middle of fall, the day seemed to be cheerful and bright with only a light breeze. Yvonne counted herself lucky since she didn't have to cover her legs at all. Making her way to the coffee shop Blake worked at was easy. Yvonne took in the dewy, brisk air, the fashion of others who rumbled along, and the trees that waved in harmony with the breeze. She wished Hyouko would walk with her under such a beautiful landscape and view, giving a cheery smile like he usually would. There was no sense daydreaming about him. It made Yvonne desire him more. The yarrow entrance was soon in sight, and Yvonne became distracted with the thought of coffee.

"I almost thought you died!" Blake's voice reached Yvonne as soon as they saw her.

Yvonne chuckled and gave a quick wave.

"No, just busy! How have you been?"

Blake shrugged while drying the cups they had just washed.

"Oh, you know, milk, coffee, sugar, and all. People love their beverages during the fall and winter seasons." Blake leaned over the counter, face-to-face with Yvonne. "So, what can I get fer ya?"

It was pleasant to have such a casual, warm, and friendly person to interact with. Yvonne looked up at the menu where a list of new drinks had been scribbled onto the chalkboard.

"What's the, uh, Mulberry Express?" It sounded intriguing and Yvonne felt adventurous.

"You've got good taste, Yvonne. I knew I liked you for some reason!" They snapped their fingers and gave a wink before spinning around to prepare. Almost instantly, a wave of mulberry engraved itself in the shop, along with a stream of dark espresso scent. It was fascinating to see and experience the artistry Blake had with coffee. They lightly shook the mixture, spritzed peppermint concentrate, and coated the cup with white chocolate sauce before pouring the drink in.

"Allow your taste buds to be blown away." Blake smoothly passed the cup to Yvonne as the peppermint filled her nostrils.

It was refreshing, a mixture of tart, sweet mulberry, and the sprinkle of peppermint. The white chocolate balanced out the tartness and coated her tongue with a layer that protected it from the spikey essence of the mulberry.

"You've done it again," Yvonne declared, gleefully smiling as she gripped the cup. Blake gave another wink, acknowledging their talent.

"Hey! Welcome, what can I get started for you?"

Yvonne glanced over her shoulder, and her heart dropped. Luther. What were the chances?

"Yvonne?" Luther seemed just as surprised.

Yvonne felt unbearably awkward, especially after the text from earlier. She gave a forced smile with no teeth.

"Oh hi, Luther," Yvonne began.

"Well, while you're here, why don't we take a moment to chat?" he interjected, afraid of letting Yvonne slip through his fingers again.

Blake gave a bewildered look and slowly turned around, pretending to be preoccupied.

"Let me just order first," Luther continued. "Hey sorry, can I get a chestnut macchiato?"

Blake spun around in a dramatic way. "Right on, you got it boss!"

Yvonne snickered a little bit. It was humorous and she knew Blake had an obvious discomfort for tense situations just based on the couple interactions they'd had. Luther pulled a chair across from Yvonne and sat down, taking off his navy blue wool trench coat and hanging it on the back of his chair. Yvonne noticed his outfit and gave credit for his fashion choice. He wore a merino sweater in a gentle shade of oatmeal, along with his usual black dress pants.

"Oh, you like this?" He tugged on the sweater while smiling. "I'll wear this stuff more often."

Yvonne quickly shook her head and tried to profusely deny it.

"Anyway," Luther was in a better mood after taking notice of her admiration, "I think you should really reconsider. Why don't we try?"

Yvonne glared at him. Blake tip-toed in between the two and quickly sat Luther's drink in front of him.

"Your order, sir," Blake whispered, then slowly walked backwards to their base.

Yvonne gave an awkward smile to Blake, who raised their eyebrows in response. "Luther, really. I really am not interested." She had her heart and mind set with Hyouko. He seemed like everything she wanted and needed so far to start a relationship.

"What's so good about Hyouko anyway? I can take care of you just as well as he could—no, even better."

Yvonne sighed. She clasped her drink, interlocking her fingers and tapping her thumbs on the lid.

"It's not like I didn't consider it, but you are too rogue. And besides, you acted like I owed you something, getting defensive and possessive over me when we weren't even a thing."

"I got ahead of myself, I'll admit. I just didn't want you to slip away from me." He inched closer to the middle of the table, attempting to get closer to Yvonne.

"Sorry Luther, but right now, Hyouko is who I want to be with." Yvonne looked up at him, staring into his hopeful eyes. He slowly lowered his view, accepting the reality. Luther grabbed and squeezed her hand firmly.

"I will be here, waiting for you to give me another chance." It was the first time Luther had ever pleaded this much for a woman to take a chance on him. He got along with the ladies just fine and Yvonne knew that.

"You'll be fine, don't hold your breath."

"Yvonne?" Hyouko grabbed Yvonne's hand out of Luther's and pulled her towards him.

"Hyouko?" Yvonne was frazzled. Where had he come from? Hyouko's eyes loomed with jealousy. Haruka was just a few steps behind him, watching the situation unfold.

"Oh, hey Luther!" Haruka exclaimed. She wasn't oblivious to the obvious tensity in the air, but rather wanted to simmer the situation down.

"Hey," he replied. "I am leaving now, but that's all I wanted to say."

Hyouko's eyes followed him as Luther left the cafe, squinting as he descended further away.

"Haruka, Hyouko! What brought you here?" Yvonne's hand was getting slightly suffocated due to the grip strength Hyouko had on her, but she wasn't sure how to get out of it. Hyouko noticed how hard he was holding her hand after a couple seconds and released it.

"Yvonne, sorry," he said sincerely.

"We were strolling by and thought to see what's up and about here! It's a weird coincidence that you and Luther were here," Haruka responded as she looked over the menu options.

"What were you doing here?" Hyouko asked Yvonne, not breaking eye contact with her.

She tried looking away as if she was guilty.

"I came by to get a coffee but Luther coincidentally came in after me." Yvonne was telling the truth, but her avoidant eye contact made it seem otherwise.

Hyouko stayed silent for a moment before holding Yvonne's arm and pulling her in for a hug.

"Whoa," Yvonne began. "What's this?" She didn't know how to react. He must've felt jealous.

"Are you free?" Hyouko's lips brushed against her ear as he hugged her. She could smell his sweat off his neck and chest area, and Yvonne found it somehow arousing.

"Get a room!" Haruka yelled from the cashier. She was disturbed by this public display of affection. Blake snickered in the background, almost in agreement.

"I can make time," Yvonne said a little too eagerly. "I mean, if you want."

Hyouko released the hug, still holding her shoulders, and smiled.

"Can we go back to your place for a bit?"

Yvonne examined Hyouko's body language. He was obviously still on guard about Luther, and was being more intimate out of jealousy. It was a good time for them to talk about their situation, so Yvonne nodded and agreed to go back.

"Haruka, I'll be right back," Hyouko said aloud. He wrapped his arm around Yvonne's waist as he guided her to the exit.

"Sure you will. Don't bother coming back here, I am not waiting!" She rolled her eyes as she took a sip of her drink.

Hyouko seemed out of character. He was silent and had a stern face he had tried to mask by giving a feeble smile. His hand was still riveted to her waist as they entered her apartment.

"Everything okay?" Yvonne asked, putting her hand on his forearm. Her eyes glimmered in the overhead lighting, concerned, worried. Admittedly, she felt a bit of angst seeing Haruka and Hyouko together again, but she put her feelings aside for a moment.

"Of course, now that I'm with you." Hyouko grabbed her hand and rubbed his face on it as if to comfort himself. She grinned and cupped his face. He seemed to relax a bit and let a deep sigh out.

"Let me make you some coffee," Yvonne chimed, spinning around to fix him a drink. There was only the sound of grinding coffee beans and aromatics that hung in the air for a while. The spoon tinkled as she stirred the coffee and condensed milk.

"Iced or hot?" Yvonne asked, glancing over to see Hyouko sitting on the couch in front of the fireplace.

"Hot is fine," he said absentmindedly. His eyes wandered around her complex, then out the window. Yvonne pulled out a coaster and placed it on the table.

"It's probably too hot for you right now," she said, placing her hand over top of his. "Drink it whenever you feel like it." He smiled and pinched her cheek lightly.

"You're too sweet, thank you." He brought his body closer to hers and embraced her with a tight hug. His structure was comforting and substantial compared to Yvonne's. She wrapped her arms around his neck, catching wafts of his scent. She closed her eyes momentarily to envelope herself in comfort.

"Sorry, I really needed that," he said, pulling away slightly to see Yvonne's face. Her eyes were half lidded, coming out of that space.

"Don't apologise, I think I did too." Yvonne's stomach felt heavy and her heart slowly pounded. It reminded her of the days she would spend watching the rain from her window, curled up in a blanket, alone listening to music. It made her nostalgic, and she hated it as much as she loved it.

"To be honest, I think something came over me when I saw you with Luther." Hyouko stared into Yvonne's eyes, desperate for her connection. She reciprocated and shook her head.

"I promise you, it was a coincidence. I honestly was telling him how I wanted to be with…you." Her voice faltered. She didn't want to seem needy or desperate and was afraid of deterring him. His eyes brightened up, but saw that she felt vulnerable.

"Me too," he whispered, bringing her in closer. He led her to lay down on him on the couch, in which she hesitantly complied. She could feel his heart beating, and his breath inhaling and exhaling. Subconsciously, she began following his pattern. Being in Hyouko's arms made her feel protected and invisible somehow. She felt childish thinking that, and wanted to push away from the feeling, but felt herself giving into the warmth.

The night sky had set into the room, like a siren that had capsized a boat. It was whimsical and daunting, being in a different atmosphere. Yvonne woke up abruptly on the couch, Hyouko still under her. The coffee laid cold on the table, only a couple sips taken from it. The room was dark and only illuminated by the night sky. She stared at Hyouko's resting face, calm and winsome. His eyes fluttered open, feeling Yvonne move about on him.

"Sorry, I didn't mean to wake you," she said gently, coming back down to rest her head on his chest. He pulled her into a firm hug.

"Stop apologising." His breath heated the top of her head, voice reverberating. "I wish I could stay like this forever."

Yvonne peered at him. His eyes were closed again as he slowly rubbed her back.

"Why can't you?" Her hands rested on his chest, watching it go up and down with his breathing. She could barely see his face in the dark, but could see he'd opened his eyes again to stare at the ceiling.

"Don't be silly." He pinched her cheek. "We have work!" He supported her back up to a sitting position and stretched himself. "Good god am I stiff."

Yvonne blushed red.

"I'm so sorry!" She massaged his shoulders desperately to help his cause. He chuckled and reassured her it was okay.

"If I had to do it again, I'd do it a million times." He clung onto her hand and gave it a peck, something Yvonne began to love and yearn for. Her lips pursed as she thought about seeing Haruka and Hyouko together so often.

"What's wrong?" Hyouko noticed her tense expression and guided her chin up so that her eyes met his.

"It's just…" Yvonne took a deep breath, knowing how frustrating it was for her to seem like such a simpleton, like such an insecure woman. "You and Haruka…"

Hyouko gave a worried look.

"Hey, please don't worry about anything between me and Haruka. She's just my co-worker, there's nothing between us. I'm sorry if I made you feel jealous or anything like that."

Yvonne felt the earnest emotion through his words and grip. She relaxed a bit, letting the tension from her shoulders and chest drop considerably.

"Sorry, you must think I'm stupid." Yvonne shied away from his gaze, cursing herself in her head.

"No, don't say that. You are valid for having those thoughts. I will give you all the reassurance you need."

Hyouko held her hands tightly and gave them a smothering kiss, deep and tender.

"I'm all yours."

# Chapter 8

Had it been only once, Yvonne wouldn't have thought anything of it. This was the second time a cryptic message had been left for her to open. It was a single page filled with timestamps and amounts of money next to it. At the end, it was tagged *Weeping Widow.* At this point, Yvonne found it peculiar and reached out to Kersa, asking to meet.

"Weeping Widow?" Her finger tapped the cigarette stump. Kersa's breath smelled rancid, but Yvonne tried to cover her disgust by sipping her tonka bean coffee. It was colder out, especially since it was the morning. The dew was more like frozen droplets alongside some fog. Kersa dressed in black slacks, a white dress shirt, and a black blazer with pointed toe mules. Yvonne shuddered thinking how cold Kersa must be. Afterall, Yvonne had bundled up with a cashmere scarf and a long wool trench coat, and even then, she was chilly. They met at a local park with older buildings around. It was early in the morning and uncommon that others would be bustling around. There were a handful of people doing their daily exercise regimes and others passing by, but nothing that raised concern.

"It's been twice now," Yvonne stated, giving quick glances to her left and right.

Kersa took another puff of smoke before responding.

"Does anyone else know?"

Yvonne grew concerned. "What do you mean? Isn't this from Vos or someone like that?"

Kersa shook her head. She threw the stub onto the ground and crushed it under her foot.

"Vos doesn't send letters." Her eyes met Yvonne's, studying her expression.

Yvonne became a bit panicked, wondering if the letters came from somewhere else. It had to be related to the case, as the recent mail had the exact numbers matching the losses from Tamocus.

"Does anyone else know?" Kersa repeated in a gruffer tone.

"No," Yvonne replied quickly.

"I think someone is trying to set you up," she sighed as she watched the thick fog move with the way of the wind. "I know you aren't part of it."

Yvonne covered her mouth, gaping at that statement.

"How do you know?" Yvonne didn't want to sound suspicious at all, but was surprised Kersa had so much faith in her.

"Only an idiot would bring it to my attention. You clearly don't have any idea what those notes really mean, not to mention if you were part of it, you'd keep it hush hush."

Yvonne looked down at the pavement, at a loss for words. It was great that Kersa had belief that she wasn't a part of the extortion, but on the other hand, someone was trying to frame her.

"It's slow, isn't it?" She lit another cigarette, flipping her zippo with a satisfying click.

"What is?"

"The case." She blew a bog of smoke out like a cumulus cloud. "It's been too slow."

Yvonne pondered for a moment. It was true. It was too slow, and nothing had really developed since she'd joined.

"Are you suggesting...?" Yvonne began, thinking the worst possible scenario.

Kersa merely nodded while spewing more strains of smoke out. "Yeah."

*Cherise: 1:03 p.m. Yvonne! Halloween party tomorrow. 7P.M Be there or be square.*

Halloween was the last of Yvonne's concerns. Great anxiety built within her, unforgivably shaking her to her very core. It was hard to think of anything else knowing that someone was trying to frame her. She frantically checked under her prison style storage unit and retrieved the portfolio. It was gaining too much weight and needed to be rehomed. Yvonne hastily took out the two cryptic messages and studied them profusely. There wasn't much she could gather from it other than what was in front of her. She sealed them in a manila envelope and tucked it into a book on her shelf. Yvonne grinned slightly at the book she'd picked up. Although melancholy, it was a book she'd adored growing up and vastly credited it for her deepest emotions. Unrequited love and longing, fostering eternal emptiness and yielding confessions. It was the type of book one hated loving. Yvonne stuffed the portfolio in a lazy susan cabinet and promptly closed it. Imagine if someone went into her kitchen looking for some spices and found a whole portfolio instead. Yvonne chuckled to herself, thinking how crazy she would seem to someone.

*Luther: 1:16 p.m. Pick you up at 6:30 tomorrow? Just friends.*

Yvonne was relieved to hear from Luther in a friendly way. She needed a distraction from all that was going on but also didn't want to lose touch of the situation at hand.

*Yvonne: 1:17 p.m. Maybe.*

*Luther: 1:17 p.m. Come on, have some fun, let loose.*

She sighed and rubbed her face, stressed, indeed.

*Luther: 1:18 p.m. Don't forget to wear a costume.*

A costume? Yvonne hadn't had time to even think of a costume. If she wanted to, she could whip up something and get a makeshift costume together, though.

*Yvonne: 1:19 p.m. Alright, 6:30 tomorrow. I'll wear a costume.*

*Luther: 1:19 p.m. Sounds like a plan! See you then~*

After some scavenging, Yvonne was able to find her old witch hat that she could pair with some clothes she already owned. She didn't have black lipstick but didn't think it was really necessary to go buy one. Hyouko seemed busy after the last time they saw each other. It seemed like a pattern that he would kind of disappear and reappear. It was like he never had time except for random splotches at any given moment. Yvonne honestly felt a bit crestfallen with the reality.

*Yvonne: 1:23 p.m. Miss you*

The heart indeed did grow fonder with space and time between them. It wasn't like she expected him to respond right away, if at all, but she really did want to let him know she was thinking of him.

*Hyouko: 1:26 p.m. Miss you more*

It was enough for Yvonne to cling onto, making her day that much better.

"Say cheese!"

Yvonne was caught off guard and had an awkward smile on her face at the time the picture was taken. Luther laughed when he saw what was captured on his phone.

"Not fair, you caught me off guard," Yvonne begrudgingly said as she fixed her hat. Luther had decided to dress up as a vampire and donned a satin black cape with a red accent underneath. He'd applied fake fangs to his teeth and wore red contacts—the whole nine yards. His hair was slicked back with just a little fringe framing his face. He wore a monkey suit style get up and had derby shoes on. It was a classic vampire outfit, and it suited him quite well. Singed orange and brown leaves cascaded through the breeze, matching the sundown that embraced the curvature of the horizon. With a blood orange color, it saturated the town in a spooky hue. It started to get slightly darker by 6:30 as the rustic color set in.

"You look cute," Luther said as he viewed the photo he had just taken. He had a half smile on his face, seeing her bewildered expression caught on camera. Her hat was uneven on her crown and her eyes were wider than usual, lips slightly apart. The dress she wore messily blew in the wind, causing a ghost effect in the photo. Even still, she was beautiful.

"I'm sending this to you," Luther said, waving his phone above his shoulder as if to tease her.

"Oh god," she said exasperatedly. The last thing she needed on her mind was an unsightly photo of herself.

"Where's your big wart? I thought witches have those on their noses." It was obvious Luther was trying to tease her, and it really made Yvonne feel more relaxed knowing that their acquaintanceship could be restored.

"Oh, please." Yvonne laughed. "As if anyone would actually want to have that on their face at a Halloween office party." They snickered between themselves for a moment in the nippy autumn air.

"Come on, let's go." Luther opened the car door for Yvonne like the gentleman he was. She virtuously stepped into the car, accidentally hitting her cork platform shoes against the inside.

"I'm so sorry!" she exclaimed, trying to rub off the residue that was plastered on the interior.

"Don't worry! Please don't worry." He said it in such a reassuring way, Yvonne slowly stopped her silly task. Luther went around the car to get into the front seat, still presenting a warm smile to her.

It was charming and befitting of him, and made him look like a stereotypical vampire you dream about in fantasies.

*Hyouko: 6:45 p.m. Happy Halloween! What are your plans?*

"Who's that?" Luther still had his eyes on the road but heard the ding on her phone.

"Hyouko." Yvonne attached a picture to the text and sent it off. It wasn't as bad as she thought and she hoped for a picture back. Maybe he was dressed up at the ramen shop in a costume as well?

*Yvonne: 6:46 p.m. Going to office party! How bout u?*
*(1 Attachment)*

Luther was quiet for the rest of the ride to the party; not that it was a long drive, but a sadness plainly hung from the air.

*Hyouko: 6:57 p.m. You look gorgeous. I'm having a work party as well! Lookie me (1 Attachment)*

Yvonne had to catch her breath when she saw Hyouko dressed up for Halloween. A masquerade mask brilliantly illuminated her screen. Decorated with silk details, sequins, and an etched design, the mask fit his face perfectly. Only his mouth and one side of his face could be seen in the midst of everything. At the edges of the photo, she could see he was wearing a real proper suit and tie costume as though it was right out of the eighteen hundreds. Her core tightened a bit, feeling an extreme attraction to this masked get up.

"We're here!" Luther said. He unbuckled himself and jogged around the car to open Yvonne's door.

"You don't have to do that..." Yvonne mumbled, exiting the car shyly. Luther just gave a slight disapproving gesture and offered his arm out.

"What's this for?" Yvonne curiously looked at his braced arm, awaiting her attachment.

"Shouldn't a gentleman always offer his assistance to a lady?" He stuck his tongue out and nudged her instead. Yvonne rolled her eyes and flattened her skirt out, making sure everything was even.

"Your babydoll dress is to *die* for!" Cherise said as she excitedly skittered toward Yvonne, arms open for her embrace. Yvonne lightly wrapped her arms around Cherise.

"Your costume is amazing, too!" Yvonne said cheerily. "A little scary though." She stared at the blood stains exuding from the corner of Cherise's mouth, and the white contacts that clung to her eyes.

"A ghost?" Luther guessed as he examined Cherise closely.

"Bingo bango!" Cherise gave a friendly slap to Luther's back. He coughed into his fist.

"Let's head in! There's a buffet of random foods and appetisers, and of course boooooooze," Cherise emphasised.

It was bustling with noise inside the hotel's rented party rooms. Their company could afford more luxurious venues and this was one of them. The high rise ceilings were embellished with crystal lighting and chandelier fixtures, while elegantly designed moulding and millwork traced the vicinity, manifesting extravagance throughout. It was a lower lighting that filled the room, allowing mystery and zeal to permeate each individual. Yvonne and Luther followed Cherise through the crowd, giving their salutations. A few held Luther up like a flock of birds. He truly looked handsome in his costume and the women were hungry tigers ready to pounce. Cherise and Yvonne mingled with a few of their mutuals and eventually dispersed to wander off.

*Yvonne: 7:30 p.m. How's your party?*

She wasn't sure if she'd get much out of Hyouko, especially if he was also at a gathering. Her stomach grumbled, alerting her to nourish herself. Some hors d'oeuvres were displayed along the back wall, stretching from one side to the other. No one would go home hungry. Yvonne took a plate and began selecting a few to enjoy.

Cucumber with cheese topped with salmon and capers was the first thing she scooped up. Yvonne took up people watching as she grazed the table like a cow.

"Haruka?"

Yvonne had to be mistaken. She walked up to the woman dressed in a baggy white gown with long jet black hair swaying in front of their face.

"Haruka?" Yvonne tapped the woman's shoulder, who jumped in surprise and turned to face Yvonne. Haruka's guise was haste and clumsy.

"Yvonne?" Haruka managed to articulate with the crumbs of a cracker and cheese snack crumbling off her lips. Yvonne spun around, looking at as many people as she could. For the most part, she recognized everyone from her office with a few outliers here and there.

"Wait, why are you here?" Yvonne asked, confused. She had to raise her voice a little due to the volume of the party. Haruka didn't seem to have an answer in mind and flippantly stuttered and shrugged her shoulders.

"Yvonne! You've met my friend before I could even introduce you two!" Cherise jumped in and hugged the two of them, obviously a bit tipsy. Haruka and Yvonne just stared at each other in shock, Cherise catching on. "Wait, don't tell me you guys know each other!" Cherise gasped and glanced between the two.

"Small world isn't it?" Haruka laughed.

Suddenly, Hyouko appeared, but when he caught a glimpse of Yvonne, he froze.

"Hyouko?" Yvonne quickly put herself in front of him. He seemed unprepared for this sudden and shocking revelation and stammered incoherent sounds.

"Oh my gad don't tell me you know him too?!" Cherise said in a drunken voice, flailing her arms around Hyouko and Yvonne.

## 404

"Strangely, yes!" Hyouko spluttered, trying to stabilise himself against the rapid flailing Cherise continued to produce. Yvonne tried to wrap her mind around the situation. Was the world really this small? Not to mention, Hyouko was with Haruka again. Yvonne made an astringent face which Hyouko caught a whiff of right away.

"No, wait," Hyouko began, but Yvonne turned around and headed for some air.

"Let me guess, a witch?"

Yvonne looked over her shoulder to see who was behind the voice. He stood over her, shadowing her body from the light that hummed inside the party. Yvonne had sat herself down on the cement stairs outside the place to get some fresh air, hoping to recuperate. The man wore a halo above his head with frilly feathers waving in the air. He had light blond hair and was covered in a long white robe.

"Daniel?" she said hesitantly. His angelic face was something she couldn't forget from that brief interaction a while back. It made Yvonne cringe remembering how Luther was that night but she quickly brushed it off. Daniel's face lit up, scooting next to her and leaning back to rest his body.

"Good memory." He gave an awkward simper and removed his halo headband. Daniel really looked like an angel even without the get up. The only thing he necessarily added was the halo; all the rest was organic.

"Castor oil."

Yvonne was confused.

"What? Sorry?"

"Secret to my lashes." Daniel closed his eyes to display his long, blond, and wispy eyelashes. Yvonne chortled and nodded.

"Gotta try that out," she replied. "You're friends with Haruka?"

Daniel shrugged. "Yeah, kind of. Hey, you wanna see something cool?" He rustled around the garden that beautifully harboured a variety of flowers. He plucked a pansy and gently rolled it between his fingers. "Eat it."

Yvonne was hesitant.

"Uh…a flower?" She eyed the pansy closely, noticing some flecks of dirt splattered on the petals.

"It's a pansy. It's edible, I promise." Daniel tried to coax her into consuming the flower, in which she solely picked it up and held it in her palm. He let out a hmm and shrugged.

"I didn't know you worked here." Yvonne inspected the flower some more, hues of purple and yellow staining her finger.

"I don't," Daniel replied, looking back at the crowd. "I work at Tamocus."

Yvonne's heart dropped. "Tamocus?"

"Yeah! And before you ask, no we do not sell illegal drugs." Daniel was obviously joking but Yvonne seemed so stiff that he quickly became quiet. "Did I say something wrong?"

Yvonne abruptly shook her head in a frenzy. "No, no, sorry. I mean, you hear rumours and all." She cleared her throat. "So how'd you get in our office party if you work elsewhere?"

Daniel stretched his arms. Light from the lamps outside casted an iridescent glow on his figure and his grey eyes became more prominent and fascinating.

"Cherise is a friend of mine, we met at a party as well! Not too long ago too. Her work is tough, being an analyst and all."

Yvonne gave a hum of agreement. She heard rapid tapping of feet behind her, which piqued both their interests. Hyouko came out of the crowd in a rush. When his eyes met Yvonne's, he gave an exasperated breath and stumbled towards her.

"I was looking all over for you." His face was licked with sweat, even his masquerade mask seemed to perspire. "You didn't even give me a chance to speak."

His attention drew to Daniel and his eyes grew wide, startled.

"Hyouko, don't tell me this is the girl you've been talking about." Daniel gave a more animated face than usual.

"Can we talk privately?" Hyouko begged Yvonne, gripping onto the fabric of her dress like a lost dog. She hesitantly nodded and excused herself from Daniel.

"It was nice chatting!" Daniel exclaimed as he watched the two disappear into the garden.

Even though Hyouko had requested for them to get away and speak privately, there were no words exchanged for a few tedious minutes.

"If you have nothing to say, I'll go," Yvonne remarked, her foot pivoting back towards where they came from. Hyouko held the small of her waist and brought her closer to him. "Yvonne," he said earnestly. "Please let me explain."

Yvonne stared back at him. Even with the mask slightly shadowing his view, she could see his honest expression. "Okay."

He breathed a sigh of relief and softly held her hand, leading her through the floral garden. There were limestone and granite sculptures that lined the pathways, along with shrubs of extravagant flowers and assortments. The garden was obviously well kept and loved for; every petal and leaf looked healthier than anything she'd ever seen before. Like a watercolour painting, the florets procured soft, blushing pallets, while the leaves boldly shone their vibrant green. In the middle of the garden was a quaint fountain that spewed water and slid down the grooves of the sculpture. Hyouko wiped the water off a small portion of the bench that was in front of the fountain and ushered her to take a seat.

"Your sleeve is wet," Yvonne observed, using her pointer and thumb to rub the fabric to determine the level of water that had absorbed into his clothes.

"Rather I get wet than you," he responded, sitting next to Yvonne. "You're probably wondering how or why I'm here, but I'm wondering the same!"

Yvonne flashed a look of intimidation.

"I work here. But I gather you've come here because of Cherise being friends with Haruka, being friends with you, being friends with Daniel."

Hyouko looked lost for words, scoffed, and chuckled. "You hit it on the nose."

It would've been juvenile if Yvonne held that against him. She smiled and faced Hyouko on the bench.

"Are you gonna keep that mask on, you mysterious man?" Her hands grazed the outline of the mask, feeling the heat off his skin.

"I guess I could take it off."

He smirked just a smidge before taking it off, brazen with a small outline of red due to the imprint it gave him. Hyouko tidied his hair and swished his fringe out of his face. Yvonne assisted him by tucking it behind his ear.

"There's the handsome man I know." She grinned ear to ear, petting his head.

"I take it you're not mad anymore?" Hyouko inquired, going into the movements of her hand and accepting her affection.

"I got tired of being mad," she teased. "It's a small world, isn't it?"

Hyouko nodded in agreement and gripped her forearm, gesturing for her to stop. They stared into each other's eyes, exchanging loving looks. Yvonne didn't enjoy feeling such aggravating emotions but didn't want to just leave everything as it was. She couldn't ignore her feelings, especially when they came off so strong for Hyouko. He was tender and kind. He was someone she'd go through thorn bushes for.

"Did I ever tell you how beautiful your eyes are?" Yvonne rubbed his cheek with her thumb, giving it a little pinch before letting go.

"Did I ever tell you how beautiful your soul is?" Hyouko replied, holding her hand with both of his. He leaned his cheek into their hands and gave it a sweet moment of warmth.

"And what is my soul?" Yvonne cheekily asked, giving him a stink eye.

"Like a sophisticated rabbit."

Yvonne was taken aback by that response. She tilted her head, confused.

"A sophisticated rabbit?" She laughed, smacking his knee. "What does that even mean?"

Hyouko gave a look at her shoes and outfit.

"You're like that rabbit from *Alice in Wonderland*. Monocle and all."

He was just teasingly making fun of her, and she knew that.

"Jokes on you, I like *Alice in Wonderland*. So thank you."

There was a loud rustling behind the two, and they whipped around to see the cause of the commotion.

"Yvonne!"

It was Luther. His voice became louder the closer he got, but he didn't say much more when he saw her sitting next to Hyouko. His expression became unreadable as he just stood at the other side of the fountain. The splashes of water hitting each other could be heard clear as day.

"Are you guys gonna go back to the party?" He placed his hand on his hip and gave a thumb towards the vicinity.

"Oh, yes, we'll be there in a minute," Hyouko answered. He gathered his mask and placed it back on his face.

"I think Cherise is looking for you, Yvonne," Luther continued.

Her ears perked up. "What? Is she okay?" She was concerned, especially at the state she'd left Cherise in. Yvonne shot up from the bench and pulled Hyouko's arm up, encouraging him to go with her. Hyouko got up, holding each side of Yvonne's waist from beside her.

"Yeah, I think she's fine. One too many lemon drops, I think." Luther turned around and began walking back to the party.

When the three of them emerged from the crowd to meet up with Cherise, she was surrounded by Daniel and Haruka as well. Cherise was flushed in the face due to the alcohol. Even with her pale makeup, the rosie flush radiated through it all. At this point, her eye makeup was melting down her face, creating an even more horrific scene.

"What happened to you?" Yvonne was baffled by the state Cherise was in. Cherise whined and grumbled.

"Alcohol. Too many, I think." There was a hiccup between her words, and a few people were watching them. Yvonne felt safer knowing Cherise was being watched and taken care of by some mutual friends. It would've been a whole other problem if she was swept up by some drunken guy. Yvonne retrieved a cup of water for Cherise and stroked her back as she clumsily chugged it down. Water spilled onto her face and chest, allowing dribbles of water to make its home on the floor.

"Cherise, I think we should take you home..." Yvonne was concerned and gave acknowledging looks to Daniel and Haruka. They nodded in agreement and assisted her by hoisting Cherise onto her feet and walking her to Luther's car.

"Whoa, whoa, whoa!" Luther vocalised. "I don't want her to puke in my car. Besides, where does she even live?"

Yvonne rolled her eyes and poked Cherise on the shoulder. "Hey, where do you live?"

Cherise grumbled out an address that sounded familiar to Yvonne.

"Say that again? Where is it near?" Yvonne held her ear closer to Cherise.

"You know, that new coffee shop! It's a block from there," Cherise drawled, waving her fingers in the air as if to draw a map.

"That's close to my place!" Yvonne exclaimed. "I'm pretty sure that's just a building over from mine!" She glanced over to Luther, displaying a pouty face. He didn't resist and waved his hand, indicating for them to board his car. Yvonne helped Cherise into the car, glancing over to see Hyouko watching them.

"I gotta make sure she's okay going home... Did you want to come?" Yvonne extended a hand out to him.

Hyouko shook his head lightly and gave a plain smile.

404

"I'd love to, but I have to do something with Haruka and Daniel." Hyouko kissed Yvonne's extended hand deeply before raising his head again, allowing the moonlight to cast onto his face. He was charming and all Yvonne could think about was how captivating he was. She was a little upset he wasn't joining, but she just gave a slight sigh and waved him goodbye.

"Bye Haruka! And it was nice to see you again, Daniel." Yvonne called out, waving as she entered the car. They waved back and Luther drove away.

Thankfully, Cherise had been sharing a unit with another girl, so when Luther and Yvonne showed up to their door, the roommate assisted them with getting Cherise in.

"I swear it's like every other weekend she comes back drunk," the roommate complained. "Thanks for bringing her back. You don't wanna know how many taxi drivers I've had to apologise to."

Luther had a ghastly expression. He gave a look to Yvonne, who pretended like she didn't hear that.

"Well she's in good hands now. We'll get going. Thank you and have a good night!" Yvonne gave her goodbyes to the girl and Luther trailed behind.

"I told you," he jived. His elbow nudged Yvonne's side and she rolled her eyes. "I'm hungry," he continued. They stopped at the car and Luther stood beside her.

"Yes?" she asked with her hand on the handle.

"Aren't you hungry?" He cocked his head to the side, fang peeking out of his mouth.

"Not necessarily, but if you wanted company, I'll join."

"Hell yeah." Luther got excited. "Do you like ramen? I have a favourite spot I go to. It's called Warui Ramen."

Yvonne gave a confused look. "I thought you didn't like Hyouko," she said, brows furrowed.

"What does he have to do with anything? Just because he's Japanese?" Luther furrowed his brows in confusion back.

91

"No idiot. 'Cause he works there," Yvonne retorted.

"Hahaha very funny. I go there *at least* twice a week, and I have not seen that guy working there."

Yvonne had an alarmed look on her face. Luther, taken off guard, gave the same expression back.

"You're lying. Twice a week?"

"At least."

Yvonne couldn't wrap her head around everything that'd been going on. She knew he worked there. After all, that's where they met. Although she hadn't been back there for a while since things had gotten hectic, she'd gone there once a week or so before.

"No, he probably just avoids you when you enter the place." Yvonne dismissed the unpleasant feeling in her gut. Luther looked stern. He grabbed her wrist and firmly held it.

"Yvonne, I swear to you I never see him there."

Yvonne pulled away and held her arms to her chest.

"Don't freak me out right now." Her mind was racing and her head felt dizzy.

"Yvonne, what have you been working on recently? You never come to the office." Luther pressed his question, coming closer to her.

"It's just a case that's sensitive. I can't even disclose anything to you. NDA," Yvonne responded quickly.

Luther's eyes narrowed, deep in thought.

"I'm not really hungry now," he said. "Let's take you home. I think the night is over."

"And the portfolio?" The walls wept in shrouded flaxen stains.

"Why do we even need it?"

The woman gave a sharp breath before exhaling more smoke.

"Haruka, I thought you'd know by now," they said disappointedly.

Haruka grimaced, hating the feeling of disappointment. She scratched her neck aggravatingly.

404

"We all have the same information, so that portfolio would have no importance," she lamented.

"Yes, in theory. Except they have more access and information than us. Not only that, but I need to find Sophia," they snapped, tossing the butt of their cigarette towards Haruka. Haruka jolted at the sudden assault but quickly regained composure.

"Okay."

# Chapter 9

Worrying was all that was on Yvonne's mind. After hearing what Luther said the other night, Yvonne became more quiet to think about everything. She had to be vigilant, especially when she was on an important case., It seemed she didn't truly know Hyouko. He did send his usual morning text and then became busy. Would it be too much to go over there to see for herself? Yvonne had to contemplate what to do but couldn't spend too much time thinking about him. She had a pile of letters that flooded her inbox over the weekend. Most were aligned with the case, and some were junk letters and bills. Unfortunately, the reports that came in, primarily from J.J., did not provide much optimism. It was like a headless chicken running around an acre. Even though there were times J.J. seemed like they had a grasp on St. Sylke, they would get lost almost just as fast. St. Sylke always seemed to be purposely misleading them into thinking they were the target, and then there was Hemlock. Hemlock was persistently on J.J. 's ass, driving them away from St. Sylke and diverting almost every possible notion. It got slightly more intense when J.J. finally decided to be a bit riskier than usual by invading St. Sylke's privacy and digging into the files they left on their desk. The file, however, did not contain what J.J. hoped for, and they were back to square one.

*Bzzt. Bzzt.*

Yvonne was startled from the sudden disruption from the rhythm in her head.

"Hello?" Yvonne said uneasily into the phone. She took a quick look at the caller ID after saying that and realised it was Hyouko.

"Hey, what's this beauty doing today?" he said cheerily.

Yvonne was glad he wasn't right in front of her, afterall, as she couldn't hide her dismay.

"Oh, just work," Yvonne responded flatly. She thought it would be a good time to ask a few questions surrounding the suspicions she had about him. "Are you at work? I was feeling like some ramen."

There was only a brief moment of silence before Hyouko responded. His voice was slightly different, but not too noticeable.

"Yeah! If you wanna come by, I'll be here."

Yvonne quickly gave a "Yes!" before clearing her throat and looked over at the pile of letters, changing her mind. "Actually, I can't. I have too much work. What time are you off?"

"6:30," Hyouko responded. "But I'm not sure if I'm able to meet up with you after work. I have some personal things to tend to."

Yvonne grew unsettled. "Are you okay? I can help you if you need it."

Hyouko didn't give much time to ponder her offer. "No, no, don't worry. It's just some personal stuff."

Yvonne wanted to talk to him more, but he abruptly apologised and said he needed to be out on the floor. After hearing the end call tone, she put down her phone and glanced at the stack of letters. Although there wasn't too much for her to do except update her reports and review the new pages, she made the decision to go see if he really was working. She usually wasn't the type to be so sceptical, but this was truly an outlier.

Warui Ramen was only a few blocks from Yvonne, but it was too far of a walk for her, so she took a taxi. She requested to get out a block before her actual destination so that she could approach the place cautiously. It did seem busy from the outside, so she peered in the window that had been slightly fogged up due to the temperature difference. All the tables were full and two waiters could be seen bustling between the commotion, but neither were Hyouko. Yvonne frowned slightly and entered the shop.

"Irashaimase!" The two waiters loudly greeted Yvonne. One of them made eye-contact and gave a startling look. Yvonne patiently waited at the front to be approached, surveying the place for Hyouko.

"Yvonne?"

It was Hyouko. He came out from the back of the restaurant kitchen, holding a notebook and bun. Yvonne felt ashamed and cleared her throat.

"I missed you, and felt like ramen," she explained, examining him in his glistened demeanour. He looked like he worked hard enough to get slightly sweaty, but not disturbingly sweaty. Hyouko smiled slyly and waved her over to a table designated for staff. She sat down and Hyouko followed, sitting next to her.

"It's nice to see you so randomly." He put down the notebook and munched into the bun. "Your usual?"

Yvonne nodded and stared into his eyes. How could she have believed Luther? She felt hot headed thinking about how he made her question Hyouko's honesty. Hyouko leaned over the ordering machine and plugged in her order before sitting back down.

"You smoke?" Yvonne asked, smelling the slight tobacco coming off his shirt. She gave a wry face, indicating her disdain for it. Hyouko sniffed his shirt and took it off quickly, leaving him in his tank top. Yvonne almost drooled, seeing his muscular pecs teasingly making themselves known through the shirt.

"No, sorry, a lot of my coworkers smoke and I'd join them outside to chat. I don't smoke. I know you don't like it," Hyouko replied, throwing his outerwear to the side. He kept sniffing himself to make sure nothing else was saturated in the poison.

Yvonne giggled. "I see, and stop sniffing yourself. You don't smell like smoke anymore." She leaned in to take in his natural scent on his neck. Hyouko slightly jolted at the sudden intimate feeling. He blushed and allowed her to finish her action.

"Sorry if I stink," he said, rubbing the back of his neck. Yvonne shook her head and smiled.

"You smell good to me."

Hyouko nervously laughed. "Most people think I smell a little strange, especially after working all day. Maybe your sense of smell is off."

Yvonne shrugged. "Maybe." It was comforting to her, especially after the roller coaster of emotions she had felt earlier.

"Hyouko, food's ready!" Jun hollered from the kitchen, clashing noises reverberating through into the main floor. Hyouko got up and slid his hand across Yvonne's shoulder as he passed her.

"Come on, eat up." The bowl clacked in front of Yvonne, containing the same ramen she always loved.

"I feel like it's been ages. Not since that spicy ramen incident." Yvonne's eyebrow raised playfully.

Hyouko smiled, remembering the memory. "Don't worry, I could never forget."

Yvonne indulged in the rich broth and scooped some into Hyouko's mouth.

"Hey, just give me a second." Hyouko's attention seemed elsewhere. Yvonne looked past her shoulder to see what it was. It was the lady again from the wine tasting date. She stood with her arms crossed, obviously angered at Hyouko. He got up from his seat again and the two left the restaurant.

"Who's that lady?" Yvonne took her bowl over to the kitchen to Jun. Jun peered over to see them chatting outside the window.

"Hmm? Ah, old friend?" He wasn't sure by the sounds of it. "I heard you couldn't handle the spice well." he ragged, wriggling a fresh red chilli pepper in between his fingers.

"Oh please, what normal person would subject themselves to that level of spice?" Yvonne rolled her eyes. She kept taking glimpses at the window of Hyouko and the woman. It didn't seem like a pleasant conversation. Hyouko turned back toward the restaurant door and made eye contact with Yvonne.

"Is everything okay?"

Hyouko shrugged. "Sorry, I should get back to work. Let me walk you to the door." His hand melded to Yvonne's back as he guided her. Yvonne so desperately wanted to ask who that was, but didn't want to burden Hyouko with more stress. He already seemed frazzled as it was.

"Text me when you're free… I miss you." Yvonne stared into his eyes.

"I will. I miss you more," he whispered into her ear. He gave her a quick peck on her cheek before swivelling her around to leave. She caught a glimpse of Hyouko staggering to the back of the restaurant before disappearing behind the curtains.

Boutique shops were one of her favourite places to go for her wardrobe necessities. Brand names and luxury items were of course a staple, but they were extremely pricey and sometimes overrated. Yvonne passed down the strip mall and peered through windows, seeing if anything was of interest to her. She urged herself not to spend too much money on clothing as she didn't have the adequate amount of space for more. Whenever she went through her closet and found pieces that she no longer wanted, she'd bundle it up and donate it to womens' shelters. She never talked about it much, but her mother was a victim of domestic violence. It contributed to Yvonne's disinterest in relationships for most of her life until now. Her mom tried protecting Yvonne the best she could, but when the nightmare was finally over, the damage had already settled into their bones. It was hard for Yvonne to talk to her mom sometimes, especially when she'd ramble on about her trauma and instil paranoia and fear into her. He was a real rough guy. Got into the wrong crowd at a young age and participated in substance abuse, the common factor in most cases. Yvonne only remembered him as 'that guy' and nothing else.

Not a father figure, not a caregiver, just that guy. It was partly her mom's influence that made Yvonne cherish fashion and clothing. Whenever there was a moment of fear, she would scoop little Yvonne into her arms and plop her in front of her vanity mirror.

"Look at all this makeup, these clothes, those shoes," she would say, pointing at the various items she had. Her mom would hand her a lipstick in a mauve color and allow her to paint her lips with it. "Play dress up for me, show me your style!"

It was a way to distract Yvonne from her belligerent father, who was banging on the locked door after hitting her mom. She was the strongest woman Yvonne knew.

Yvonne stopped in her tracks when she saw the most beautiful sheath dress displayed at a boutique shop. Definitely vintage. She *had* to try it on.

"Gorgeous, gorgeous, gorgeous! A must buy. You cannot leave without it."

Yvonne raised her eyebrows as she pivoted in front of the mirror. The shop keeper hounded her and encouraged Yvonne to buy the dress. Luckily, it really was gorgeous and something Yvonne *would* buy.

"Haha, you're a great salesperson," Yvonne snorted. "I'll take it." It was an easy decision. After all, it had the most rich fabric and feel. Not only did the tailored seams feel like second skin, but it elegantly traced her body. The fitting rooms were a makeshift solution, made from shoji screens and antique decorations. It was tidy nonetheless, and contained a lot of character. Vintage items and clothing filled the place and added uniqueness to it all. Yvonne ran her hand along the rows of intricate clothing as she headed to the register.

"I'm so glad someone as beautiful as you came in to buy this. It's meant to be!" The woman carefully wrapped the dress in tissue paper, placing a dainty sticker to seal it.

"Thank you, but you flatter me too much." Yvonne accepted the bag from her, and gave a little nod and wave before departing.

"Come back soon! I'm expecting a new batch from overseas from a good friend. I think you'd be interested in looking." The shopkeeper waved enthusiastically, making Yvonne warm inside. Yvonne felt giddy knowing she had a new piece to add to her wardrobe. The bag hung from her hand as she walked along the sidewalk, swaying to and fro. Blake's shop wasn't too far from where she was, so she decided to pop in for a coffee.

"You seem to be the flavour of the month." Blake passed the coffee to Yvonne, smirking while they pulled the chair next to her.

"What do you mean?" Yvonne eyed Blake curiously. She took in the new decorations placed around the shop. It was quaint.

"Two guys fawning over you? Not to mention they're attractive." Blake pulled out their phone to respond to a text that had just come in. "Hey, I hope you don't mind, but my partner is coming by. I'd love for you to meet them!"

The coffee went down her windpipe as she coughed.

"Absolutely!" Yvonne exclaimed. She wiped her mouth with a napkin as a few strangling coughs forced their way out. Blake patted her back to help.

"Thank you," Yvonne said weakly, recuperating. "What are they like?" She nudged Blake's arm teasingly.

"Pfft, only the best person on earth! I love them so much… they're just the sweetest, kindest, and gentlest person I know." Blake's mind dazed off, reminiscing. "One time, when I was newly out to my family, I had strayed to a park to cry. My family doesn't really accept who I am. It was really hard and I felt alone." They fidgeted with a napkin in their hand. Yvonne didn't know whether to console them or let them ride their wave. "I met my partner when we were in college, you see, and we were only new friends at the time. Anyway, I briefly told them what was going on, and said I needed to go somewhere to cool off from my home. I turned my phone off and ran off into the night. It was snowing out and I remember my nose and fingertips threatening to freeze off. Somehow during the time I was curled up laying in the snow, they found me. I was unconsolable, and it was even more crazy they found me. It was like they were an angel… they *are* an angel." Blake smiled with melancholy. Yvonne's heart ached hearing such a heartfelt experience.

"I'm glad you found someone like that." She rubbed Blake's shoulder comfortingly.

"Babe!" a voice called out from the front of the shop, bringing a chilly breeze in from outside.

Yvonne's jaw dropped. It was Kersa. Kersa looked like she had just seen a ghost. Blake giddily ran over to her and embraced her with a kiss. Kersa stood there like a mannequin as Blake kissed her lips like a doll.

"Babe! Meet my friend Yvonne!" Blake led Kersa towards the booth they were seated at. Kersa hesitantly stumbled along, watching Yvonne, who was just as shocked. Yvonne wanted to run but knew it wasn't a good idea to do so. She held her stomach as an intense amount of anxiety flooded her. Kersa's lips were firmly shut and her eyes never left Yvonne's face. It was as if she was threatening her.

"Hello?" Blake waved their hand in between Yvonne and Kersa. They looked into Kersa's eyes worriedly. "Hey what's going on?" They seemed concerned.

"Oh, nothing babe." Kersa patted their head and assured them. "Nice to meet you Yvonne." Kersa stuck her hand out.

"Nice to meet you as well." Yvonne shook her hand. "I've heard lots of good things about you." She wasn't sure if she should've said that, but it felt like there was nothing else to say.

Kersa gave a wanton look to Blake, who only replied with a tongue sticking out as if they were oblivious.

"I need a smoke…" Kersa itched, feeling the crawlies through the amount of unfortunate coincidences. Blake smacked her hand and urged her to stay at the table.

"Hey! I thought you were gonna try to cut back." Blake crumpled their face in protest.

Yvonne tried not to stare too much at them, since it made her just as uncomfortable to be there. Luckily, another customer came in, allowing Blake to shoot up from their seat and scurry behind the counter to take their order. Kersa darted a look at Yvonne.

"Come with me."

The pebbles ricocheted off the pavement as Yvonne slid her feet, looking down and avoiding eye contact. A waft of smoke entered her nostrils which made her nauseous.

"What a fucked up world," Kersa muttered under her breath, releasing a stream of smoke.

"Hmm?" Yvonne timidly looked up, only to look down again after seeing how scary Kersa looked. Kersa's expression was more intimidating than usual, and it looked like she hadn't slept well in days. Bags ran down her eyes like shadows of hell, and the whites of her eyes were covered in veins of red. Those cigarettes weren't helping her cause either.

"Didn't Blake say—"

"Shut it." Kersa whipped out another cigarette from her pocket like an addict feening for their next hit. "Don't tell Blake anything. They don't and *can't* know anything." Kersa eyed Yvonne's stature, who was still shaking like a feeble fawn. Yvonne nodded. She didn't know if she meant anything specific, or overall, but ended up going with the safest choice of 'overall.'

"I'm assuming they don't know what you do for a living?" Yvonne didn't dare make eye contact but could feel Kersa shoot a look up and down at her.

"No, and I'm going to keep it that way."

It wasn't like Kersa had a shameful job or anything, but Yvonne could tell Blake was a gentle, worrisome person. Kersa's job was high-profile and taxing. If Blake found out, all hell would break loose.

"While I have you here," Kersa grumbled, "there's an update I have, specifically for you."

Yvonne turned her head to face Kersa. Kersa's expression changed slightly to something resembling more of a worried person. "There might be something more nefarious going on than we anticipated." She looked Yvonne in the eye as smoke hovered between them.

"What do you mean? Yvonne breathed, trying not to inhale more smoke than air. "You've already indicated that, but you're saying it again. Is there more?"

Yvonne had an amazing memory. Maybe it was the adrenaline rushing through her that engraved that memento into her, but she had deja vu hearing it again.

"This job isn't easy, ya know?" Kersa seemed like she was talking to herself at this point. Yvonne couldn't imagine the amount of stress and responsibilities she had. "So much to remember, track, and take care of." At this point her cigarette was a mere stub, just barely enough to prevent Kersa from burning her fingertips.

"Everything okay?" Yvonne was worried and stepped closer to her. Kersa stepped back with a grimace.

"Whoa, hold on now," she said, throwing the butt onto the ground. "Yvonne, be vigilant. Contact me if there's *anything* out of the ordinary."

Yvonne became frustrated. She wasn't cut out for ominous adventures and danger.

"Why can't you just tell me what's going on?" she exclaimed, bursting into a more offensive posture. Yvonne looked like she was squaring up to Kersa, but it was obvious Yvonne couldn't even land a punch if that were to happen.

Kersa didn't even bat an eye.

"I have duties to withhold as well. *If* the time comes, you will know."

Kersa was good at her job. Extraordinary in fact. No wonder she smoked so much.

It had gotten busy at the cafe, so Yvonne waved a good bye to Blake and Kersa before leaving. Kersa only gave an acknowledging nod, while Blake enthusiastically waved their arms. It was like night and day, those two. Yvonne's mind was displaced and she couldn't bring herself back to her baseline. Work was burdening her shoulders and covering her like a weighted blanket. Most people didn't realise how taxing her work could actually be. There was a reason why cyber security and analysts make so much money. It was especially difficult for Yvonne to have this case only by paper and nothing else. She was constantly on edge about her portfolio and the security of it. It was time for an upgrade.

The one she currently had wasn't ideal. Though it had a manual lock and code, it could be pried open if someone was desperate enough. It was easy to obtain in the city, as it seemed to be a trend to keep things as tightly secured as things could be. Yvonne picked up a discrete case that was embedded with highly patented security features, including the ones she had before. It gave her ease of mind as she hurried home, making sure to keep the receipt to get reimbursed.

"Oh! Sorry—"

Yvonne had been bumped off balance, clashing into Cherise. Cherise gawked as Yvonne's eyes went awry, trying not to compromise her new case. Cherise grabbed onto her as they did a silly little dance to balance themselves.

"Oh my god, Yvonne! Are you okay?" Cherise supported Yvonne into a stable stance, bag swinging against her.

"Yes! Sorry, thank you." Yvonne replied, brushing herself off. She heaved a sigh of relief and looked at Cherise. They had a little giggle fest before anything else.

"Why do I feel like I see you at the oddest times?" Yvonne chuckled, placing a hand on her shoulder. Cherise shrugged, smiling. She enjoyed being around Yvonne and looked up to her as a mentor and friend. Yvonne never got that from her though.

"I don't know, but I'm glad to see you! OH! Right, thank you for helping me the other night." Cherise went in for a sudden hug, leaving Yvonne bewildered. Yvonne patted her back in reciprocation.

"It's no problem, I couldn't just leave you like that." She let Cherise hug her for another few seconds before she finally let go.

"It's so embarrassing when I get drunk!" Cherise whined. "Hey, I'm heading to this place Haruka suggested. Wanna come?"

Yvonne cocked her head to the side.

"I have to get home and drop this off… It would be too much of a hassle."

"Please?" Cherise whined, gripping onto Yvonne's sleeve. "I don't wanna go alone…"

Yvonne felt bad.

"What is the place you're going to?" She didn't want to go anywhere that would take her away from her work too long. Even though the case was at a stalemate, there had to be something she was missing.

"Some place Haruka heard of! It's some sort of activity…" Cherise looked around before leaning into Yvonne's ear. Yvonne hesitantly leaned in to listen. "Bondage class."

Yvonne's ears singed with red. Cherise giggled and hid her mouth behind her hand.

"What? Wait, why?" Yvonne wasn't necessarily opposed, but felt it was strange.

"You see, I might have mentioned to Haruka that I was interested in it, and she suggested this place. I've already made my reservation and paid for it, so I can't back out now!" She fidgeted with her hair, making sparse eye contact. "I'd feel safer if I was doing it with someone I know."

Yvonne wanted to chew her out for being so unprepared. Cherise was naive and simple minded and obviously didn't think to get someone she knew involved before the day of.

"Well I don't have much of a choice now, do I," Yvonne exasperatedly whispered. Cherise gleefully hugged her again.

"You're the best! Let's get a cab, drop off that beaut, and head there. We still have time!"

Cherise had advised Yvonne to wear something skin tight so that they didn't have to be in underwear for the class. Obviously, Yvonne complied and donned biker shorts and a padded undershirt, along with a long cardigan to cover herself. While Cherise excitedly rambled about the class, Yvonne took in every landmark in case they were in danger. The class was located in a secluded building with basically no indication of it. There was a group of about ten, including them, inside the class. It had bleak lighting and tons of fixtures all around the room. There were snacks, water, and other various things at one corner. Everyone buzzed restlessly amongst themselves, most in pairs with a few lone stragglers. Thank god Yvonne agreed to come with Cherise. Everyone went silent once a man slowly walked to the front of the room. He was calm and had a plain smile on his face. His eyes were barely visible, as he walked with his eyelids mostly closed. Only a small slit could be seen, and even then, they couldn't tell.

"Welcome, and please take a seat. Get comfortable with one another." He rested on a small cushion at the front of the class, waiting for everyone to get settled. Yvonne gave a 'what the fuck' face to Cherise, who only awkwardly shrugged.

"I assume everyone knows why they're here, or what this is all about," he continued, surveying the group. Everyone gave some sort of acknowledgement; a nod, a hum, or a 'yes.' Yvonne made eye contact with the instructor, then he made eye contact with Cherise, then carried on.

"I urge everyone to be open and optimistic. If you feel uncomfortable at any point, make it known." He clapped his hands together which startled most people. "Let's get going now, shall we? I have two helpers in this class today, Kim and Seth. They are here to help and be my eyes in the room!" He gestured to the side of the room, where they stood. Nobody had even noticed them before. Someone chimed in and asked what their name was.

"How rude of me, of course, my name is Axton but most call me Ax."

Ax began walking around the room towards the equipment. Yvonne noticed how tall he was. Not only was he tall, but his muscles rippled through his shirt. She averted her gaze and looked over to the two helpers who were dressed in tight black clothing. They began moving as well, handing out bundles of rope to each individual.

"Feel the rope, and play with it. I'll give you a minute." Ax passed a bundle to Cherise, who seemed mesmerised by this hunky man. She gave a big smile with a tinge of pink on her cheeks, slightly subduing her body posture. He lingered at her for a second longer than he did for others, then passed to Yvonne. She accepted the rope and just nodded, avoiding eye contact from the primal man that exuded dominance and confidence.

"Consent is crucial. Ask your partner if they have consent and vice versa." Ax paced the room as the exchanging of consent wriggled through the room.

"Very good," he said loudly, returning to the front of the room. "In the art of shibari, we want to restrain and control the body in the will of the rigger." He wrapped the rope around his hand twice and pulled. "We also want to avoid hurting or killing someone."

There were a few laughs, but the majority had pale faces.

"That was a joke, but seriously, we do want to avoid hurting someone. We wrap the body carefully and avoid any vulnerable areas such as vital organs or veins." He paused for a moment, making sure to look everyone in the eyes. "Now, who wants to be my volunteer?" A few eager people shot their hands up, but Cherise was ultimately more excited to be a volunteer, twiddling her fingers in the air and practically screaming 'Me! Me! Me!'

"You." Ax pointed at Cherise and gestured for her to come up. She ran up, full of butterflies, and stood next to him.

"Now introduce yourself," he instructed, placing his hands on her shoulders. Cherise straightened up, putting more of his gravity onto herself.

"My name is Cherise, nice to meet you all!"

Yvonne was astounded by the amount of confidence this woman had. Never in her wildest dreams would Yvonne volunteer in front of a crowd, nevermind something so unorthodox as this.

"The lovely Cherise will now be at my mercy, willingly," he announced, organising the rope in his hand. He split the rope in half and folded it. "Cherise will now put her hands in front of her as I demonstrate a basic tie." He interlaced the rope through Cherise's arm, wrapping it a few times and doing various intentional ties. It was all purposeful, with design. Everyone watched diligently, including Yvonne. It looked sturdy and strong.

"This is a simple tie," he remarked, pulling Cherise's hands above her head so she was unable to retaliate. She was in a vulnerable position, arms in the air, bound by the hands.

"You can try to escape, but I assure you, you cannot," Ax continued, swaying her by the binds. Her body lifted just barely off the ground as he held her up as though he'd caught game. Yvonne watched, conflicted with enticement and embarrassment. Cherise was beet red, avoiding eye contact from the bunch of voyeurs.

"Let's all get to it, shall we? Get into pairs if you aren't already." He clapped his hands powerfully before turning to Cherise. Yvonne watched as the two exchanged words amidst the rumbling in the room. It was obvious Cherise was attracted to Ax. Yvonne didn't want to bother her, and let them mingle a few minutes more.

"Do you have a partner?"

Yvonne turned around to face a taller man. He had hazel eyes with a firm demeanour. He wore a sleeveless turtleneck top, all black and skin tight. His hair looked soft even in the lighting of the class. It was a pleasant shade of brown, reminding her of a lush leather sofa.

"Er, sorry, I do." Yvonne pointed up to Cherise, who was giggling with Ax. The man glanced over and smiled.

"I see." He tousled his hair a little before looking back at Yvonne. "That's too bad. Well, maybe next time then. It was nice to meet you." He winked before searching for another partner. Yvonne was admittedly a bit flustered but thought nothing else of it. Cherise had ended the conversation with Ax and was making her way back to Yvonne.

"Omg sorry for leaving you for so long!" she exclaimed, still high on elation.

Yvonne shook her head and grinned. "It's alright, I didn't want to disturb." She raised an eyebrow towards Ax, who was now going around the room to observe everyone.

"I already got the chance to be bound, so it's your turn," Cherise eagerly said, already leading Yvonne through the motions.

"W-wah…" she wanted to protest, but didn't. It did entice her, the idea of being bound, and at least it was with Cherise. Her form was lacklustre to say the least. Cherise had a loose first tie on Yvonne, and the following steps were more difficult than anticipated. Yvonne and Cherise shared the same blank expression as they examined the pattern on her wrists.

"Looks like you've got some practising to do." Ax peered over and chuckled. "Let's get someone to help you. Kai has been exceptional, do you mind?" He gestured for Kai to come over. Yvonne's face turned red. It was the guy from earlier. Kai gave a sly smile when seeing who he was asked to help.

"I don't mind, do you?" Kai asked Yvonne. Yvonne shrugged lightly and mumbled.

"It's okay, I guess."

Cherise backed away to allow Kai and Yvonne adequate space. Ax watched as Kai tightened the binds and followed the pattern to perfection, garnering an approving hum from him. Yvonne had to tell herself not to make anything more than a blank expression. She felt good having the binds against her flesh. The ribbed rope that held her so securely and submissively was something she had never felt before. Yvonne's eyes lingered on the ropes longer than before, getting Kai's attention.

404

"You like it?" he asked, following her eyes. His arms held the long strands firmly, giving more friction in the bind.

She jolted out of her trance and coughed lightly.

"Yeah, definitely better than Cherise's," Yvonne managed to tease, trying to seem nonchalant.

Cherise gave a garbling annotation but then simmered down after seeing just how *much* better Kai's skills were.

"Well, Cherise, I think you're gonna have to practise a lot more to get to his level. Did you want to try again? We're going to try to build off this foundation." Ax sat his hand on Cherise's shoulder supportively. Her eyes wandered between Yvonne and Kai.

"No, it's okay… I'll try my best!" Cherise leaned towards Yvonne. "Besides, I don't think Hyouko would really like the fact that Yvonne's being bound by another man."

Yvonne was surprised that Cherise was so mindful, even putting her own desires away to keep integrity at good standing. Yvonne nodded in agreement, almost prying tears from her eyes as an expression of appreciation.

"Oh, totally understandable," Kai responded, backing away as though a wall had erupted from the ground.

Yvonne's hands were still bound, and she looked to Ax.

"Should we unbind this tie and restart, or…?" Yvonne gingerly asked, showing her wrists.

"It should be fine. Besides, I think Cherise needs a stable foundation to get a head start."

Cherise awkwardly laughed, swaying back and forth on her feet.

"I'll go back to my partner then," Kai said, giving a courteous wave before leaving the huddle.

"What else do you know?" Luther's jacket hung from his shoulder as he leaned against the brick wall. The air was thick in the midst of autumn. The sweat acted like a styling agent, wicking his hair back into a slick style. His cellphone was sandwiched between his shoulder and ear as he caught his breath. His fingers were tinted red, fighting the bitter cold from engulfing his flesh completely.

"What do you mean?" he mumbled, listening to the voice on the other end.

"It's someone within your company, that's what I mean dimwit." The phone gave a static sound, reverberating the words from the other side.

Luther refrained from lashing out in agitation, breathing in sharply.

"Who? Do we know?" Luther pried, furrowing his brow. He grabbed the phone to hold with his hand, beginning his trek once more.

"Someone on the reporting and analytic side."

Luther stopped in his tracks.

"Come again?"

"Don't make me repeat myself. You know I hate repeating myself."

Luther loathed conversing with this person, but he had no choice.

"Who from the analytic side? Give me a name. Name!" Luther almost yelled, repeating the word *name* again.

"Don't get saucy with me, young man," they warned. "If I had a name, I would've told you."

Luther's heart pounded heavily as he thought of Yvonne. *It couldn't be.*

"Keep me updated. Anything. Tell me right away," Luther urged, checking his left and right side before jaywalking across the busy streets.

"Don't tell me what to do."

*Click.*

By the time Yvonne got back to her place, she was exhausted. Too much had happened in one day for her to process. She glanced over to the new case she'd purchased and thought to reorganise everything. Yvonne wasn't keen on leaving urgent matters until the last minute, nevermind something that would haunt her if she didn't do it as soon as possible. She begrudgingly recovered the portfolio from the lazy susan cabinet and sprawled the various papers and information onto the lacquer floor. At first, Yvonne had actually paid attention to what she was filing, but eventually, she started stuffing them into the pockets so she could finish and head off to bed. She recklessly threw the portfolio into her closet, piling other clothes overtop of it before closing the doors. She glanced over at the clock and realised it had been some time since she'd last had a self care session. The day itself was a daze, so it was befitting for her to soak in a bath and enjoy a face mask while freely dancing around her flat. She busted out a fuzzy robe with a cute, embroidered design at the pocket square. It resembled a cartoonish cat, with its large, sparkling eyes and its blushing face. The material itself was lush and soft. Any woman would enjoy being wrapped in something like that. Yvonne enjoyed embracing her femininity as most would observe, but like most, she had her human traits. She slipped off her bra and outerwear, cozying into the luxurious wrap. Yvonne hummed her way to the bathroom and retrieved a calming hydration mask from her cabinet before placing it meticulously onto her face. She played some oldies jazz tunes that would serenade her through the night. Before she knew it, she fell asleep with the mask stuck on her face and the music drowning out the night.

# Chapter 10

*Luther: 9 a.m. Coffee? My treat.*

Yvonne's eyes flickered at the screen as she begrudgingly awoke. A slight panic settled into her as she realised that she was late to her in-office day, and she groaned when she realised she'd slept with the sheet mask on. It laid on the floor, deserted and dried up, mouth and eye holes agape.

*Yvonne: 9:06 a.m. Yes please… much needed.*

"I can't believe you're late." Luther sipped his coffee, hovering over Yvonne's desk.

"Enough, forget about it." Yvonne was bothered at the fact she was late too. She only had time to dress in her plain office attire—black slacks and a dress shirt with loafers. There were two reports she had to review at her desk. They weren't really important, but were assigned to make her look less peculiar. Yvonne's eyebrow raised at Luther cowering over her.

"Do you mind?" She eyed him, confused.

Luther glanced at her reports then back to Yvonne.

"Whatcha got there?" Luther inquired as the coffee aroma wafted into Yvonne's space, making her crave the bean.

"Where's my coffee? I thought you said you were gonna buy for me," Yvonne mumbled, slightly disappointed. Luther laughed and jokingly smacked her shoulder.

"Come on, you gotta work for it. Let's go down the street and get you a coffee."

Yvonne wanted to groan, but held her composure.

"Fine…"

Luther's stature was strong and confident. Yvonne absorbed the ambiance of the cafe as he ordered. They had swapped the lights out to something more luminescent and bright, following with fairy lights that hung from every corner.

"What do you want?" Luther gripped Yvonne's sleeve, gaining her attention.

"Oh, sorry. May I get a hot macchiato with a pump of caramel?" Yvonne glanced at Luther, who was surprised.

"What?"

Luther shrugged.

"I never thought you would order something hot. You love iced drinks." He pulled out his card and tapped the machine.

"It's cold out… I wanted something to warm me up," Yvonne responded, pulling out a coin to toss into the tip jar.

They waited in the corner, watching the barista brew the espresso shots and mix the drinks.

"What did you get?" she asked Luther, nudging him with her elbow. He enjoyed feeling her brief touch, even if it was a friendly one.

"I got a black coffee. I already had a sweet beverage today." His eyes lingered on Yvonne the entirety of the time. She didn't even realise he was staring at her. She was too busy taking in the view of the cafe; the wooden chairs, the scent of the beans stirring and roasting, and the dainty tea cups that lined the walls, cased in glass.

"One day, I will make you the best coffee you'll ever taste," Luther said as Yvonne whipped around.

"What?" It was endearing. She was caught off guard, but knew how to counter his candour.

"Haha very funny, I doubt you even know how to brew a single bean."

"One day you will see." His eyes focused on her face, lingering at her eyes.

They stood there for another few minutes, Yvonne anxiously waiting for her drink so they could leave the heavy mood.

The drinks were placed on the pick up counter, and Yvonne darted to retrieve them. She handed Luther his coffee.

"Let's go back to work, I don't want to get fired," Yvonne joked, pivoting towards the exit.

Luther just nodded, watching Yvonne get a head start back. Luther walked two steps behind her, watching her every move. She looked graceful and beautiful. His chest ached as she fluttered in front of him, unattainable. Her gait, her smile, her eyes. It was all so beautiful to him. He watched as she pulled out her phone to text *him*.

Yvonne was cheery for the rest of the day. Hyouko asked her to meet after work for a date; something she had been waiting for. She craved his touch and embrace. Yvonne found herself longing for comfort and security from him more often than not. Hyouko exuded that nature and knew exactly how to be there for her.

"Where are you guys going?" Luther's voice jolted her out of her daydream.

Yvonne cleared her throat, resuming her posture at her desk.

"I'm not sure, it's a surprise. He just told me to dress up a little bit more, but still somewhat comfortable." She began clacking away at her keyboard, typing a whole lotta nothing. Luther knew she was trying to shake him off, but he needed to do some more investigating.

"Can I help you with your case?" He leaned into her computer space, reading the scrabble on her monitor. She blushed and began deleting her gibberish.

"No, it's fine." She minimised her report and moved her chair to face him. "I don't think they'd like it if another person saw their details."

Luther hummed in contemplation. He knew better than anyone how sensitive cases could be, and how much trouble someone could get in if information was disclosed to the wrong person.

"Alright, goody two shoes." He blew a raspberry and put his hand on his hip. "Let me know if there's anything I can do."

Yvonne shook her head and rolled her eyes. "I'm more than capable."

It was vital to Yvonne that she dressed nicely to see Hyouko. She wanted him to find her attractive, beautiful. As soon as she got off work, she rushed home to get dressed up. Yvonne was normally meticulous with her closet, but the rush she had in that moment overrode her usual self. She threw piles upon piles of clothes on her bed, stooping down even to the floor. Eventually, she decided to stick with a long, silk dress with a high slit up to her right hip. It had a pleasant creme color that went exceptionally well with a quaint pearl necklace and earring pairing. Yvonne decided to wear her hair down, styling it with a curling iron to create gentle beach waves. Effortless and elegant. Yvonne tried her best to remain calm and settle her heart rate, to no avail. She was beyond excited and nervous to see Hyouko and experience what he had planned. Quite honestly, she'd never had a man go out of their way to make extensive plans for her without her asking.

*Hyouko: 7:53 p.m. Are you almost ready? I'll be there in about 5.*

Yvonne's pulse quickened, and she hurriedly double checked everything. Her nerves got the best of her, as she spent far too much time on her makeup than she wanted.

*Yvonne: 7:53 p.m. Sounds good! I can't wait to see you.*

She hoped she didn't sound too needy. Yvonne peered out her window to see if Hyouko could be seen in the distance. Luckily, he wasn't, which gave Yvonne time to go down to the mailbox and retrieve her mail before the date. She shimmied into slides, causing her stockings to bunch up in the crevice of her toes. She quickly descended down the flights of stairs and opened the door to the mailbox area located near the lobby.

"Hyouko?" Yvonne was dumbfounded. She was slightly out of breath from the staircase adventure and stood at the door, supporting her body weight with her hand against it.

Hyouko stood there in shock and stuttered for a brief moment before responding.

"Yvonne? I mean, sorry, I didn't mean to surprise you." He shuffled a stack of letters in his hands and presented them to her. "I thought to bring your mail up again since I was passing through." He was dressed quite proper, wearing black oxfords, black dress pants, leather belt, and a white dress shirt with suspenders. Yvonne wanted to focus on his attire, but couldn't help but feel uneasy.

"How did you even get my mail? There's a key to every mailbox." She got closer to Hyouko, taking the pile of letters and closing the steel door.

"It was being dropped off at the same time I was getting here, so I just saved them the trouble of putting it in your mailbox." Hyouko gave a smile and laughed. "Odd time for a postal worker to be delivering, hey?"

It was odd, but not all that odd for Yvonne, especially if it was to do with the case. The letters would be dropped off at various times and odd hours of the day since it wasn't executed through the normal postage routes.

"You seem quite popular," Hyouko added, clearing his throat. "You get a lot of letters and mailings." His eyes lingered at the stack.

Yvonne glanced at the first letter that faced her. Her last name was written with nothing else. Kalman.

"Just friends and family; I enjoy writing them letters." She tucked them behind her back.

"I need to go upstairs and put these away. I'll be back. Meet me outfront." Yvonne eyed Hyouko past her shoulder before quickly running up the stairs. It was difficult for Yvonne to wrap her head around what had just happened. It was innocent enough, but why did he lie about how far he was? Yvonne felt like she was being cynical for no reason, so she stuffed the letters in the case and locked her doors.

"Honestly, I didn't know you had a car."

Hyouko drove carefully as the husky dark blue sky began to morph into darker hues.

"I don't usually use this car, maybe that's why," Hyouko responded, noticeably checking his mirrors.

"I mean, it's not an expensive car, but certainly isn't a cheap one either," Yvonne noted, looking over to Hyouko. He had two hands on the wheel, never letting his eyes off the road.

"It's expensive to drive everyday, that's why I usually walk or use the bus. Eventually, you save enough to get a car."

Yvonne hummed, watching the trees flash by.

"Where are we going?" Yvonne asked, seeing that Hyouko had travelled further than the usual areas they ventured into. It was on the outskirts of the city where the glowing lights halted at the peripherals of the night life. He had driven at a slight incline, higher than an average hill. Hyouko slowed down and parked the car onto a rocky gravel road. There were no indications of individual parking reserves, confusing Yvonne.

"Where are we?" She squinted in the moonlight, trying to make out shapes in the dark. Her eyes focused on a secluded building, hidden in shrouds of bushes and trees that overlooked the city. She looked over to Hyouko, who was getting out of the car. She watched as he walked around the car to open hers, assisting her out with a gentle hand.

"Trust me," he said lowly. Yvonne abided, nodding slightly as she reached for his hand. Rocks and gravel crunched under their feet as they made their way to their destination. It was an older building, made up of aged bricks and cement. The birch door was vast and large, as if built for a giant. The cosmic windows were iced with glass, accentuating the moonlight that created soft spotlights inside.

"I passed by this place the other day and thought of you. Turns out it's a little old building managed by an older guy." Hyouko locked eyes with Yvonne, gleaming with heart. "He doesn't get visitors often, and I asked him if I could arrange a time and day where I could plan a special date night for the two of us. He gave me the go ahead, so here we are." He opened the wooden doors, hinges creaking loudly. The smell of old timber danced in the vicinity, cherishing the age and love over the years. A thick chandelier hung from the ceiling with intricate, delicate design.

"Do you like it?"

Yvonne was breathless. It was beautiful and filled every cell of hers with serotonin. She lapped up the merit of antiquities and character. Everything there had a story, a life, and she adored it. She whipped around to gaze into Hyouko's eyes. He was staring at her longingly, waiting for her response.

"I love it," Yvonne breathed. "I don't know what to say… thank you…"

Hyouko bathed in the buzz that set in the room. He could feel how much she enjoyed his choice of place.

"That's not even the best part," he said eagerly, guiding her further into the building. Yvonne's dress glimmered in the shine of the moonlight and window, creating wispy patterns that flickered as if it were enchanted. They hurried up the stairs, and for a moment, Yvonne felt like time had slowed. Hyouko pushed open the balcony doors, exhibiting the night sky. Dreamy didn't justify it. It was as if they were in the milky way, absorbed into the city view. The stars shone brightly as the city lights glistened in the background. A soft wind hummed against the two, allowing Hyouko to bring Yvonne's body closer to his, hugging her from behind.

"You're beautiful," Hyouko whispered into her ear, placing a warm kiss on the edges of her lobe. She felt the blood rush to her ear, causing a blush to form.

"When did you become such a romantic?" she poked, holding his strong arms that held her, harmoniously swaying to the rhythm of his body. Hyouko grinned against the feel of her cheek, nuzzling into her face. Yvonne's eyes met his, and she embraced him with a slow kiss. Tender, soft, and warm. Yvonne wanted to know Hyouko more and more. She wanted to know him like the back of her hand.

"What's your favourite colour?"

Hyouko laughed at the sudden question.

"Playing twenty-one questions now, are we?" He held her tighter as they watched over the view.

"I'm being serious! I want to know," Yvonne said earnestly. She pouted slightly, which only made Hyouko melt more than he had before.

"Okay, okay. If I had to choose…" He looked up into the night and rubbed his chin. "I like salmon pink."

"Salmon pink?"

"Yes, why?"

Yvonne laughed. "Not just pink, but *salmon* pink? Why so specific?"

Hyouko rubbed her shoulder as he moved next to her, standing over the railings.

"It's just a familiar colour. It's nice, bright, and has no ill feeling."

"I didn't realise colours could feel," Yvonne teased, leaning onto the railing. "What about… hmmm… What's your favourite dish?"

Hyouko's ears perked up.

"Why? Are you planning on cooking for me?" He nudged her and winked.

"Who knows," she said. "Tell me!"

"Alright, alright. If I had to choose, I love lasagna." He leaned against Yvonne for a brief moment.

"Tell me why! I wanna know."

Hyouko cleared his throat and went into thought.

"It's sharable. Filling and warm." His smile had a pained expression that Yvonne couldn't decipher. She hugged him and lightly kissed his cheek. Hyouko caressed her face before retracting slowly and heading back into the ballroom area, rummaging in a corner.

"What are you up to?" she asked curiously, trying to get a peek as she walked toward him.

"You'll see," he said, bringing out an antique gramophone. Yvonne's eyes fluttered at the sight, excitement embellishing her face.

"Where did you get that?" she exclaimed, eagerly tracing her fingers against the drops and grooves of the fine piece. He set the pin down as a classic tune began to play.

"It's the owner's," Hyouko explained, taking her by the waist and swooping her onto the ballroom floor. Yvonne watched Hyouko's face as he tenderly guided her into a waltz. Her abdomen tightened, trying to contain the absolute woo and swooning feeling.

"Who *are* you?" Yvonne gasped, going with the rhythm of the waltz. Hyouko gave a sly smile.

"I'm the man of your dreams, of course," he teased, bringing her closer to him. Yvonne rolled her eyes, knowing he was being his usual cunning self. They swayed and danced closely, the soft music bubbling with sporadic static from the gramophone. Yvonne basked in the feel of his warm body against hers, his large fingers interlocking with security. Hyouko began to hum to the tune of the music, allowing Yvonne to feel the vibrations of his sounds. The stars could be seen twinkling overhead out the skylight window, willow trees dancing in the light breeze.

"Have you been to Paris?" Hyouko's eyes gleamed longingly. His hand was firm against her back, continuing to lead her in their dance.

"Paris?" Yvonne pondered. "No, I never thought to go."

Hyouko seemed a little taken aback and smirked.

"I'm surprised you, of all people, haven't thought of going to Paris. Your style and demeanour totally fits Paris." His eyes lingered on the silk dress material, as well as the coordinating components that garnished her look. Yvonne cocked her head to the side. It was rather odd she had never thought of Paris, but it wasn't like she had thought of travelling at all before this conversation.

"I never really thought of travelling," Yvonne murmured, looking toward the patio window. "Everything I need is right here. Besides, work has me on a tight leash." She immediately regretted mentioning work.

"Work can't be all *that* serious, right?"

Yvonne stayed silent, which only made Hyouko prod more.

"Yvonne?"

They stopped their waltz and stood in the dimly lit ballroom, shadows casting on half of their faces.

"It's just busy work. Always busy, and always demanding," she responded, trying to make it sound as casual as possible. "Maybe it's more like I'm a workaholic. I don't know, I just never thought of actually going out of the country for any reason."

Hyouko breathed a sigh of relief.

"Gosh, I thought you were like some sort of secret spy or something dangerous. Yeah, I can tell you're the workaholic type. You gotta learn to have some fun in your life before it's too late." He pinched her cheek lightly and gave a big smile. "Let's go someday, just the two of us."

Yvonne's eyes glittered in the dark, feeling a sense of excitement at hearing those future plans.

"Okay," she responded lightly, trying to mask her melancholy happiness. She was happy to hear he was thinking of them in the future like that. Yvonne had feared that maybe she was the only one who'd thought of them like that.

"I have something for you." A gentle rattling sound came out from Hyouko's pocket. He held his hands behind his back. "Close your eyes for me." He shuffled sideways until he was behind Yvonne. She grinned and obeyed, closing her eyes in anticipation. Yvonne felt a cold metal touch her neck as Hyouko clasped the necklace in place.

He rubbed her shoulders and embraced her for a moment, a light tune still playing.

"You can open them now," he whispered into her ear. Yvonne opened her eyes and tried to view the necklace that had been placed onto her.

"Hyouko…that's too kind of you. Thank you," she whispered, feeling the precious stone between her fingers. "I can't see it, but I know it's beautiful."

Hyouko laughed and rubbed the back of his neck.

"Sorry, I totally forgot you wouldn't be able to see it without a mirror."

He pulled out his phone and took a picture, Yvonne standing as still as she could while baring her neck. With a click and soft flash, Hyouko stared at the photo before presenting it to Yvonne.

"It's so beautiful…" Yvonne gasped, taking in the modest luxury. The necklace was a simple ruby stone in a small round shape. It shone brilliantly in its exhilarating, dark blood red tone. The silver dainty chain hung delicately on her neck, placing itself symmetrically and emphasising her collar bones.

"You deserve something as gorgeous as you," Hyouko said, caressing her face softly. Yvonne thoroughly enjoyed the feeling of his masculine hand touching her face. It was comforting and warm.

"I don't know about you, but I'm hungry," Hyouko chimed, patting his stomach. Yvonne giggled and gave an agreeing nod.

"Let's go get some food. My treat." Yvonne wanted to repay his kindness somehow.

"No, don't think you owe me anything just because I got you that." He pointed at the necklace. "It was my choice. Besides, I wanted to buy us some dinner." He jutted out his bent elbow, waiting for her to latch on. She accepted his gesture and clung to him, her heart and abdomen feeling an intense pang, a void she never knew she had. It was as if Hyouko was filling it.

# Mabert Mazyck

# Chapter 11

Luther's leather oxfords ravaged the puddles that were in the way. He was aggrieved and wanted to settle everything. He grumbled to himself as he wrapped the trench coat closer to his body, fighting the breeze. It was the most desolate time of the night, fitting for a secret rendezvous. Luther glanced in all directions as he stormed through the light, spitting rain. He always thought it was inappropriate, the places they made him meet at, as they were junky or sketchy. Littered with garbage, vagrancy, and negligence, there was always at least one of those characteristics. His eyes set onto a figure in the distance, standing still under the lamp post.

"What else is there?" he asked the person. His foot tapped, flinging droplets into the air and soiling the lower parts of their pants.

"There's more than just the money." The person made a disgusted face at the dirt marks that coated their slacks. They made a knowing look at Luther, giving him a one-up.

Luther contorted his expression. His body shifted closer to them.

"It's them, isn't it?" Luther's voice was low, his eyes darkening. The person handed Luther a cardstock paper. Luther's hand crinkled the edge, gripping it roughly.

"Yvonne."

The aroma of arabica beans stimulated Yvonne's senses as she woke up. It was her day off and it had already started pleasantly. Hyouko had his back facing her, grinding the coffee beans with a manual grinder in the kitchen. Her heart fluttered watching his muscular back work as he rotated the instrument.

"Hey." Yvonne came behind him, giving him a tight squeeze. He chuckled as he peered over his shoulder to see her holding him in her pyjamas.

"Good morning, beautiful," he said, rubbing her hands as he continued to prepare the coffee. Yvonne speculated as Hyouko carefully ground the beans, inserted them into the press, and then turned back to her.

"Someone's happy," he said, rocking them together side to side while holding her body. Yvonne playfully punched his arm before nuzzling back in. A smothered buzzing ruminated in the room, causing the two to look around in confusion.

"It must be my phone," Yvonne said, pacing around the living room to locate it. The phone buzzed once more before stopping. She found it on the counter near the entrance of her place.

*Luther: 10:06 a.m. Where are you? We need to talk.*

*Luther: 10:15 a.m. Hello?*

*Luther: 10:30 A.M I'm coming over. It's important.*

Yvonne's hair stood up at the back of her neck. She rushed over to Hyouko, taking in the time on her phone. It was 10:43 a.m. He could be there any minute.

"Luther said he's coming over, but I don't know why." Yvonne furrowed her brow, accepting the cup of coffee Hyouko finished making. He leaned in to see the text messages. He gave a shrug.

"Maybe it's actually urgent..." Hyouko sipped his coffee, making his way to the large window to peer out. "Should I leave?"

Yvonne shook her head.

"No, it's fine. I feel safer with you around." She looked out into the street and spotted Luther.

404

Luther made eye contact with the two and stopped in his tracks.

*Luther: 10:50 a.m. I need to speak to you alone, not with him around.*

Yvonne grimaced.

*Yvonne: 10:51 a.m. Why? Can't he just stay up here?*

*Luther: 10:52 a.m. No, it's confidential.*

*Yvonne: 10:52 a.m. Then technically I shouldn't know then, right?*

*Luther: 10:53 a.m. It's not binded by contract.*

Yvonne cursed under her breath. Hyouko glanced at her and understood what was happening.

He placed his hand on her shoulder.

"Hey, it's okay. I gotta go anyway, just text me."

She reached out to embrace him by the neck before planting a kiss on his cheek.

"I'm sorry. It's work."

Hyouko shook his head and smiled.

"You need to stay away from Hyouko." The birds cawed in the distance, harmonising with the sounds of the wind. Luther and Yvonne sat across from each other in the patio area at a nearby bistro.

"Excuse me?" Yvonne was agitated. "If this is another one of your ploys to try and get me—"

"I'm serious. This isn't a joke," Luther warned. His face was stern and his eyes never left hers. Yvonne cleared her throat uncomfortably, crossing her legs.

"Can you explain?"

Luther stared blankly at the circular table, his coffee neglected.

"I can't disclose a lot of things right now." His eyes met hers once more. "Does Tamocus mean anything to you?"

129

Yvonne tried her best to sustain a poker face. "No. But Daniel mentioned he worked there."

Luther raised an eyebrow before going into thought.

"That angel looking guy?" He asked.

Yvonne nodded.

It was quiet between them. Goosebumps rose on every surface of Yvonne's skin. She *also* couldn't disclose that she was working on a case regarding Tamocus. It took her some time to wrap her head around the blurbs and cliff hangers Luther threw at her.

"What does Hyouko have to do with Tamocus?" Yvonne sputtered, realising that Luther had mentioned Hyouko in the beginning.

Luther shook his head. "I told you, I can't tell you. But I just don't have a good feeling."

Yvonne nearly burst out in anger. "You're going off a *feeling*?!"

Luther's eyes widened in shock. Yvonne usually had a stoic and calm demeanour, but now, in front of him, she was vexed. Yvonne quickly regained her composure, self-soothing herself by flipping her hair away and letting the cold air hit against her neck.

"Sorry, I didn't mean to do that." She glanced away, sipping her latte.

"It's okay," Luther assured. "Just trust me… I don't want to see you get hurt."

That only made Yvonne more upset.

"What do you mean? You can't just say these cryptic things and not elaborate." She scowled, emphasising her disdain.

"Please, I'm begging you to trust me."

Luther was going out of line, but Yvonne felt a pang of insecurity. It was odd that Hyouko's actions were shrouded in mystery… especially after the mailbox incident.

"I don't know what to think right now, but I'm not going to stop seeing someone I love because you have an issue with them."

Luther's face went pale.

"Love? You *love* him?" His eyes zeroed in on the necklace that was peeking through her shirt.

Yvonne practically slapped her mouth. She was taken aback by her own words. Did she love him? Did she actually love him? She must've if she said it out loud unintentionally, right? It was as if she was in shell shock, unable to react. Luther had a grim aura about him and looked down at the pavement.

"I gotta go." Yvonne jerked up, grabbed her latte, and set off into the street. Luther didn't even attempt to run after her.

Yvonne wasn't always the best at sorting her feelings. She walked aimlessly, blinded by the blaring sun that only saturated the color of the leaves more. It was becoming more bitter and cold as the days went by. Forlorn as she was, she tried to keep her expression controlled so that passersby didn't look at her strangely. Just when Hyouko had slid through the walls of her heart, something had to jeopardise it all. As much as she hated to admit, Luther wasn't someone who would make something up or joke about something serious. On top of that, there had already been statistics of instability in Hyouko.

Yvonne passed by a specialty store that sold different items of interest to those that partook in BDSM. She glanced at the bundles of silk ropes displayed in the shop's window. It reminded her of Cherise and Ax, as well as Kai, who had made a lasting impression. It wasn't her intention to look longer at the shop, but it caught the eye of Haruka, who was passing by.

"Interesting," Haruka said, closing in on Yvonne's space. Yvonne whipped around, coming almost nose-to-nose with Haruka.

"Haruka!" Yvonne exclaimed, trying to divert her attention from the explicit store.

"That's funny. Cherise also mentioned she wanted to try this type of thing." Haruka gestured to the display. Yvonne shook her head, linked arms with Haruka, and tried to walk away from it.

"No, no, don't get the wrong idea," Yvonne protested. "I was just observing."

Haruka laughed. "Alright! If you say so… I know a place if you ever wanted to try."

Yvonne would've rather been caught dead than to let Haruka know that she had already ventured into that turf. Haruka would most likely tip off Hyouko about this newfound kink, and Yvonne was not ready for that discussion. They walked together along the sidewalks, enjoying the fall weather.

"Wait, you're not working today?" Yvonne asked, looking over to Haruka.

Haruka shrugged. "Needed a day off."

Yvonne gathered that Haruka seemed a little less enthusiastic than she usually was.

"Wanna go shopping? I've been looking at some winter stuff now that it's getting colder," Yvonne proposed, hoping to cheer her up a little.

Haruka nodded and gave a weak smile. "I guess, why not?"

They were at a vinyl store. Yvonne paced around, touching the raised edges of the vinyls and admiring the various gramophones and such in the store. Haruka suggested they go inside after spotting it in the distance. Yvonne watched as Haruka picked up a few vinyls, carefully holding them in her arm.

"You like vinyls?" Yvonne peered over Haruka's shoulder, noticing the different genres of music she chose.

"I love music," Haruka replied. "I wanted to be a singer when I was younger." Her eyes never met Yvonne's.

Yvonne was shocked, but could see that. Haruka had a nice, soothing voice. Delicate, without a hint of misandry.

"Why don't you?" Yvonne liked to imagine people pursuing their dreams. It gave her a sense of hope and fulfilment, vicariously living through people's stories.

Haruka shook her head and gave a light chuckle. "I can't."

404

"Why not?"

Haruka faced Yvonne this time and took a deep breath.

"My family wouldn't support me. Actually, I got punished if I even tried to sing."

Yvonne felt an immense sense of sadness. Haruka was always so bright and cheery, and yet she didn't seem like it now that Yvonne got to know her a bit more. It was like someone clipped her wings.

"That doesn't sound like family to me," Yvonne piped, hoping to encourage and make her feel better.

Haruka gave a sharp look, causing Yvonne to take a step back.

"You don't know anything."

Haruka was dark. Scary. Yvonne could feel the blood rush out of her face. She'd never seen Haruka like this. Every second she spent with her, the less she felt like she knew her.

"Sorry, I didn't mean anything bad," Yvonne apologised, pining for Haruka to go back to her old self. "I was out of line, I get that now."

Haruka sighed and rubbed her neck.

"No, I'm sorry, I didn't mean to say it like that." Haruka looked out the window, watching street cars and people pass by. "I'm sure you know family can be difficult."

Yvonne knew alright. She nodded in agreement, patting Haruka on the back.

"Let's not think about that right now. Come on, let's go get a bite to eat."

Finally, the mood had lightened. Yvonne and Haruka giggled at the table, food and laughter filling the void they had before.

"Tell me more!" Yvonne said, trying to get a breath in after expending her air on laughter.

The fries were soggy, laying on the single sheet of parchment paper handled by a basket. Haruka had craved pasta so they went to a nearby restaurant known for their homemade gluten shapes.

"I'm not joking, Hyouko had the police called on him because he was trying to get a cat down from a tree. He was so bewildered the cat scratched him up so much. The cat even scratched the top of his head, making him bald for a few weeks!" Haruka was flailing her arms around; she was a big body language type of person, looking erratic and lively.

"Oh my god, you're joking. Do you have a picture?" Yvonne's mouth hung open in shock, imagining Hyouko with a small bald spot like a harvested plot of hay.

"No, he would smack the phone out of my hand whenever I tried!" Haruka snorted, wheezing uncontrollably. "Daniel might've gotten a picture but risked his life for it." She wiped away a small tear.

"Speaking of Daniel, he tried to make me eat a pansy!" Yvonne laughed at the memory. "It was so random, I was no way gonna try to eat it from someone I just met."

Haruka snorted, water spilling out her mouth.

"NO! Omigod. I've told him so many times to stop getting people to ingest random stuff, even if they're edible!"

"Speaking of which, did you want to finish off the fries? I'm not a huge fan of soggy fries." Yvonne held one up, fry drooping down and getting grease on her hand.

Haruka waved her hands in front of her.

"No way, I'm the same as you." Her eyes lit up. "Why don't we get dessert!"

Yvonne excitedly agreed as they called for a waiter.

"I love their creme brulee here." Yvonne pointed at the picture in the menu.

"Yes, it's our best seller!" the waiter chimed in. "I am guilty of taking some home every week."

Haruka nodded animatedly. She gave the go for creme brulee as well as the house made vanilla bean ice cream.

404

"I had no clue you had such a big sweet tooth," Yvonne noted, resting her face in her hands. Haruka smiled while glancing around the restaurant.

"I used to get scolded for it all the time, but now that I'm an adult, I can indulge whenever I want." She stared blankly at her reflection from the window. "I still don't though, in front of my family."

Yvonne got the hint that it was something about body image or weight. She could understand that type of pressure and consoled Haruka by petting her arm.

"Let's enjoy our dessert without guilt."

It was an odd phenomenon where people felt the need to discuss or spill deep things when the moon was shining and the sky was dark. They both stared out, catching glimpses of the shining stars.

"You know, you're special."

Yvonne looked at Haruka, puzzled. Haruka was still looking out the window, arms crossed, finger tapping.

"What do you mean?"

Haruka gave a smile that resembled something more of a prickle. For some reason, Yvonne felt like she could smell cinnamon in the air. Spiced, confrontational.

"Hyouko. I've never seen him be like this to anyone. There must be something special about you."

Yvonne gave an uncomfortable laugh, adjusting her posture.

"I'm not sure about that. It kind of just *happened*, but I also really like him." *Love* him. Yvonne coughed to ease the tension in her throat.

"No... you don't understand. I know Hyouko. It's like he can't rest easy without hearing from you. It's kind of annoying." Haruka laughed, trying to mask her animosity that had become apparent. Yvonne fidgeted in her seat, unsure how to navigate this.

"Oh hahah you know, relationships do that to you." Yvonne didn't want to make eye-contact with Haruka anymore. It was weird to her. Haruka seemed like a generally chill, gentle person, but right now it was different. "How long have you known him?"

Haruka looked back out the window. A slow wave of snow began falling, melting at the touch of rough gravel.

"It's snowing…" Haruka pointed out, staring at the blur of white. Yvonne watched as well. Although the snow was beautiful, it reminded her of the more difficult times.

"I've known Hyouko long enough."

"Two creme brulees and one vanilla bean ice cream!" the waiter exclaimed, balancing the plates perfectly. He gently set them down in front of Yvonne and Haruka, who gave their thanks before he left again. Was there something between them? Yvonne couldn't tell. There must be, after all, as she'd felt the thorns in her voice.

Yvonne whacked the sugar glass that sat on top of the creme brulee, shards scattering.

He typed vigorously, angered by the news he had just heard. His eyes fluttered between typing and writing. He could hear his heart beating, mumbling words under his breath. Though he was not shackled to his post, it was as if he was. He grunted, looking at the pieces of mail that came in. It was easy to report things, but it was a hassle getting them sent.

*St. Sylke has many locks. Cannot figure out which one is the one. Hemlock has taken more of the time I've had alone with Sylke.*

There was a banging at the door. He slowly turned his head, gripping the edge of his seat. Endymion.

# Chapter 12

*St. Sylke has many locks. Cannot figure out which one is the one. Hemlock has taken more of the time I've had alone with Sylke. A note was found at their desk—it gives an indication of their involvement. Was this on purpose?*

*J.J. Cruz*

Her head began to pump with blood. The case was finally picking up. Yvonne reread the report again before stuffing it into the case. It was good to see things were being uncovered. At this point, she had no work to do besides playing the waiting game. She looked at the clock and decided it was adequate for her to be in the office. Maybe she could work on other reports during this slow time.

"Ax? Really?" Yvonne stared at Cherise with concern.

"Yes! Can you believe it? It must be fate." Cherise believed it was kismet. Based on her story, Cherise was at a bar by herself after getting stood up by a date, and there Ax was. It was evident that Chereise believed Ax and her were meant to be. Lasting impression.

Yvonne gave a weak thumbs up. After all, who was she to tell her otherwise?

"He paid for all our drinks and I ended up getting drunk as fuck, of course," Cherise continued, laughing at herself as if that was something to laugh about. Yvonne became even more concerned.

"Like drunk, drunk?" Yvonne couldn't shake the bad feeling. "Do you remember *anything*?"

Cherise pondered for a moment before giving a ditsy face.

"Honestly, no, but I do remember him taking me back home! My roommate was so mad at me this time. Probably because Ax was a big burly man she had never seen."

Yvonne wanted to scold her, but refrained from doing so.

"You have to be more careful… If Ax wasn't a good person, he could've taken advantage of you. You barely know him!" At this point, Yvonne was considering entering Cherise into an AA meeting. A flash of concern crossed Cherise's face before she quickly returned to her usual self.

"No. Pfft, I got good vibes from him."

Yvonne just shook her head as she resumed her work. It was refreshing to pull numbers and analyse reports without unnecessary stress and unorthodox methods. She gleefully tapped away, going with the rhythm of her mind. Her eyes somehow wandered after entering the last column, looking over in Luther's direction. At least, the direction he should've been in. His desk was empty without a single indication of life.

"He hasn't been in for a couple days." Cherise gestured to Luther's desk.

Yvonne scoffed and looked back to her screen. "I didn't say anything."

Cherise gawked before pretending to do work.

"Okay, okay," she said, fiddling her fingers against the keyboard. It was obvious without saying that Yvonne was curious of his whereabouts.

Luther waited long enough for them to show up. He became impatient, huffing and puffing the longer he waited. He kept checking his watch, the window, and the watch again. They must've felt fancy since they made the destination at a higher class establishment. Luther's loafers gleamed in the brisk light, emphasising the care he took for them. He wore a blazer today, accommodating some classy plaid slacks. The hair he usually kept trimmed had grown out a bit, sweeping his forehead more than usual. He tried to fix it by using some hair wax while brushing it up and to the side.

"It suits you."

Luther looked towards the woman who was dressed in white. "Can we hurry up, please. Give me all the details so we can get this over with, Nova," Luther sneered. He was tired of playing games and being held by a leash.

Nova made a sharp sound with her mouth.

"Don't say my name in public." She took off her sunglasses, red lipstick spotlighting her pearly white teeth and decorative lip ring. "Weren't you the one that said *'not to talk to me so familiarly?'"* Nova sat down across from Luther.

"I see you got yourself a drink, but not me?" She pointed to the americano that sat in front of him. Luther took the americano and sipped it, not breaking eye contact.

"You're petty."

Luther shrugged and handed her a menu. She glanced over the items slowly. Painfully slow.

"Oh, come on." Luther called the waitress over, knowing Nova was doing that on purpose. "She'll get a cappuccino." Nova glanced up at Luther.

"Any sugar?" the waitress asked, looking between the two.

"No, bitter like her." Luther smiled.

The waitress uncomfortably laughed before retreating to make the drink.

"You make it obvious that you don't fancy me." Nova lazily tossed the menu back onto the table while crossing her legs, skimming Luther's calf with her stiletto. Luther was not humoured by her attempt in enticing him.

"Get to the point."

Nova sighed and brushed her hair with her fingers.

"It's a ruse." Nova made circular motions against the table with her pointer finger. "Endymion is behind it. We got a tip from a reliable source."

Chills ran up Luther's spine. He could feel the tips of his toes buzz with numbing sensors.

"Endymion? You're sure?"

Nova gave thanks to the waitress who had slithered in and dropped the cappuccino down before running back.

"Oh this is a cute cup. I wonder if they'd let me keep it."

"No, now finish your thought," Luther urged, staring, leaning, listening.

She sipped the edge casually, taking in the frothy, bitter coffee.

"You just love speaking for others don't you. I didn't even ask! Maybe they will let me keep it."

Luther gave a stern *'ahem.'*

"Fine. Peter spoke to an old friend of his and got a scoop about Tamocus. Yes, there are funds being extracted, but from who? That's where we got the lead. After some gentle digging, a woman named Nyla was found to be directly in cahoots with this whole thing. She actually isn't part of just Endymion's team, but the direct secretary of Tamocus. That's how they got the *in*. I'm certain her real name isn't Nyla, but anyhow."

Luther scrunched his face. How typical.

"How does that tell us it's Endymion? Just one person that links it? What about the list Peter gave me the other day?" The americano laid stale in anticipation.

"Oh that list." Nova smacked her lips. "It's a hazy one. It has some definite information but also a couple unconfirmed."

Luther wanted to feel relieved but couldn't.

"Do you know the reason?" Luther needed to get to the bottom of this. That way, he could pull it from the roots.

Nova cackled with buoyancy.

"You think we aren't all trying to get to the bottom of this? Good job, hot shot." She pretended to wipe a tear from her eye.

"So what do you want me to do then? Just wait around?" Luther clenched his fists on his thighs.

Nova smirked, knowing he was getting riled up and frustrated.

"Do you like danger?"

Danger wasn't what he had in mind when he agreed to pursue this. It was important that he got it done and over with. Not only was it a pain in his ass, but he was also looking out for Yvonne's welfare. His heart ached whenever he thought of Yvonne…her beautiful eyes, her lips, her composure. The way she worked, walked, talked… His heart fluttered whenever she looked at him with those calming eyes. He enjoyed talking to her, even over coffee. Luther first took notice of her when she walked into the office on her first day. She was clean cut, proper, and elegant. He remembered what she wore—a pencil skirt, silk button up blouse, and stilettos. Classy, of course, but it really struck a chord within him. He would watch her focus on her work everyday and admire her maturity, responsibility, and agility. Even when work was tough, she never complained.

Luther was peeved knowing that he was working alongside his brother. Not many people know that Luther had a brother, only because Luther chose not to disclose that as a fun fact of his. His brother was rogue, unpredictable, and usually only doing things for his own benefit.

"Where are you now? We need to meet." Luther leaned against the red brick wall in an alleyway. He held the phone to his ear, watching his breaths disperse in the frigid cold. Luther heard his brother chuckle on the other end of the phone.

"Oh, so eager to meet now? After not seeing me for over a year?" The static aggravated Luther's eardrums.

"I agreed with Nova to go with you on this. Make it quick. I want this over with." Luther looked at his watch, making sure he could go back into his work office to wrap a few things up before the end of the day.

"I have a class first, let's meet after."

Luther groaned.

It was refreshing for Yvonne to finally be done for the day. She logged out of her computer and stretched in her chair. It felt like everything was back to the normal routine, but of course she knew that wasn't the case.

"Where are you off to now?" Cherise asked, pulling her bag over her shoulder. She walked towards Yvonne's desk and rested her face in her hands. Yvonne hummed and looked over to the clock on the wall.

"Maybe go eat some ramen. Want to come?"

Cherise giddily got up and gestured for her to follow.

"Let's go! I'll treat you. After all, you helped get me home safe that time."

Yvonne smiled.

"It wasn't just me. Luther actually *drove* you home. I just came along."

Cherise shook her head.

"I remember you actually suggested that I get safely transported home, so thank you. Without you, I doubt I'd be saved by Luther." She gave a knowing wink.

Hyouko wasn't there. That was the first thing Yvonne noticed when she arrived at the ramen shop. She kept looking around, hopeful, waiting for Hyouko to peek his head out from the back, but it never happened. Haruka wasn't there either. Cherise noticed the upsetting face Yvonne displayed and asked what was wrong.

"Nothing..." Yvonne grumbled. Their waitermade glances in their direction every so often; it was a glance of anxiety.

"Didn't you say Hyouko worked here?" Cherise slurped the ramen as she spoke.

404

Yvonne winced. "Yeah, that's what I'm wondering about. Maybe it's his day off."

*Yvonne: 8 p.m. Hey what you up to?*

Yvonne continued to eat her ramen but couldn't indulge as much as she had lost her appetite.

"Did you hear that there's a new stationery shop opening near here?" Cherise pointed across the street where there had been a leased storefront for a while.

"No, that's real neat," Yvonne replied half-heartedly. Cherise could tell something was bugging her and assumed it was about Hyouko.

"Relationship problems?"

Yvonne let go of her chopsticks, allowing them to swim and sink into the broth.

"Somewhat, I guess." Yvonne sighed. "I just feel like maybe I don't know him as well as I thought. Sometimes I feel so connected to him, and other times, it's like he's a stranger."

Cherise laughed. "That's normal, especially in the beginning!" She patted Yvonne's arm. "Don't worry too much, men are confusing."

Yvonne smiled and nodded. She gingerly touched the necklace, remembering the night they'd had. It wasn't all that easy, but she didn't want to explain the details.

"Speaking of which, tell me more about Ax. What's going on with all this?"

Cherise beamed as soon as she heard the name. "He is *so* hot."

Yvonne could almost see the drool seep through her lips. Yvonne giggled at Cherise's thirst.

"Sure… but seriously. Are you thinking of pursuing him?"

Cherise scoffed, her hair flying in the air comically.

"Me? Chase *him*? No, he will be doing the chasing and I will gladly submit."

Yvonne wanted to cringe but held back. Cherise was such an open and honest woman; Yvonne had no clue how she didn't feel

143

some sort of resistance to her words. Yvonne raised her eyebrows and looked to the side.

"Okay then, whatever you say. Just be careful… he could probably murder you and hide it."

Cherise went pale.

"Why would you think of that?! Oh my god…" Cherise was visibly panicked, which freaked Yvonne out even more.

"Wait, did you really not think of that?" Yvonne gasped.

"No! Who thinks of that?!"

There they sat, saucer-eyed, mouths ajar. Yvonne was flabbergasted at how naive Cherise was, and Cherise was stunned at how dark Yvonne's mind was. Yvonne glanced at her phone to see if Hyouko had responded. Nothing yet.

*Hyouko: 8:32 p.m. Hey beautiful, yes sorry, I was busy earlier. Are you able to meet in about an hour?*

Of course. Butterflies. Yvonne had a smug grin on her face as she read the text, garnering Cherise's teasing expression.

"Oooh someone finally responded." She sipped on her tea, doing a silly jiggle in her seat.

Yvonne scoffed playfully. "Whatever, I'm just glad to hear he's alive."

*Yvonne: 8:33 p.m. Yes… Can we go to your place?*

Yvonne paused to think. She hadn't been to his place this whole time. It had always been her place. She anxiously waited for his response, gripping the sides of her phone.

*Hyouko: 8:34 p.m. Of course… don't mind the mess please. I'll pick you up from your place.*

Dashing wasn't the word for it. Hyouko looked like a dark knight. Yvonne's eyes fixated on him as he approached her outside her building. He wore dark midnight slacks, a fitted black dress shirt, and his hair...was messily put into a bun. His shoes clacked against the cobble stone as he came closer.

"Why are you sitting on the cement stairs?" Hyouko quickly helped Yvonne onto her feet. "I don't want you to get dirty... were you waiting long?" He worriedly patted the dirt and debris off her, carefully inspecting any areas he missed.

Yvonne shrugged. She did wait long but didn't want to bother Hyouko with that information.

"No, don't worry."

He smiled warmly, giving Yvonne an achy heart. She couldn't put off her uneasiness and gave a trembling sigh.

"What's wrong?" His brows furrowed and his pupils dilated. He raised her hand to his lips and gave it a gentle kiss.

"I don't know..." Yvonne was a terrible liar. Her eyes shifted from his, when usually she would gaze into them lovingly.

He led her chin upwards, hoping to elicit her attention.

"I know you. You're lying. Tell me please." His eyes wavered with concern and plead.

Yvonne frowned slightly before letting out her thoughts.

"You weren't at work today but said you were busy. Where were you?"

Hyouko did react with surprise for a second but responded efficiently.

"I got a new job." He cleared his throat, placing his fisted hand against his lips to encourage the phlegm to move. "I didn't tell you yet because today was my first day, hence my clothing." He struck a pose to allow Yvonne to observe his fit. Yvonne's eyes picked at Hyouko as a smile slowly crept onto her face.

"I'm so happy for you! What made you change your job?"

"I'll tell you more about it, but let's head to my place first."

He held his hand out, offering it to Yvonne. She accepted, feeling his warmth envelope her hand, thumb gently caressing her finger.

# Chapter 13

Hyouko's place was plain. It was as if he didn't live there or had just recently moved in. Messy, maybe, but only because of the miscellaneous items strewn in the common area. It was a studio flat, so there weren't any rooms besides the bathroom. His bedroom could be seen plain as day with only a single shoji screen attempting to mask the bed. He had all the basic necessities but nothing with character.

"It's like you just moved in." Yvonne's hand traced the wall as she entered. She observed the mattress that laid on the floor. Grey sheets and a single pillow slumbered on the bed as well as a blanket that looked all too basic. Hyouko chuckled lightly as he gathered their shoes to prop onto the rack.

"I'm guessing you don't like my place." Hyouko came behind to shadow her.

Yvonne looked past her shoulder to meet his gaze. He smiled at her, blissful to connect.

"No, not that... I guess I wanted to see more of your personality but your place shows nothing."

"Don't worry, I hid my porn mags under my mattress," he joked, evoking a stunned expression from Yvonne. "I'm kidding! You can check," he said immediately after, holding his hands in the air as if at gunpoint. Yvonne gave a hmph of annoyance before continuing her crawl. There was a small window next to the bed, allowing a small spray of moonlight to embrace the vicinity. She couldn't help but feel a bit saddened by the flat. It screamed sorrow, sombre, and blue.

"Did you have any questions about my new job?" Hyouko asked joyfully. He went to the kitchen to wash his hands before drying them on a plaid cloth.

"Mmm… What made you look for a new job? How come you never mentioned it to me?" Yvonne sat down on the couch. Hyouko came with a warm glass of water and handed it to her.

"I wanted to surprise you. You're no longer dating a waiter, but an office worker!" He beamed and sat next to her, rubbing her thigh. She leaned against him as she took a sip of the water. It warmed her up from the inside, calming her nerves and loosening her muscles.

"Wow, an office worker?" She sat the cup down on the small coffee stand. "I wasn't embarrassed by your occupation, you know."

Hyouko rubbed her thigh with his thumb before stretching. "I know but I wanted to do better… for us, for you."

"How did Haruka feel about that?" Yvonne thought back to the way Haruka reacted the last time they spoke. Hyouko did become silent for a minute before speaking again.

"She'll be fine. Work is work."

Yvonne nodded in agreement and hoped for no repercussions. Although he said there was nothing between them, there seemed to be some one-sided emotion that Yvonne couldn't figure out.

"I saw Haruka a bit ago. She told me you had a bald spot because of a cat! How come I never saw it?" Yvonne tucked a stray strand of hair behind his ear.

"Maybe because that was like two years ago?"

"What? No, that can't be right," Yvonne sputtered, creating wrinkles between her brows.

"I think I would remember when I was bald, Yvonne."

"No, you're definitely remembering wrong. Haruka said Daniel was there. You only met Daniel a few weeks ago or so."

Hyouko's expression changed in a flash.

"...Right, you're right. I'm remembering wrong." He rolled up his sleeves, exposing his tattoos again. "How—"

*Bzzzzz.*

Yvonne looked down at Hyouko's pocket. She raised a single eyebrow with confusion. "Aren't you gonna get that?"

Hyouko shook his head after checking his phone.

"No, it's just work. I'll deal with it later." He tucked the phone back into his pocket after silencing it. It buzzed again.

"You should just pick up, it seems important. Besides, it'll be bad if your employer already thinks you're no good in the first week." Yvonne gave space between them and sipped some more water.

"Okay," Hyouko responded, accepting the call. "Can we talk later?" he sniped at the phone, facing away from Yvonne. Yvonne heard a familiar voice on the other end. Haruka.

"Is it Haruka?" Yvonne asked, peering over his shoulder. "Hi Haruka!"

Haruka audibly sounded angry over the phone, which made Yvonne cower into herself and sit back in her spot. There were a couple more minutes of conversation between them in Japanese before he hung up. Hyouko turned to face her and exhaled deeply.

"Sorry, I have to go. It's important."

Yvonne felt like she got punched in the stomach.

"For Haruka?"

Tears stung her eyes, burning, threatening to come out. Hyouko gave a pained expression and quickly tried to console Yvonne.

"I can't explain. It's important. Please trust me."

He tried reaching for her hand but she refused.

"Do you love her?"

Yvonne clenched her fist. She couldn't see past the blur in her eyes.

"No, I don't, I swear. It's really not what you think," Hyouko pleaded, phone buzzing in his pocket again.

"Go."

Yvonne's work got busy. The case had picked up in progression drastically, causing mayhem. After last night with Hyouko, Yvonne felt riddled with frustration and confusion. He dropped her off at her place and they only exchanged simple goodbyes. He watched her ascend the stairs and disappear into her building before leaving. Yvonne's mind spun. It felt like a rock hit her head but she knew it was no good to keep punishing herself and went to bed.

*100,000 extracted overnight. Perpetrator is slipping through our fingers but we cannot stop. I will be conducting more aggressive methods to put an end to it.*

*Mackie*

Yvonne couldn't believe it. Her ears pounded and rang loudly as she read the stack of letters that had been sent to her. It was delivered overnight, something that was happening more and more frequently. Their services must be getting better.

*Code: WW40240430404*

Definitely a red flag.

"I have a feeling something is off in our team." Kersa said, dragging Yvonne to a convenience store to buy two packs of cigarettes. Yvonne gave a disapproving look as she followed behind. Kersa paid and snatched the packs up, slipping them into her blazer pocket.

"You've gotten bolder, ya' know." The lighter flicked, followed by a flame. Kersa held the cigarette between her lips, fueling the cigarette with the fire.

"What do you mean?" Yvonne asked, staying a slight distance away from her. She had unfortunately become more accustomed to the smell of tobacco and did not enjoy it.

"You're being more expressive." Kersa exhaled a long strain of smoke. "More human." She gave a sly smirk.

It boggled Yvonne's mind that Kersa could actually smile in front of her.

"You just smiled," Yvonne spat, inching closer. Kersa rolled her eyes as she continued to smoke.

"Enough of that. Tell me what's up." Kersa rested her body weight against the cement wall. They met at a park in a nearby neighbourhood, usually bustling with local people. The oak trees provided shelter and coverage for the wild life that existed in that area. Although the weather was cold with a light sheet of snow here and there, children and families still came around.

"I don't think you dressed appropriately for the weather. I don't think you ever have," Yvonne noted, eyeing Kersa's dark navy cigarette pants, flats, and blazer. The flats had been soaked through by the melted snow, creating pools of water in the fabric.

"Answer the question," Kersa said sternly, looking at her watch. "I don't have much time."

"Another code," Yvonne said. She handed the piece of paper to her. "It came this morning."

Kersa took the note and examined it. The cigarette ashes splat on the paper as she stared at it.

"Thank you for this." Kersa tucked it into her pocket, giving company to the cigarette packs.

"That's it? Do you know anything about this?" Yvonne knew it technically wasn't her problem but it *did* directly come to her.

"Don't worry about it." She lit another one. "What you *should* worry about is your fellow teammates."

Yvonne had a crossed expression on her face.

"Elaborate…?"

Kersa busted out laughing.

"See? That! That right there, expressive." Another puff of smoke. "I think we've been sleeping with the enemy."

"You mean…?" Yvonne listened intensely, waiting for the ball to drop.

"Besides you and Vos, I don't know the other two. Never met them." Kersa huffed. "I wasn't technically called to meet them; they were hired externally, J.J and Mackie."

Yvonne wanted to laugh.

"You mean, the two biggest factors in our team? You don't know them?" Yvonne scoffed.

Kersa just stared at the wall and shook her head.

"Not my rules." Kersa strung a long breath, burning through the cigarette at an impressive speed. "I think they're the ones infiltrating Tamocus."

Yvonne didn't want any of this. Yvonne wanted to work and go about her day. It became increasingly clear that the case was becoming more and more complicated, if not hazardous. Coffee was something she wanted to enjoy, but knowing that Blake might catch onto her woes, she decided to wander to another place. Like a stray, she followed the pavement paths after departing from Kersa. Not even staring at her immaculately clean Mary Janes made her feel better. Watching her shoes crush the rocks, snow, leaves, and mixture of mud, she continued her stride. After about twenty minutes of wandering, she found a cafe. Locally owned, locally loved. Yvonne felt like she was in a trance as she opened the cafe doors, letting the unforgiving cold burst into the room. A few people sat in their respective seats; the majority were seniors, and a couple of them were students, studying.

*Luther: 10:08 a.m. Hope you're doing well.*

For some reason, it was comforting to hear from Luther.

*Yvonne: 10:10 a.m. I hope you are too. (1 Attachment)*

Her phone captured her in the coffee shop, the display case of pastries tempting those that viewed it. Yvonne ordered herself a hot macadamia latte, hoping the nutty taste and the warmth of the brew would make her feel something other than uncertainty and anxiety.

*Luther: 10:11 a.m. Hey, I recognize that place. Say hi to Helen for me!*

Yvonne looked over to the counter where an elderly woman worked, sorting the pastries and restocking the coffee beans.

*Yvonne: 10:12 a.m. Helen? Do you know her?*

Yvonne stared a little harder at the name tag that was pinned on her chest. *Helen*. It was indeed Helen.

*Luther: 10:13 a.m. Yeah, I grew up in that neighbourhood. Helen took care of me sometimes. She makes the best cookies.*

Yvonne smiled, warmth filling her from her stomach and spreading around until it reached the top of her head and the tips of her toes.

*Yvonne: 10:13 a.m. I bet she does… What a coincidence. It's a nice neighbourhood.*

*Luther: 10:14 a.m. Are you free? There's a place near there I wanna show you. I think you'll like it.*

She hesitated, but only for a moment.

*Yvonne: 10:15 a.m. Ok, yeah, let's meet.*

*Luther: 10:15 a.m. Meet you in 15.*

Yvonne got up from her seat, carrying the cup carefully to the front.

"Thank you, Helen, for the coffee." Yvonne passed the cup to her.

Helen beamed with amiability.

"You're most certainly welcome." She spun around to put the cup into the sink to wash. "Is there anything else you needed dear?"

Yvonne stared at the pastry case and hummed to herself.

"Oh, by the way, Luther says hi." Yvonne peered over to see Helen's expression.

Helen illuminated as soon as she mentioned Luther.

"You know little Lulu?" Helen asked, inching closer. She was visibly excited.

*Lulu?* Yvonne thought to herself. *How cute.*

"Yes, I work with Luther." Yvonne giggled as she examined the different pastries in the case.

"Oh, please tell me he's well." Helen sounded so genuinely sincere. She opened the pastry case and packed two cookies in a bag. "Please take this. Have one for yourself and one for Luther."

Yvonne felt embarrassed. She was going to buy one for Luther anyway and couldn't accept without paying.

"Oh, please let me pay for those."

Helen violently shook her head.

"No, I insist. That boy is just the sweetest ray of sunshine. Take good care of him, will you?"

Yvonne almost choked.

"Take care of him? He's very much capable... and he doesn't seem like he needs anyone's help." Yvonne carefully accepted the little baggy of cookies.

"He's always little Lulu to me. Thank you for stopping by, I hope you both will come next time."

Helen waved a sweet goodbye, wrinkles creasing at her eyes and mouth. A lifetime of smiles and laughter.

"Hey Lulu," Yvonne teased, entering the car. The exhaust created a smog around them as he idled, waiting for her.

Luther's ears turned red. "Oh my god, don't tell me Helen told you."

Yvonne smirked and nodded. "Don't worry lil' Lulu, it's our little secret." She handed a cookie to him. The scrumptious chocolate chunk cookie scent wafted into his nostrils. It brought him back, truly.

"Fine..." He reached for the cookie and held it with care. It was as if he was transported back in time.

"I should visit her soon. I've just been so busy." Luther sighed. He stuck the cookie in his mouth and started driving.

"Whoa, whoa!" Yvonne exclaimed. "Isn't it dangerous for you to drive and have a cookie in your mouth?"

Luther couldn't coherently respond, so he gave her a mischievous look instead, a glint in his eye.

Yvonne awkwardly handled the cookie that dangled off his lips. Her fingers grazed his lips, feeling a plump and plush feeling. She jolted, cookie falling onto his pants.

"Hey!" he said, trying not to take his eyes off the road.

Yvonne flustered, scoffed, and tried to protest as well.

"I'm not the one driving dangerously!" She grasped her hand that touched his lips and pretended like nothing happened. The warmth off his lips still lingered on her fingers.

"At least it didn't fall on the floor," Luther said with a smirk. "They're just as delicious as I remember."

Yvonne smiled at the window, staring at the trees that flew by. It began to snow again, very lightly.

"Where are we going?" she asked, turning back to him. He was driving confidently as usual with a calm demeanour. Yvonne took a moment to look at what he was wearing. Admittedly, he was well dressed. He wore leather boots, black slacks, a waffle knit pullover, and a black trench coat.

"I know you're staring," he said lowly.

Yvonne's face burned like a sore thumb.

"I know you like it." He winked, giving a dark look.

"I like fashion, okay," Yvonne grumbled, spinning her head back to look out the passenger window.

Luther chuckled as the car started to slow down.

"We're here." He got out his seat and gestured for Yvonne to stay put. She hastily stayed, watching him go around the car to open her door. "Now you can get out." He offered his hand to her while not expecting anything, but surprisingly, she took it. It was a soft embrace of hands. Luther looked slightly surprised as he helped her out of the car. She didn't look straight at him but around the area instead. The first thing she saw was a gazebo in the midst of a limestone pathway. There were shrubs of red and white chrysanthemums as well as baby's breath. They were slightly wilted due to the frost in the air but yet they sustained as much as they would. It was a decadent arrangement that blessed her eyes; mystical, like *Narnia*.

"What is this place?" Yvonne asked, following Luther down the path. They sat together on the bench inside the gazebo. Her feet got cold after being outside longer than she usually would be on a normal day.

"It's like a fairytale, right?" Luther said, giving a cheeky eye. He looked down to check his phone and gave a satisfied smile. "It's almost here."

"What's almost here?" She looked around curiously. Another car had started to approach ever so slowly. Luther got up to greet the person in the car, in which Yvonne became a little bit anxious about. She wasn't prepared to meet anyone new at this moment. Luther accepted a bag and waved goodbye to the person before they drove away.

"I got us some food to eat together." Luther unpacked the bag and set the takeout boxes on the table. "What?" he asked, noticing her gawking expression.

Yvonne breathed a sigh of relief. "Nothing, I got nervous that we had unexpected company."

Luther smirked and gave a pat on her back.

404

"No, I know how you are. It's just us, so be comfortable." He passed a fork to her while offering one of the takeout boxes.

"Cake?" What she had expected was some sort of savoury food, but rather than that, it was a red velvet cake. Luther grinned and dug into his own piece of cake.

"Isn't it enticing?" he said, icing on his lips as he spoke. Yvonne stuck her fork into the dense, spongy cake saturated with cream cheese frosting and shavings of chocolate.

"It is," she replied, putting the fork in her mouth. Bliss. Pure bliss. The frosting was just mouthwatering and light. The sponge melted in her mouth as her saliva coated it in eagerness.

"Wow," Yvonne gasped. She went in for more.

Luther enjoyed watching her delve into the cake like a child. He watched carefully and longingly, putting aside his chase for taste.

"What are you looking at..." Yvonne mumbled, noticing his stare. She tucked her hair behind her ear and wiped the residue of cake off her lips.

"Nothing, I am just glad you were able to join me today."

"We need to leave soon." Haruka paced back and forth in the room, grumbling while causing a stir. Hyouko sat on the chair, watching her as if he was her babysitter. His eyes glanced from Haruka to the door and back.

"You should sit down before they come. It's no good to let them know how much anxiety you're in." Hyouko said, pulling up a stool for her. Haruka lumbered over to take her seat.

"You're an idiot." Haruka spat, her eyes stabbed Hyouko as she spoke.

Hyouko gave her a side-eye. He clenched his jaw and sighed. "You don't have to tell me."

"She doesn't deserve this, you know." Her arms crossed across her body as she leaned back into the chair.

Hyouko looked straight at Haruka this time. She wasn't phased at all and stood her ground.

"I've known you longer than anyone has. You're being selfish."

Hyouko knew that. They both sat, waiting impatiently and staring at the door.

# Chapter 14

Cherise had become more ecstatic at the fact Ax had asked her out on a date. She asked Yvonne to go do some shopping together beforehand.

"I wanted to buy this dress after going to buy some binders and stickers but I ended up spending too much time there and the dress shop closed."

Yvonne and Cherise walked around the outdoor strip, trying to get to their destination before they became too cold.

"Cherise, you can be a bit of an airhead sometimes," Yvonne stated, rubbing herself to warm up.

Cherise cackled and shrugged. "I know, I know, but hey… at least it gave me the opportunity to hangout with you now!" She pointed over to the boutique shop where she had seen the dress.

They entered the shop and were greeted by a warm burst of air. The heating system was more than efficient and kept the cold at bay.

"You see that?" Cherise pointed over to a grungy purple dress. It was sleeveless with a unique sash design that was styled bound around the mannequin's neck. It was definitely an inviting look.

"It looks beautiful," Yvonne said, feeling the fabric of the dress. Chiffon; just as she had suspected. "Feels beautiful too."

"I'm gonna try it on!" Cherise squealed as she grabbed the hanger along with the dress and disappeared into a fitting room.

Yvonne needed this type of energy; the lights, clothes, the girly thrills. She wandered around the shop to view other articles of clothing before coming back to the fitting area.

"How is it?" Yvonne knocked at the fitting room door.

The door flung open, showing off Cherise's attire. Cherise was head over heels with the look and flounced around in the dress. The sash laid delicately along her neck and across her collar bone as the dress hugged her figure perfectly.

"It is ah-mazing," Cherise articulated. Her eyes were like a sugar high child's, wide-eyed and restless. She admired herself in the mirror with awe. Yvonne nodded and hummed in approval of the dress. It really suited her.

"Cherise, you look stunning in it!" Yvonne spun her around as Cherise laughed in joy.

"I know! Ax would go wild, I think." She snickered and went onto her tiptoes to imitate the look of heels.

"That settles it, you *must* get it." Yvonne felt the rush of excitement just by watching her. It was refreshing to be out with a friend and do such mindless, puerile activities such as shopping, giggling, and talking about first dates.

"Ax seems to be a little bit more of an experimentalist," Cherise announced while changing into her clothing.

"What do you mean?" Yvonne responded, browsing the palooza pants that were on display next to the mirrors.

"I mean," Cherise grunted as she shimmied into her pants, "he keeps talking about this supplement that's been trendy. Some sort of company called Tamocus. Have you tried?"

Yvonne's throat felt tight. Her attention flew back towards Cherise's fitting room.

"No, why?"

"Well, he said it's real popular and all. I don't know if he's trying to get me to try it, but I'm not really a fan of psychedelic trips."

160

Cherise popped out of the fitting room, dress hung over her arm. "You okay?"

Yvonne's face was pale and ghastly. It frightened Cherise as she didn't think it was that big of a deal.

"Yeah, I'm fine, sorry." Yvonne managed to muster the words past her constricted throat. It could just be a coincidence afterall.

"Oh my gosh, guess the price of this dress." Cherise gripped the dress in her hands and keeled over slightly. What an expressive woman.

"I don't know…fifty dollars?"

Cherise scoffed.

"As if! This cut, material, and design…it's over a hundred. But worth it!"

By the time Yvonne had departed from Cherise, who lived fairly close to her, it was already past four. Yvonne rummaged through her purse to locate her keys before entering the building. From the corner of her eye, she spotted a familiar face. Those cheeky eyes, that firm demeanour. She nearly dropped her keys as she met eyes with him.

"Kai?" Yvonne almost jumped at the sight of him. She didn't want to gain attention from others unnecessarily so kept her tone down.

"I knew that was you." He then jogged towards Yvonne from the pathway over. Yvonne quickly remembered who the man was as soon as she laid eyes on his beauty mark. Kai. Kai from the workshop.

"I couldn't forget a face like that. Eve, was it?"

How cunning.

"It's Yvonne." She hid the key back in her purse. "Do you live nearby?" Yvonne was hasty with her words and cautious of the distance between them. She held her purse close to her body in front of her. Yvonne sorely wished she had put on more layers, as she felt extremely vulnerable.

"No, just here for work," Kai said, staying an adequate distance from Yvonne after noticing her body language. "Do you have time for dinner?"

Yvonne glanced back to her apartment, realising that Kai now knew where she lived.

"Uh, no, it's okay... I should really see my friend." Yvonne gestured to the door behind her.

Kai raised a brow. "Your friend that lives in the same complex as you?"

Shivers. Yvonne's feet grew cold and her face started to spasm in stress.

Suddenly, Yvonne was pulled with a great amount of force.

"Enough."

Yvonne's dumbstruck expression met Luther's chest. Luther stared at Kai with malice.

"Long time no see," Kai said with a cocky tone in his voice.

"You didn't show up," Luther responded angrily. His grip was strong against Yvonne's wrist, holding her close to him. She could smell the white musk off his body mixed with the overpowering intensity of his emotions. Yvonne felt like she was being smothered in a thick cloud of tension. Kai glanced at Yvonne.

"That your girl?" He smirked, zoning into Yvonne's expression.

Luther looked down at Yvonne, who was staring at Kai nervously.

"...no. What are you doing here?" They could hear the disheartening tone in his voice.

"I see." Kai licked his lips playfully. "I'm just doing my job. What about you?"

Yvonne gave Luther a worried look. She had no clue what was going on and was rather baffled at the fact that they knew each other. Not to mention it seemed like there was some history between them.

Luther let go of Yvonne's hand and gestured for her to go behind him. She did, but didn't want to go into her building.

"No, no, I think she should join. This'll be interesting." Kai had an ominous voice. He knew more than he led on; it was obvious. Luther tensed up and looked over his shoulder to meet Yvonne's eyes. She was slightly afraid, worried. Not to mention the fact that they had met at an anomalous event.

Sitting with them was not something Yvonne would've imagined to happen, even in her wildest dreams. They sat at a booth; Luther and Yvonne in one, and Kai in the other. Kai was humming to himself as he perused the menu, sipping water from the cup the waitress had just set down.

"I think I will go with the noodle soup." He looked over to the two. "Feeling a lil' chilly."

"Why are you acting so casually?" Luther was still tense. Yvonne hadn't ever seen him like this before.

"Why aren't *you*? Come on, it's been a while. Lighten up." Kai sat the menu down and leaned into the booth.

"Sorry, how do you guys know each other?" Yvonne was tired of waiting. She was too curious.

Kai gave a look of pity. "Luther, don't tell me she doesn't know."

Yvonne glanced over to Luther. He had an expression that could only be described as annoyance and grievance.

"Know what?" Yvonne asked, egging him on.

"He's my brother." Luther clenched his fist against his thigh. Yvonne watched the creasing on his pants get deeper.

"Brother? Really? Brother?" Yvonne never knew Luther had a brother. Nevermind the fact that Kai had partook in something peculiar with her.

"Big brother, might I add," Kai said with pride. He gave a knowing look to Yvonne again. "Whatcha gonna get?"

Yvonne didn't even take a look at the menu. How could she be hungry in this situation?

"Er… maybe their club sandwich…"

They ordered, except Luther, as he refused to dine with his brother.

"Okay, now let's get serious." Kai leaned into his interlaced fingers, resting his chin. "Does Yvonne know she's in a little bit of a pickle?"

"No, I haven't really gotten there yet."

Yvonne had an unsettling feeling in her stomach.

"Yvonne, please give us the details of the case you're working on right now." Kai was stern.

"No… I can't." Yvonne would if she could, but at this point, keeping her job was more important than a potential problem that wasn't even confirmed yet. Luther placed his hand on hers.

"Please. It's serious." Luther had never looked so serious before. Yvonne's heart felt heavy. Could she even handle all this stress?

"All I'm going to say right now is that it has to do with Tamocus."

"BINGO!" Kai pointed a finger gun at her. "It is you, I knew that."

"Kai," Luther said through his teeth.

"Hey, what? Endy boy is an idiot," Kai said in a mocking laugh. "I'm sure they almost gotcha though."

"Endy?" Yvonne asked. She was getting more confused the more he spoke.

"Mmm yes, our favourite little boy. The Joker to the Batman."

"I don't think they're *a little boy*," Luther added. "In short, your case is a fraud."

Yvonne furrowed her brows. "Excuse me?" She glanced at Kai, who was distracted by the food arriving.

"Hyouko is part of it," Luther said lowly. "Do you understand now?"

Yvonne's mind spun. There was no way this was happening. Would Hyouko actually lie to her like that? Did he even know?

"There's a good chance he doesn't know you're the analyst on the case. On their records, they think it's Cherise." It was as if Luther read her mind.

Cherise.

"CHERISE?" Yvonne almost yelled. She jumped out of her seat. "Why Cherise? How could they have gotten that wrong? What else is there to it?" Yvonne felt a throb of guilt knowing that Cherise could be caught up in this mess.

Luther got her to sit back down and whispered in her ear. "Don't cause too much of a scene. You never know who's watching." His warm breath caressed her ear as his voice reverberated deeply.

"Sorry," she mumbled. "I'm worried about Cherise. How dangerous are these people?"

"Not that dangerous."

"Very dangerous," Kai interjected. "Hyouko and Haruka are part of Endy's team."

Luther gave a warning look to Kai.

"How do you know?" Yvonne asked breathlessly. She didn't know what to believe. In fact, she might've been in denial about it all. Also, Haruka?!

"A reliable source. Also, they're known for these types of kerfuffles." Kai dove into his noodle soup. "Oh, delicious. Want some?" He offered it to Luther, who immediately rejected it.

"Like, they've done this before?" Yvonne was beyond riddled with anxiety. She needed to know more.

"Oh yeah, they're like Endy's kids basically." Kai slurped a noodle up that had fallen stray. "Poor guys."

Luther grumbled. "I knew there was something wrong with him." He eyed Yvonne.

"How can I believe you guys?" Yvonne said shakily. She darted looks between the siblings, feeling cornered with all this information.

"I mean, you could ask him yourself," Kai proposed with a challenging look.

Luther seemed disturbed by that proposition. "I don't trust him alone with you."

"I will." She glared at Luther. "I need to talk to him. Alone. *I* trust him."

# Chapter 15

People were stirring about the sudden snowfall that happened over night. Yvonne watched out her window as children and adults ventured out to play in it. It got increasingly frigid in her place so she lit the fireplace in hopes of warming up. Yvonne had bags under her eyes after the conversation the three had the night before. Unable to sleep, she stared at the ceiling in bed and wandered to and from the living area until she could finally fall asleep. Even though she said she trusted Hyouko, she only half believed herself.

*Yvonne: 10:00 p.m. (Yesterday) I need to talk to you. Are you free?*

She hadn't heard from him at all. Yvonne looked at the antique clock to check the time. It was 9:00 a.m. He read the text, she knew that. Yvonne sauntered to the kitchen to prepare herself a coffee, though only for the sake of it; she had no intention of actually drinking it. She stared blankly as she absorbed the aromas of the coffee roast, cup hot against her grasp. Suddenly, a vibration jolted her wide awake.

She cleared her throat.

"Hello?"

It was Hyouko. *"Sorry, I was busy last night. Everything okay?"*

Yvonne paused for a moment to recollect her thoughts. "No, not really. We need to talk."

A fumbling sound could be heard from the other end.

*"If this is about Haruka, I can explain."*

"It's not. Can we meet in about twenty minutes? Gargoyle grove."

Hyouko was silent this time.

*"Okay. Yes, I'll see you in twenty minutes. Gargoyle grove."*

After hanging up, Yvonne peered out the window one last time before getting dressed. It was really quite lovely, the weightless, feathery snowflakes that danced in the air before landing on a surface. The brilliance of it, the feel and the enticing chill.

Gargoyle Grove was a well-known attraction in her neighbourhood. By the title, one could suspect there would be gargoyles. There were a few, as well as many statues and fir trees. Poinsettias were planted all around the attraction for the winter season. Their blistering red colors bled and highlighted themselves in comparison to the white snow. Yvonne sat at a bench with her long, tweed coat. She shivered against the cold in her knee high leather boots and knitted dress. It wasn't long before she heard a crunch of snow behind her.

"I'm surprised nobody else has gotten to this part of land," Hyouko said, embracing her from behind and giving a soft kiss on the top of her head. Yvonne tried not to display her worries but Hyouko knew her better than that.

"What's wrong?" he asked worriedly. He knelt down before her, disregarding the wet snow underneath his knee. Yvonne was choked, hoping to form words appropriately.

"Are you lying to me?" she breathed, hoping to keep her emotions at bay.

Hyouko was solemn. He thought for a moment, still in the same position. The knee of his pants began to get soaked by the melted snow. The tip of his nose became flushed pink from the chill.

"What? Lying about what?" he asked with a straight face. The wind blew his long, loose strands of hair like the vines of a willow tree.

"Who you are." Yvonne stared into his eyes, examining his expression. It was usually hard to see exactly what he was feeling, but

404

this time she saw hopelessness; surrender. Hyouko's eyes glazed with a brush of solidarity and secrecy.

"I'm Hyouko." His tone was flat. His position never waivered.

"I'm giving you one more chance." Yvonne's voice trembled. Was it fear? Sadness? Distress? She wasn't sure what was going to happen if he did confess the truth. Part of her still clung to the hope that he wasn't actually part of any of this and that it was all a misunderstanding.

"Please, I'm begging you. Tell me the truth."

"Then what?" Hyouko's voice boomed in her head.

That was the question. Yvonne already knew the answer at that point but still had no clue as to what was going to happen either.

"Then…then, I don't know!" Yvonne spluttered; her body shook with fear. Her face burrowed into her hands in grief. Hyouko offered his hand but quickly rescinded, knowing this wasn't the time for it.

"Yvonne, I love—"

"Don't!" she yelled. Tears burned the edges of her eyes despite her best efforts of keeping them in. "Don't. I don't want to hear that right now." Yvonne looked up to see Hyouko again. Hyouko's eyes were singed with the same sorrow that burnt through Yvonne.

"It wasn't meant to be this way," he breathed. His voice was softer, subdued. He got off his knee to stand, hovering over Yvonne like a shadow.

"Why?" Yvonne cried. "Why would you do this to me, to us?"

"I don't know how much you know, but trust me, I never meant for this to happen."

"I don't know much. Tell me everything. Maybe we can work it out." Yvonne was becoming desperate. She wanted to find any reason to pull him out of the *villain* title.

"Who are you?" she repeated. Hyouko sat next to her on the bench; his knee was sorely saturated with the wet snow.

"I'm Hyouko Sanaka. I'm the adopted son of Endymion." His eyes glanced to meet hers.

169

*Endymion.* Yvonne tried to stabilise her shaky breath, closing her eyes as if to meditate. Hyouko felt almost like a stranger. The person she once knew and found security in now became a blurred, fuzzy shadow.

"I just want you to know that I did not get to choose my life path." His fist bunched up tightly. "Endymion is not a pure person, nor are his intentions."

"And what about Haruka?" Yvonne asked, trying to hold her strength.

Hyouko stared down at their feet, looking at the mud that had soiled the bright snow.

"Sister, by adoption. Daniel too."

It all made sense now.

"So you know then," Yvonne affirmed, looking over to Hyouko. "You knew. You *knew* I was the analyst of the Tamocus case."

Hyouko's eyes were tenebrous.

"I only found out *after* we got together." The veins in his forearm and neck protruded out, emphasising the amount of tension he was holding. "The mail."

Of course. The mail had given it away.

"I wanted to pretend like I never saw it. Pretend to be a normal couple. I wanted to hold you, love you, and be with you as if none of this was going on."

"What were you thinking? There was no way any of this could be kept in the dark for long," Yvonne shrieked. The shrills in her voice began to crack. "Do they know?"

Hyouko shook his head.

"Cherise. Cherise is in danger because of all of this. Because of *me*," Yvonne cried.

*Ax.* Yvonne's palms began to perspire.

"Don't tell me Ax is part of this." Yvonne grabbed Hyouko's shoulder with urgency.

"How do you know about Ax?" Hyouko asked, fearful of the tenacious energy Yvonne exuded.

"Cherise was supposed to go on a date with him. Please tell me Cherise is safe," Yvonne pleaded. Her fingers gripped onto Hyouko's flesh animalistically. Hyouko's eyes were harrowing.

"They've already gone. Ax didn't harm her."

Yvonne exhaled with great relief; a light buzzing filled her head with nausea.

"I wouldn't do anything to harm you." Hyouko's voice was strained. "I want to run away with you and live a true life."

Cold and unforgiving snowflakes descended angelically. Yvonne was brought to tears again, the chill relentlessly scathing her optics. Her hands held his, feeling the cold embrace of him.

"Now what?" Yvonne drawled, her body numb.

"They can't know it's you," Hyouko said. "The plan would be to frame you."

Yvonne felt like she couldn't breathe.

"I won't let that happen." Hyouko was firm with his words. "I'll do everything I can to make sure of that."

Yvonne sunk onto the bench. In only one day, her life had been flipped upside down.

"And what about us?"

Hyouko remained silent, before eventually saying, "All that matters is that you're safe."

Cherise was frantic. After the date with Ax, she had been escorted back home safely but found that someone had ransacked her place while she was gone. Her roommate wasn't home either at the time of the event.

*"Everything is in shambles!"* Cherise cried.

Yvonne's stomach did somersaults, assaulting the lining of her organs.

"Really? Are you okay?"

*"NO!"* Cherise was one for dramatics but Yvonne knew this time was valid.

"Do you need me to come over?" Yvonne offered, hoping that it would settle Cherise.

*"Yes please! I feel petrified."*

Cherise was shaking like a Bambi in the middle of her room. Yvonne set down her bag and embraced her, getting a good look at the room. Everything was dishevelled and a mess. It didn't seem like anything was stolen, so it was definitely Endymion's doing.

"Is anything missing?" Yvonne asked Cherise, who was clinging onto her like a baby would to a mother.

"Not that I can see so far," Cherise sniffled. "But whoever did this was vindictive as fuck!"

Yvonne wanted to laugh at Cherise's potty mouth but chose to keep a straight face. "What do you mean?"

Cherise pointed to her closet. Everything was torn up.

"My stationery, my cases, portfolios, *everything!*" Cherise's eyes watered at the sight of her precious collection in complete desolate condition.

She was right, all of her items had been torn apart. Someone was looking through it desperately to find something. But *what?*

"I need a drink," Cherise moaned, massaging the temples of her head. Yvonne gave a disapproving look at first but gave leniency as she knew what was going on.

"I don't have time right now," Yvonne said with guilt. "I have to do some work. Please go be with a friend or your roommate. Don't be alone."

Cherise gulped. "What? Why? What do you mean?"

"Just trust me. What if it's a stalker?" Yvonne wanted to deter her from worrying about the actual problem so she came up with something vague but realistic.

"Oh my god. You think?"

Yvonne nodded.

"You better stay with a friend for now. Call the police too."

"Don't leave meeeee," Cherise whined, her face contorted in a funny manner.

Kersa couldn't be reached. Everytime Yvonne called her, it would ring until the call dropped. Panic settled into Yvonne's vessel. It wasn't typical of her not to answer, especially if she called more than once. Yvonne paced her living room; her eyes wandered to the lazy susan in the kitchen. She had an idea of what Endymion was after and it was only a matter of time before things came to a head. Only Kersa would have a better clue of what was actually at stake. Yvonne scrambled to the kitchen to recover the case and old portfolio. Yvonne had almost completely forgotten to place it back there after throwing it into her closet. After seeing what they did to Cherise's closet, she knew it was good that she changed her hiding spot. What was it they wanted? She let the various reports and papers loose, placing them across the floor. Besides the reports, the only outlier would've been the code with the *weeping widow* name. That didn't make sense at all. It would be Endymion sending the code over to frame her, wouldn't it? Again. She read everything again. There had to be something she was missing. Yvonne's breath was stiff and rapid. She truly didn't know what she was up against and to what extent.

*Cherise: 6:07 p.m. I'm with Sandra, she says hi! (1 Attachment)*

Yvonne was glad Cherise had actually listened and sought the company of her friends.

*Yvonne: 6:08 p.m. I'm glad. Say hi back for me!*

As it grew darker, she began to get a little bit antsy. She couldn't find any indication why Endymion would want the portfolio since they had the same correspondences as she did. Yvonne grumbled and grabbed her phone.

*"Hello? Yvonne? Is everything okay?"*

Yvonne felt solace hearing Luther's voice on the other end.

"Yeah, sorry. I hope I'm not bothering."

*"NO!"* He coughed. *"No, not at all. Did you need something from me?"*

He was eager.

"I just wanted to talk to someone I trusted…" Yvonne began. "Besides that," she cleared her throat, "I was wondering if you know why Endymion is looking for my portfolio."

She could hear him rustling and going into a quieter area. He hummed in thought.

*"It wasn't confirmed yet, but besides them trying to frame the analyst, I think there's a kill switch key somewhere. They think the analyst has it."*

Kill switch key? Yvonne had no clue what that indicated.

"What do you mean kill switch key? Why would I have that?"

*"Can we talk in person? You never know who's listening."*

Luther was right. It was stupid that neither of them thought about that till now.

"Yes, please come over."

"You brought food?" Yvonne met Luther at the front of her building, wearing only a cardigan and her silky pyjamas. Luther walked up the stairs with bags in his hands. He gave a smirk as he held one of them up.

"Of course. I doubt you thought to eat. You need to take care of yourself."

Yvonne felt flustered. How did he know? She gestured to help bring a bag up, but Luther rejected; he seemed almost offended that she offered.

"Let me take care of you."

Yvonne huddled her cardigan closer to herself. She felt embarrassed knowing she was dressed so casually while Luther was in his professional clothing.

"Let me pay you back," Yvonne insisted, grabbing her wallet as soon as they arrived inside.

"No." He was firm with his words. Yvonne's reach lowered and she just scratched the back of her neck.

"Don't mind the mess," Yvonne said, pointing out the papers that covered the floors.

"It's my first time in your place," Luther called out, setting the bags on her table. "It's really nice." His eyes wandered around, peering into her bedroom.

"WAH! Don't look in my room, it's really disorderly." Yvonne rushed to close her door. Luther chuckled and surrendered his search, heading back to the living room.

"So these are the case files?" Luther rummaged around the papers and stacked them.

Yvonne nodded and sat on her knees. Luther concentrated deeply, zoning in the information and reports. Yvonne never got to see Luther in action before. It was remarkable how intense and focused he could be. His eyes were narrowed, moody and deep. His brows remained furrowed as he read the papers in thought.

"I heard someone by the name of *Kersa* knows what they're looking for," Luther spoke, breaking the silence.

Yvonne jolted at those words. She sighed and groaned.

"Kersa hasn't answered any of my calls. They all drop after ringing a few times." Yvonne gave a concerned look, holding her phone in her hands. Still nothing.

"She might've caught wind of more action," Luther said. He picked up a piece of paper. The code. He grimaced. "This… is incriminating."

Yvonne shuddered.

"Kersa mentioned someone was trying to frame me," Yvonne said, reaching for the paper. As if *Weeping Widow* wasn't ominous enough, now she was being told it was incriminating. "How do you know Kersa?"

Luther looked out the window as if he was watching for something. "The partner we work for knows them. Long history. Kersa isn't someone to mess with either."

What did that mean?

"It's better if you don't ask too many questions right now. It's a rabbit hole." Luther patted Yvonne's shoulder. "Come on, let's eat!" Luther untied the bags he had brought in and placed them on the table.

"Have this, I thought you might like it." He handed Yvonne a little cardboard picnic box. Yvonne accepted it and looked at Luther.

"Come on, open it," he urged excitedly.

Yvonne obliged and carefully popped the top off. Inside was a small chocolate mousse cake. A small bear design was on top of it, intricately placed to catch anyone's eyes.

"What's this for? You keep feeding me cake." Yvonne giggled, admiring the mousse cake. She could smell a faint note of tonka bean, which made her incredibly happy.

"I just thought you'd like it. Tonka bean is your favourite after all." Luther had begun eating a sandwich from the bag. He smiled at Yvonne, giving a push into her heart. Yvonne took in the gracious gesture and made sure to put it in the fridge.

"Hey, it seemed like you knew Kai. How'd you meet?"

The moment Yvonne dreaded finally came. Yvonne turned around to face Luther.

"Uhm… I don't know if I want to say."

This only piqued his interest more. He stopped eating and set the sandwich down.

"What do you mean?" He swallowed his bite and wiped his hands on a napkin. Luther looked at her expectantly.

"I really don't think we should talk about it," she said, rubbing her wrists. Yvonne could almost *feel* the ropes against her skin again.

Luther noticed her motion and zoned in.

"Don't tell me…" He got closer to Yvonne and grabbed her wrist.

"W-what…" she stammered, avoiding eye contact. Her face heated up with a blossoming flush.

Luther wasn't dumb. He knew what Kai's special interest was and he knew the signs.

"I know how to, too," Luther declared jealously. He was jealous at the fact that Kai had engaged with Yvonne in that type of thing. Not to mention he got to see her in tight fitted clothing…sensual and private.

"What?" Yvonne blurted, trying to play coy. "What do you know how to do?" She was hoping he didn't know what had happened, or what she was thinking.

"Bondage. Shibari. Kinbaku. I know it." His grip tightened against her wrist. Yvonne didn't know what to do. It was enticing, the feeling of restraint against her, but she was in a predicament. This wasn't the time for it.

"It's not like that…" Yvonne said, releasing herself from his grasp. "I just went along with Cherise that day, that's all."

"Did you like it?" Luther asked, hovering over her with his big stature. He could see her face was blushed with interest. He knew Yvonne did, but he wanted to hear it for himself. He could see her shaking ever so slightly under his grip.

Yvonne gulped.

"That's not the point." She peered over to the stacks of paper. "We should stay focused."

Luther sighed and put his bitterness aside. His hair was a mess as well. He brushed it upwards and made a mental note to get it trimmed.

"I don't feel good engaging with you, especially when everything is so fresh. I don't think Hyouko would like it either."

Luther bit his tongue. He grimaced and shook his head.

"Do you really think you two will be able to come out of the woods with this?" He wasn't even thinking for his own interest at this point. He was genuinely concerned for Yvonne's safety and mental well-being.

"I don't know yet," Yvonne admitted, giving a distant look. She didn't—*couldn't*—give up on Hyouko yet. She was being unrealistic but needed time for it to sink in.

"Maybe it's not realistic…but I really deeply liked him. *Love* him, if you will," Yvonne said under her breath.

"Forget about him! Let me help you forget about him," Luther exclaimed, grabbing Yvonne's shoulders. He was breathless from exerting and suppressing his emotions.

"It's not that easy…" Yvonne began to tear up again. She didn't think she had anymore tears left in her. "His hair, his eyes, his face, his smile. The way he held me, comforted me, spoke to me." Yvonne's voice cracked and pitched the more she went on.

Luther embraced her into a tight hug.

"Let me do that for you. Let me be the centre of your infatuation and love. Let me be the one to hold you, comfort you, and love you. I'll wait for you. However long it takes, I will be by your side." His voice was pleading and genuine. He wanted Yvonne more than anything.

"I-I don't know…" Yvonne said. She tried to snap out of her sorrowful, pitiful demeanour. She needed to be strong.

"Let me show you. I'll be here." He was earnest, calm, and determined.

"Let me say this once: even if I knew where they were, I wouldn't tell you." Kersa's fingers crumpled the cigarette she was working on, agitated while she spoke on the phone. She hadn't slept for days and it didn't seem like she would get much anytime soon. Her teeth clenched tightly as she spoke. It was clear what Kersa had to do. There wasn't much time left. Kersa mumbled under her breath before hanging up abruptly. She stared into the muggy sky that was shrouded in neverending clouds. A ringing came from her pocket again. Kersa cleared her throat and combed through her hair before answering.

"Hey babe, don't worry. Sorry, work got me caught up again. I'll come soon." Kersa's fingers suffocated the phone in her hand as she tried to converse normally. "I love you, Blake."

# Chapter 16

Yvonne hadn't heard from Hyouko for a couple days. Nothing had moved since then; even Ax seemed absent, which Cherise didn't mind. It wasn't like she expected to marry him. Kersa had been missing in action as well, which certainly didn't bring any peace of mind to Yvonne. It was difficult for Yvonne to go about her day as if a heavy weight wasn't on her shoulder. She dragged herself out of bed and anxiously stuck to her phone, hoping Kersa would call. No letters had come. That was expected; afterall, everything was out in the open with Hyouko. Assuming that was being dealt with, Yvonne managed to get herself together and head into her office.

Cherise watched Yvonne walk in and tried not not to make any strange expressions. She had never seen Yvonne look so dead. Her outfits that were usually on point and meticulous were lazy and mismatched. Somehow, even with staple clothing, she managed to pick all the wrong things.

"Hey, are you okay?" Cherise asked, rolling her chair over to Yvonne's. Yvonne plopped herself into her seat and gave a ghoulish exhale.

"No, but I think a coffee might fix it," she lied, hoping to ease Cherise's concern.

"It's almost Christmas season. You know what that means!" Cherise chimed in a sing-song tune. "New coffee flavours!" She did jazz hands.

Yvonne knew Cherise was trying her best to cheer her up despite not knowing the circumstances. Yvonne gave a half-hearted chuckle and smiled factitiously.

"It sounds like a date," Yvonne cheered, wincing at the amount of energy it took to muster that positivity.

They both gathered themselves to head over to the coffee shop across the street. Yvonne complimented Cherise's cashmere scarf that she had flung over her neckline, drooping one side longer than the other. It was idiotic of Yvonne to have not dressed appropriately, as she almost instantly regretted it as they ventured over.

"It's a Christmas party. You have to come." She reached over to grab her coffee, pouting at Yvonne. Yvonne gave a tiresome sigh and bit her chapped lips.

"It's not like I don't want to…" That was a full-fledged lie. "But I have a lot going on right now. Some personal issues." Yvonne thanked the barista for the drink and held it between her frostbitten hands.

"Oh my god. Is it Hyouko? What happened?" Cherise loved gossip. This time it wasn't gossip and Yvonne didn't know how to navigate it.

"No, just other stuff. It's nothing juicy." Yvonne tried to laugh it off. Quite honestly, she was tired and was ready to head home.

"You really don't look well." It was imminent that Yvonne was going to become sick in some way or another. "Have you gotten enough sleep lately?" Cherise noticed the gloomy bags that sunk into Yvonne's under eyes.

"Just a lot to think about," Yvonne admitted, brushing off her concern. "Are you bringing Ax to your Christmas party?"

Cherise dismissed his name, waving her hand in the air.

"I had my fun but honestly, I don't think he was into me like that. After that night, he basically ghosted me!"

Figures. It was really too bad but it gave Yvonne relief knowing he wouldn't tear her apart for the sake of their case.

404

"Anyway, you have to come! It won't be fun without you," Cherise persisted. She really knew how to tug on heartstrings. Cherise gave those pleading, cherished eyes.

"Fine…" Yvonne groaned, checking the calendar on her phone. "What day did you say it was for?"

"The twenty third!" Cherise was ecstatic just from the sheer hope of Yvonne coming. "Don't bring anything! I just want you to come. Be my Christmas gift." She winked playfully.

Hyouko sent one message. He was just checking in, seeing how Yvonne was doing. It was a brief message. Quick and to the point. He did add a tender comment at the end of the line. *Hope you're well, missing you.* Those were the words. Yvonne responded as quickly as she could but it didn't matter. Hyouko wouldn't answer. Dismayed, Yvonne held her phone close to herself everywhere she went.

*Luther: 5:47 p.m. Dinner?*

How dearly she wished that it was Hyouko. Dinner wasn't a thought in her mind, but she desperately needed a distraction. She longingly touched the necklace that hung perpetually on her neck. Yvonne never took it off, even in the most uncertain times.

*Yvonne: 5:49 p.m. Why not.*

Yvonne agreed to have dinner. Luther became more excited at how compliant and agreeable she had been lately. He knew it was because of the troubling scenario that was ongoing, but he took it as a blessing as it gave him an opening. Besides him being jealous over the event that happened between Kai and Yvonne, he overlooked it and was optimistic of the future. Luther displayed a playful grin as he got himself tidied up before meeting her. He knew he had to be careful with Yvonne and how he proceeded, especially in a messy situation like this. He slid on some chino pants, a knitted sweater, a long coat, and leather boots. The snow danced in the air as he opened the door, getting blinded by the sheer, bright light. Even with the sun setting, the snow reflected the beams off its pure form, illuminating all that went around it. Luther brushed his hair with his hands, taking in the length of his locks and realising how desperately he needed to get a trim. Afterall, long hair was never his fancy, unlike Hyouko.

How could one feel anything? Yvonne stared in the mirror before leaving her flat, feeling the chill permeate from outside. She closed her curtains to retain the leftover heat and shadows that remained. The cold from outside withered her soul, invading from the tips of her fingers down to the soles of her feet. As if all the stress and chaos made her numb, she couldn't recall what it felt like before. Usually, the winter weather would drive her to dress in intricate layers; however, her mind was elsewhere as she threw on a sweater and then a hoodie before heading out.

Juxtaposition between the two was obvious. Yvonne seemed lost, unwell, while Luther displayed a suppressed but giddy expression. It wasn't ideal that he looked so happy across from Yvonne, as it garnered glancing looks. Yvonne picked apart the cod in front of her, using the fork to separate every individual flake. Luther watched ardently, swishing his beverage and sipping it occasionally.

"Is the cod not to your liking?" Luther gestured to the piece that had stuck itself onto her fork.

Yvonne snapped out of the trance she was in and shook her head, biting at it gingerly. She was not hungry at all.

"No, it's good." She offered a strained smile. It was good, just not something she could rejoice about through the aching in her body and mind. Taking tiny tears of the cod's flesh, she savoured the flavour and appreciated it the best she could. Luther, knowing that her mood was primarily being affected by Hyouko, knew he couldn't avoid it for long.

"So, how is he?" Luther inquired, narrowing in at her expression. Yvonne's gaze softened knowing that he was asking about Hyouko.

Softened, yes, but not in a good way. It gave her pain thinking about everything. She had never been given the opportunity or life experience to dwindle in big relationship problems, nevermind one like this. It wasn't everyday a girlfriend found out their lover was actually the enemy.

Yvonne shook her head. "No word," she breathed, still peeling away at the cod. It was painful to watch.

"Let's pack this up and take a stroll through the park," Luther suggested, bringing the plate closer to him while waving for the waiter. Yvonne didn't resist and gnawed at the edges of the fork. It made Luther frustrated knowing how helpless he was. Nothing seemed to cheer Yvonne up or bring her attention elsewhere. It angered him, knowing how much Hyouko had Yvonne on a leash like a dog. He grit his teeth, tasting the faint irony spell peruse his taste buds.

They walked side-by-side. The air was beyond frigidly cold and relentlessly scowled at Luther's cheeks, making them blush pink. It didn't seem to phase Yvonne as she trekked on, staring into the forever nothingness. The watch tower clock could be seen overhead, letting Luther know it was getting late. Even the beds of water frosted over, encapsulating any living organism within its icy walls. "Alaska."

Yvonne's eyes met Luther's. He was looking down, eager to catch her gaze.

"Excuse me?" she asked.

"That's where I was from," he continued, matching Yvonne's slow pace. "We moved here from Alaska. It's even colder than this." Luther stuck his hand out to catch a stray snowflake. It landed on his palm for a millisecond before melting from the heat of his hands.

"I had no clue," Yvonne commented. She tried her best to engage in the conversation. "So, you like snow?"

Luther chuckled.

"I actually hate it. But that's only because I enjoy the sun, the trees, and the warm breeze." His eyes closed as he tried to imagine the summer heat against his skin. Of course it didn't work so well as the chill stuck to him like a grappling hook.

"I love the fall and winter," Yvonne spoke, staring up into the sky. The snow bombarded towards them, creating a surreal snowy scene. The corners of her mouth flicked up as she felt the snow melt against her cheeks. They walked along the pathways running against the lake, passing a couple benches here and there. Most of the time it was just the sound of their breathing that took up the air. Yvonne knew she should've dressed in more appropriate layers, as her nose began to run and her body became numb. Luther took notice and instantly reached towards Yvonne. He drew his coat off himself and slung it around her. His coat was warm and large, acting like a blanket on top of Yvonne's smaller stature.

"I don't want you getting sick," he said with worry in his eyes. He tugged on the edges of the coat to bring it closer to her body, keeping the heat in. Yvonne was slightly hesitant but couldn't deny the gesture, as she felt a cold threaten her wellbeing.

"Thank you," she said quietly, glancing down.

In the dark, she could see a figure further away from them. She squinted into the distance, causing Luther to also become curious of what she was trying to look at.

"Do you know them?" Yvonne asked, taking note of how suspicious this person was. Despite it being cold, the person was covered from head to toe, wearing circular glasses that reflected whatever light that hit them. As soon as they saw Yvonne zoning onto them, they faced a different direction as if they were looking at something else.

"No... I also was wondering the same. They've been following us for a few minutes." Luther took a protective stance in front of Yvonne. His head thumped, trying to think of anyone that would be tailing them. The executioner? Maybe? Hard to say. So far no indication of threat or ally. "I should take you home," he said, guiding Yvonne's waist towards the pathway out. Luther took observant glances back and around, making sure no one else was tailing them.

"I need to make a quick phone call." Luther opened the car door for Yvonne, carefully letting her settle in before pulling out his phone. "Yeah, it's me. Any updates?"

Yvonne could hear the murmuring on the other end. It was probably Kai. She watched out her window for any sign of life. Maybe it was Kersa's connection? She checked her phone to see if Kersa had tried getting in contact with her. Nothing. Yvonne sighed and sunk into the car seat, praying for this anxiety riddled nightmare to end. Luther got in the car and gave a deep sigh of frustration as he closed the door. Yvonne looked at him expectantly, waiting to hear an update.

"Not really much. Apparently they started to shut everything down and *fast*." Luther started the car and reversed out of the parking spot, using Yvonne's headrest as leverage as he looked back. "Tamocus is in a frenzy, as well as our company. Obviously this is out of our control, so now there are bigger fish after them." He glared at Yvonne's expression. He knew she was still thinking about Hyouko as a saviour, as a lover. "You need to forget about him. He's a bad person." Luther's words stung Yvonne's ears as he said them. She darted a look over to him.

"*He* is not a bad person." She broke, balling her fists tightly. "He is not a bad person. Endymion, or whoever the hell that guy is, *is* a bad person."

Luther scoffed as he continued to drive. He knew it was pointless to keep egging her on about Hyouko. If he wanted to be a good guy to her, he would have to lay low and be someone of support. He rolled his neck and made a slicing sound as he inhaled.

"I don't know, Yvonne, but whatever you do, I am here for you."

The rest of the car ride was silent. As Luther drove up to her place, he grasped her forearm and pulled her closer to him.

"Get your things. I'll be waiting here."

"Excuse me?" Yvonne said as her brows furrowed with angst.

"It's too dangerous to leave you alone at your place. God knows what they'll do to get what they want, whatever it is." Luther's eyes were warning her as if he knew something bad was bound to happen.

"I can't just abandon my place… Besides, where would I go?"

"To my place."

Yvonne sat in her seat, marinating in his words.

"You're joking. I am not going to sleep over at your place."

Luther gripped harder against her skin in a pleading manner. It was scary yet earnest.

"Please," he begged. "This way I know you'll be safe."

Yvonne really didn't think much would happen to her, nevermind someone coming *after* her. She didn't feel like she was in imminent danger at all. What? The worst they could do was scavenge her flat like a mad man.

"I don't know… I don't really feel comfortable sleeping at your place." She glanced over to her window, noticing the curtains blowing in the wintriness. It was dark inside of course. Eerie. "Maybe I can sleep at Cherise's. I'm sure she won't mind."

Luther couldn't protest that suggestion. Endymion's critters had been all over Cherise's apartment, so he doubted they'd come back to pick another bone.

"Alright." He nodded. "Call her and ask."

Luther dropped her off at Cherise's. As one could imagine, Cherise was over the moon to have a sleepover with Yvonne. She met Yvonne at the door and jumped around like a child, hugging her like they were best friends. Luther smirked as he waved the two good bye. Yvonne waved with an uncertain grin before entering the building. Luther gripped the coat that remained on the passenger side, holding onto the warmth that lingered from Yvonne's body. Luther knew more than Yvonne did, in terms of the case. He didn't want to frighten her, so he'd withheld some information. Yes, there was someone following them and while it could've been anyone, he had suspicions it was the executor. In each team, there was usually someone they would refer to as an 'executor.' Their role was mostly law ridden whether that be for the bad or good. They intercepted when needed and could usually determine whether or not the case went as expected. Luther had a feeling that Yvonne's team would have one but so far he had no leads. While it was the standard, it didn't necessarily mean they had an executor. After all, Luther's team had only consisted of him, Kai, Peter, and Nova. Peter was no executor, he was just the intel. It wouldn't be a surprise if Endymion's executor decided it was time to cut things once and for all in order to salvage what was left of their plan. Luther drove into the city night life, hoping to catch something. His eyes were riveted to the blurring street signs and lights as he grumbled to himself. It was time to visit an old friend.

# Chapter 17

Yvonne clung onto her phone as if it were her baby. Admittedly, it made Cherise a little uncomfortable to watch. Yvonne was so uptight and silent, it was as if she was having a bit of psychosis.

"Hey, you okay?" Cherise held Yvonne's shoulder and sat next to her. Cherise was beyond worried. She'd never seen Yvonne like this before. Yvonne sighed and let go of the phone. It fell to the ground, making a clattering sound before laying dead.

"Sorry. Thank you for letting me stay over without question." Yvonne glanced at Cherise. Cherise didn't question why Yvonne asked to sleep over. As soon as she heard the words, she said yes. Cherise smiled and gave Yvonne a tight, loving hug.

"You don't have to explain anything you don't want to. I'm just happy to be able to be someone you can turn to!"

Yvonne's lip quivered ever so slightly. Cherise was so comforting, which was something she desperately needed.

"I hope you were able to save some of your collection." Yvonne nudged towards the closet where she had last seen the mess. Cherise groaned and opened up the closet. Some of the collection was neatly stacked, and there was a pile that resembled that of a carcass.

"I could only manage this much. The rest are goners. Who shreds this type of stuff anyway? Lunatics!" Cherise exclaimed, holding a maimed portfolio in her hands. It was an eyesore really; it was torn to pieces with dangling strips helplessly floating against gravity. "The police said that nothing was stolen and there were no footprints so they couldn't do anything about it. '*Consider yourself lucky*,' they said. Can you believe that? These were priceless!" Cherise scoffed and rolled her eyes. She plopped onto her plush bed, sinking into the soft mattress. She gestured for Yvonne to join, patting the vacancy next to her.

"My clothes are dirty," Yvonne said, pulling the fabric of her sweater. "I should probably shower. Can I use it?"

Cherise jumped up from her laying position and made a mischievous expression.

"No, you can't shower," she joked. "Of course you can. It's down the hall, to the left. Towels are in the linen closet. You can use my washed PJs." Cherise tossed a bundle towards Yvonne. "Say hi to Nora for me!"

"Nora? Your roommate, right?" Yvonne held the clothes tightly, pivoting towards the hall.

"Yessirreee!"

It was much needed; a hot, sudsy shower. Yvonne walked back into Cherise's room, who was sprawled across her bed, mindlessly watching some videos. Cherise looked back at Yvonne as soon as she smelled the soap scent come into her room.

"Where'd you get this soap?" Yvonne asked, sniffing herself. It was magnificent and delicate. Rose petals, jasmine, and refreshing linen lapsed into her nose and coated her body.

"You like it?" Cherise said excitedly. She pulled out a bottle from under her bed and handed it to her. "It's this real nice brand I recently found. It's from an import shop nearby. We should go someday! Here, take this for now."

Yvonne hesitantly took the bottle. "Here, let me pay for it. How much?" She grabbed her purse and took her wallet out, ready to exchange products. Cherise huffed and rejected the gesture.

"Absolutely not! Just take it. A gift! Don't worry about it." Cherise smiled and gave a thumbs up. "It really suits you anyway."

404

Yvonne blushed and gingerly placed the bottle in her bag.

"Thank you. I'll get you back." Yvonne picked her phone up, hoping to see a message or something. There was.

*Hyouko: 11:10 p.m. Can we meet?*

Yvonne had to remind herself to breathe, forcing a gulp down her restricted airway, She typed as fast as she could.

*Yvonne: 11:11 p.m. Yes*

*Hyouko: 11:11 p.m. I'll meet at your place. 10 mins.*

"I have to go," Yvonne said abruptly, shaking as she fumbled her purse strap onto her shoulder and brushed her wet hair behind her ears.

"Wait, what? Where are you going? Should I come?" Cherise became erratic with the same energy Yvonne was putting out.

"No, no. I'll only be a few minutes. I gotta do something really quick." Yvonne left faster than Cherise could comprehend. Dumbfounded, Cherise stared out her door, watching only the air that had once held Yvonne. Yvonne bolted, scared she'd miss Hyouko's appearance. Never had she run as fast as she did, becoming out of breath rather quickly. She made it to her house within eight minutes. When she arrived at her flat door, she realised there was a small crack. Did she haphazardly leave it ajar? Yvonne carefully opened the door wider, peeking in through the gap. The lights were off as they were before she had left, and she felt a small draft from the window. Yvonne worriedly split the crevice wider, allowing herself in to close the window. It was biting; the snow from outside made its way in, creating its own winter wonderland inside her apartment. Yvonne cursed at herself not only for leaving it open so carelessly, but for also leaving without a coat. She was freezing in the pyjamas she had borrowed from Cherise. They were flannel pyjamas with a small cat detail at the pocket of her shirt. It was cute and cosy, but not nearly warm enough to keep her sane. Yvonne shivered as she typed, her body trying to fight the cold.

*Yvonne: 11:22 p.m. Are you here? Let me know so I can come down.*

Yvonne flicked the light on in the living room. That's when she saw them. A ding rang through her flat as their phone screen lit up. Yvonne began to scream for help before the person lunged towards her, tackling her to the ground. Yvonne was pinned under the restraint of the intruder, helpless against their weight.

"Shut up."

She recognized his voice. It was Daniel. Yvonne tried to escape his grasp, thrashing under him. Daniel remained calm with his hand planted against Yvonne's mouth. She could barely breathe against all the pressure from being subdued under him, along with her mouth being covered. His light eyelashes reflected the dim ambiance, displaying an angelic look. How deceiving.

"I'm not one to complain often, but you've really fucked things up." Daniel spoke with a malicious tone. He sighed as he checked Hyouko's phone with his other hand. "Eager to see him. So eager, you didn't even stop to think of the danger you could potentially be in." At this point, Yvonne stopped fighting against his grip as she knew it was pointless.

"It's simple. Tell me where the kill switch is and I'll be on my way," Daniel whispered in her ear. It sent shivers down her spine in contrast to the cold that danced in her flat. "Don't scream. I'm gonna let go of your mouth, but if you scream, I'll make you regret it. Understand?"

Yvonne nodded.

He let go of her mouth, allowing her to take deeper breaths than she had before. She held back tears and tried to calm herself down, not wanting to display the true fear coursing through her body.

"I don't know what you're talking about." Yvonne tried to enunciate through his weight. She slid her arm out from under her body, grasping her phone.

"Ah ah." Daniel snatched the phone out of her hand. "I doubt calling 911 would do you any good. I'll be outta here quick. I just need to get what I came for."

"I don't know anything about a kill switch," Yvonne continued, realising that her legs had gone numb between his weight and the frost-bitten floor. "It kinda hurts."

Daniel got off Yvonne while holding her wrists between his hands, then led her to her couch, gesturing for her to sit. Yvonne warily sat on the couch and faced him. He leered over her with a menacing expression.

"I bet you'd know where your case files are."

Yvonne crossed her arms, simultaneously in defiance and to try to warm herself up.

"Where's Hyouko?" Yvonne shouted. "What did you do to him?"

"Who cares about Hyouko right now. Where is the case?" Daniel jeered.

"What good is that? I've got what you guys have got."

Daniel smirked with annoyance.

"You're not really in a position to be so cocky." Daniel lifted her chin towards his direction. "I can ransack your place instead if you'd like."

Yvonne wasn't a fan of that idea, but she didn't know what she could potentially be compromising. If only Kersa would answer her!

"How do you know *I* have it?"

"I don't. Can't hurt to check." He grinned slyly, coming in closer to Yvonne's face. "Let's get this over with, huh?"

Yvonne rebelled against his command and sprung up from the couch, trying to make a quick grab towards her phone. Daniel immediately caught wind of what she was attempting and slammed her body back against the floor. Yvonne shrieked in pain, feeling the crack in her joints from impact.

"Look what you've made me do. This didn't have to happen." Daniel flicked a knife out from his pocket. "You try a fast one on me again and this thing will become friends with your skin." It was terrifying hearing that from someone who seemed so lanky and displayed themselves as cherubic. Yvonne heaved as she tried to manage the pain electrocuting her veins. Tears formed at the edge of her waterline, ready to dive down. It blurred her vision tremendously and had a cooling effect due to the chill in the room. Suddenly, Yvonne heard a hard punching sound, followed by an uneven weight and shift on top of her.

"You fucking bastard."

Yvonne could hear Hyouko, but could barely see him from the view she was stuck in. Daniel was still on top of her, debating on whether or not to face Hyouko head on or to stick with trying to subdue them both. He wasn't given much of a choice, as Hyouko socked him again in the face this time. Daniel got up and decided to fight back. Petrified, Yvonne took this as an opportunity to escape the warzone. She fled to the kitchen area to grab the case. Hyouko's sleeves were rolled up just to the elbow, displaying his strength as he pummelled Daniel. Daniel swung in retaliation but eventually cowered to defensive positions to block his hits.

"What did you expect? What *do* you expect?" Daniel shouted under Hyouko's attacks. "You think you can live a normal life as if you're not a part of this, a part of us?"

Hyouko glanced over to Yvonne worriedly, ushering her to escape. Yvonne felt her knees give out in fear, but she pressed on with adrenaline.

"I don't want her to get involved," Hyouko said firmly. He grappled Daniel's collared shirt and drew him closer. "I told you not to go after her." His eyes were dark with hurt and fury.

Daniel smirked. There was blood on the crevices of his lip, a startling contrast to his pale complexion.

"Like I have a choice?"

Those words fell hard on Hyouko, Yvonne could tell. Even though she couldn't possibly fathom the burden they had, she knew it wasn't necessarily their choice. She inched closer to the exit, carrying the two cases. Daniel hung onto Hyouko's grip, preventing him from gripping harder onto his shirt. He made eye contact with Yvonne, and contemplated pouncing on her. Hyouko gave a warning motion to Daniel, eliciting Daniel to smirk. His long, wispy blond hair was tainted with crimson blood as he swung to look at Yvonne again.

"You're lucky this time." Daniel directed his stare back to Hyouko. "I think I've gotten enough proof that I tried to obtain it. I'll leave for now." He held his hands up in surrender. He wasn't dumb enough to think he could overpower Hyouko with the difference between their builds.

Hyouko aggressively let go of Daniel and wiped the blood from his own face. Yvonne was still struck with fear as she gazed at Hyouko's frightening demeanour. His face was bruised from what looked like a striking that happened beforehand, and his lip had a gash on its side. His bun stayed messy at the back of his crown with a few stray strands sticking out as usual. Hyouko stuck out his hand, gesturing for his phone back.

"Get out," Hyouko ordered.

Daniel scoffed before swivelling around and exiting the flat. He gave an intense glare at Yvonne as he passed, eyes gleaming against the light. Yvonne held her breath, hoping he would walk away and never come back, but she knew she was being too hopeful.

"Are you okay?" Hyouko started towards her, reaching out to caress her face. Her eyes watered at the sight of him with overwhelming emotions. Despite the blood and hardened fingers, Yvonne leaned in towards his embrace. It was a foolish move. Afterall, he was the enemy. It was obvious there was some apprehension in her moves. Hyouko couldn't blame her.

"I need you to trust me," he mouthed slowly, cupping her face with a sheer sense of will. "Give me the case."

Yvonne's face paled, matching the draught that had swung in the room. His hand burned the skin on her cheeks as her heart pounded vigorously. How could she trust him? What would he do? Then what? Then what?

"I know it's hard for you to trust me," Hyouko said, taking notice of Yvonne's fearful expression. "I wouldn't do anything to hurt you. I know it's scary, but I have a plan. We need to get through this together and never look back."

She wanted to, she really did, but it was a matter of many things. Her job, Kersa, Hyouko, Endymion, Luther, and even entities she didn't know about. Yvonne stuttered and retracted herself from his hand a little. What if he actually was as dangerous as Luther said? What if he lied to Yvonne to manipulate her the way he needed to? Was this all a hoax?

"I can't do that." Yvonne shook her head, stepping backwards to retrieve the cases. "I don't know what I'm supposed to do right now, and I can't fully trust you after everything that's come out." She clung onto the cases and held the old one tight to herself. She knew that Hyouko wasn't a bad person at heart, but needed to retain a professional mindset, knowing that she was responsible for the cases. The best person to give them to was Kersa.

Hyouko breathed a deep breath but nodded.

"Okay, " he said, "I understand. I'll figure out another way." Hyouko headed towards the door, looked at his phone, then took one last glance towards Yvonne. "I'll see you again, beautiful." There was a pained smile on his face, his eyes barely able to stay on hers. Yvonne watched out the door, listening as his footsteps descended, until the entrance doors clacked.

# Chapter 18

*5:04 a.m. Meet me, same spot as before, twenty minutes.*

It was Kersa. Yvonne couldn't sleep after she retreated to Cherise's. Cherise was oblivious to anything that had happened, as Yvonne didn't disclose the interaction she had just had. Yvonne tossed and turned on the bed she shared with Cherise, catching glimpses of Cherise's drooling slumber. She turned away to face the wall. She helped cover the two of them with the thick, fluffy blanket. It had pillowed details with an embroidered design. It truly felt cosy. Yvonne knew Cherise would be mortified if Yvonne mentioned the drool that had now darkened the edge of the quilt. Besides her unrelenting brain and train of thoughts, Yvonne couldn't ignore the pounding and aching pain resonating throughout her body. For a lanky guy, Daniel had a lot more weight and muscle than he seemed. That's when Kersa texted. Yvonne choked on her spit when she got the notification and tried to slowly ease her way out of the cot. Twenty minutes barely gave her enough time to get there. Yvonne wasn't even sure if a taxi would be available around her area at this time. She scrambled out and made sure to bring her coat this time, scooping the cases in her arms before departing.

"Where have you been?" Yvonne asked, shivering through the unabating cold. Kersa seemed unphased as usual, wearing her common professional attire. It was like she couldn't care less that her feet were inches deep in the snow with flats on. Kersa patted her pockets frantically before realising she had no more darts. She sighed and rolled her eyes, a hefty black shadow following the movement of her eyeball. Yvonne grimaced, knowing that Kersa hadn't slept well, if at all.

"I ran out of cigs, but no matter." Kersa stuffed her hands in her pockets and looked at Yvonne. "You brought the case?"

Yvonne nodded as she clung onto one case in her fist, and the other to her body. Honestly, she was wary of bringing it after what happened with Hyouko and Daniel.

"Yes." She leaned closer to Kersa, trying to avoid the steep pits of snow between them. "I don't know what to do. What to do with this, the investigation..." Her voice faltered as she thought about her own personal affairs. Kersa seemed just as frustrated as she strung a deep breath.

"The investigation is done. No investigation. It was a hoax from the start. Tamocus hired us, yes, but since J.J. and Mackie, our most crucial components, are fakes and are part of the perpetrators, the case is dissolved." Kersa cracked her knuckles, taking out her anger and frustration through her joints. "I can't believe this has happened. What a joke. As for the physical case, I need to see something." She gestured for the case, raising her brow expectantly. Yvonne carefully handed it to her.

"No, not that one." Kersa dismissed the newer case and pointed to the previously owned one. "That one."

Yvonne gave a disorientated expression before giving the other. Immediately, Kersa sprang open the case and slammed it down onto the snowy cement. Yvonne made a startled sound but shut up quickly to watch the rest of the show. Kersa felt the seams of the case and went over it again before slowing down. She etched the edge of the seams with her fingernails before digging in and popping the stitching off.

"Before you," Kersa spoke as she continued to rip the stitches, "there was an investigator under the name of *Sterling*. They had a lot of dirt under major organisations, black market industries, dark web connections, and god knows what else more. Fact is, they were on a big bounty list because of that, as well as the kill switch." Kersa paused as she examined Yvonne's face, riddled with intrigue and fear. "Sounds like you've heard of it already. Anyway, after a big incident, they decided to go AWOL. It was for the best. The dust settled, and eventually no one really caught wind of where they were or where the kill switch was. Until someone tipped Endymion off. You see, Sterling's last case was with me. I'm the only one that knew about this kill switch, I just didn't know where. Idiotic, maybe, but to hide it literally in a case is beyond me." Kersa's face lit up as she uncovered the kill switch. It was a tiny memory device neatly cased in slim cellophane and tape. It was the size of a fingerprint with microscopic divots and patterns. Kersa was careful when taking it out because of the ridiculously tiny size. "I'm going to have to keep this in my hands." Kersa clicked it into what looked like a safety lock mechanism and stuffed it into her pockets.

"I have a favour to ask of you."

Yvonne's ears perked up. She never thought of Kersa to be one to ask anything of anyone. "Yes, what is it?"

Kersa sighed and stared up into the dark sky. Billows of clouds formed from her mouth due to the cold, which masqueraded her view.

"Take care of Blake, please."

She said it as a statement, a command, a plea, not a request. Yvonne stood in the soiled snow, taking in the information.

"What do you mean?"

Kersa shrugged and laughed weakly.

"Blake will need you." She grabbed Yvonne's shoulder and shook it a little. "Thank you, in advance."

Yvonne wasn't dumb. She knew that meant something ominous and dreadful. It was like a cliche from a movie. It was a great relief for her to know that she was no longer responsible for the welfare of the kill switch, but now she had foreboding thoughts of being responsible for something more delicate. Yvonne's fingers were sorely frost bitten, and her lips cracked against all the stress and cold. She didn't think what to do after such a great deal of weight was removed from her shoulders. It only made sense to go to Blake's coffee shop after Kersa's request. Yvonne took a few deep breaths before entering the yarrow doorway. Again, that familiar burst of arabica bean air flooded her senses. Yvonne was met with a beaming smile from Blake, who was overjoyed to see their friend again.

"Yvonne!" Blake clamoured, speed walking towards her. "I've missed you so much! Come, try this new flavour I've created." Blake led Yvone towards the barstools and sat her down. They eagerly scurried behind the counter and started grinding a good amount of espresso beans. They hummed to themselves, giddy and glowing.

"Someone's happy," Yvonne said, unable to pull herself out of the mood Kersa had dragged her into.

Blake smiled even wider, which Yvonne didn't think was possible.

"My love surprised me with a blossoming bouquet of honeysuckle, can you believe it? I mean, our anniversary isn't until next month, but she's been extra sweet to me. This morning, she even woke up early to surprise me with breakfast in bed. Sunny side up eggs, sourdough bread lathered in honey butter." Blake shivered at the thought of the piquant notes they had enjoyed earlier. "So I was thinking, maybe, to close up shop early and go shopping for our anniversary. If you could, could you join? I'd love some company, especially when Christmas is rolling 'round." Blake poured the espresso over what looked like a malted honeycomb. They stirred it vigorously to mix the flavours together before pouring oat milk and a sprinkle of sea salt on top of the foam. Blake had a special talent for foam art, which Yvonne hadn't gotten the chance to appreciate until now.

"Wow," Yvonne breathed, taking in the beautiful yet simple design engraved into the foam. "Blake, this is amazing. Thank you." She slid her thumb against the cup, wanting to delve in, but she felt guilt rise inside of her.

"It's my pleasure, besides, I'm the one imposing on you to join me." They winked and spun around carelessly. Of course, as Christmas festivities commenced, Blake's cafe was regularly visited by tourists and people around. Yvonne didn't get the chance to respond before a bustling few came in, ready to order their beverages.

"Be right back!" Blake said, dismissing themselves from Yvonne. Yvonne hesitantly nodded and began sipping on some of the foam. Surprisingly, it was not as sweet as she thought it would be from the malted honeycomb. It could've been the sea salt that offset its sugary taste, or it could've been the melodic symphony of all the flavours of the espresso, oat milk, sea salt, and malted honeycomb together. Yvonne was constantly impressed by Blake's indisposable talent. She had to think how to navigate all of this, especially if she were to join Blake on their shopping spree *for* Kersa. How could she pretend like everything was okay, that Kersa was okay, and that their anniversary would go as planned? A stinging pain lingered in her chest as her own issues began to arise. Thinking of relationships and heartache only fueled her own. Of course Hyouko hadn't reached out, but still, Yvonne checked her phone.

*Luther: 6:45 a.m. Breakfast? Or lunch later?"*

Persistent. Yvonne grumbled with less than sufficient energy to think. There was no way she'd give up Blake's invitation for Luther's.

*Yvonne: 6:47 a.m. Sorry, I have plans. Thanks for asking.*

She watched Blake happily greet and chat with their customers, while simultaneously making their drinks with precision. Although

Yvonne didn't know exactly what was going to happen, she knew it wasn't good.

*Kalman: 6:48 a.m. Can we meet for more details?*

Her message bounced right back. Kersa had disconnected their phone line. Maybe it was even a burner phone. Yvonne's nails dug against her palm as she tried to remain calm under all of the uncertainty.

"So, what do ya say?" Blake's puppy-like energy came full on towards Yvonne. She faked a chuckle and nodded.

"I'd love to."

They wouldn't stop telling Yvonne more about Kersa, and what Kersa meant to them. Yvonne always thought Blake would be the sunshine in their relationship, but everything they described and spoke about made her realise it was the other way around. It took every cell within her body not to show the true solemn feeling she had.

"...and one time, when I was still getting good at this coffee stuff, Kersa insisted on trying every single concoction I made, even if it was distasteful! I remember they drank all of this one flavour that I knew was terrible, but Kersa said it was decent, trying to protect my feelings." Blake was head over heels for Kersa, smiling uncontrollably as they spoke. They walked down a shopping strip in their bundled up attire. Blake was actually stylish and had a nose for contemporary aesthetics. They wore an environmentally conscious puffer jacket, skinny jeans, merino sweater, and leather boots. To keep themselves warm, they donned a cashmere scarf in a beautiful plaid pattern. Yvonne returned the happy memories with a smile, a melancholy smile.

"Let's go in here, Kersa *loves* stuffed animals." Blake tapped at a window display with an assortment of adorable and equally fluffy toys. Yvonne didn't expect Kersa to have such a soft side, and in all honesty, that only made her feel worse. Blake played around and picked up a few of them, examining their ears, face, and button noses. Yvonne did the same, gently playing with their soft and plush bodies. She almost wanted one for herself. A bunny stuck out to her. It was exceptionally cute and reminded her of Hyouko.

"This," Blake declared. "*This* is the one." They showed off a grizzly bear plush with the most dopiest eyes. Yvonne giggled at the sight and patted its head.

"It's so cute," Yvonne said, encouraging Blake to buy it.

"I know! I have to get it for her. She's gonna love it." Blake proceeded to the checkout and picked out a little red bow for it as well. "I'll name it Bean."

Although their shopping wasn't as successful as they had planned, Yvonne and Blake enjoyed their time together. Yvonne almost forgot about the foreboding series of events that was bound to happen. It would be difficult to pretend like she knew nothing about Kersa, as well as what Kersa had been up to leading to the hilt of the event. Yvonne viewed her phone as she swung her shopping bag while walking back to her apartment. It seemed futile to sleep elsewhere when she no longer had the kill switch. She assumed that Endymion would catch wind of the change in ownership and disregard Yvonne as a target altogether. Yvonne jingled her keys before going inside, being extra cautious as she entered. She didn't want to take the chance that there was an uninvited visitor waiting for her. She was met with the familiar scent and view of her space and quickly became comfortable. It was still cold like the last time she was there, so she decided to fuel the fireplace. The crackling sounds were therapeutic once Yvonne finally got it started. It was a drag for her, as it had been a while since she had tended such a thing. She gathered scrap wood that had been lying dormant next to the fireplace, underneath an ottoman. It was handy, since the ottoman served as an extra storage space. Along with that, she managed to scavenge old newspapers and recyclable items and threw them in as extra subsistence. Yvonne was satisfied with the fire she had raised and comfortably sat in front of it, feeling the kisses of the flame's heat against her skin. The warmth was so snug and inviting, Yvonne almost fell asleep.

*Luther: 8:16 p.m. How's a late dinner sound?*

Yvonne's tired eyes forced themselves to focus and respond. She had forgotten about dinner and thought a bit of company might do her some good. Besides, Luther probably had more of an update than she did about the case.

*Yvonne: 8:17 p.m. What do you feel like?*

*Luther: 8:18 p.m. Sushi? Your place I'm assuming?*

*Yvonne: 8:18 p.m. Sounds great. Let me know how much, I'll pay half.*

*Luther: 8:19 P.M. Shut up.*

Yvonne rolled her eyes at his response. There was no way she'd give up that easily. She got up from her chair to tidy her hair up into a claw clip and rummaged through her purse to retrieve some cash.

"I told you no." Luther put the bags of sushi down on the table, refusing the handful of cash Yvonne offered. He unwrapped the scarf from his neck and hung it on the coat hanger.

"Come on, I don't feel good accepting something expensive like this. We're both eating it anyway," Yvonne urged, trying to stuff the cash into his pockets or hands. She was on her tip-toes, trying to stuff it in any way she could like a squirrel. He dodged effortlessly and shimmied away to wash his hands.

"No, just accept it, my treat." He grabbed a hold of her flailing wrist and held it firmly. She stopped, of course, in part due to how resistant his strength was, as well as the fact that she knew she wasn't going to get past him. Oh well, at least she tried.

"Fine," she said, giving a huff of defeat. "Next time, my treat."

Luther watched her eyes carefully before letting her wrist go.

"We'll see about that," he said under his breath. They continued to the living room and sat across from the fireplace, indulging in the sushi. It was a perfect scene, enjoying such lavish food in front of the comforting flames, along with the dim lighting from her adjustable fixtures. It was silent for the most part, except for the crackling sounds. Yvonne watched out the window a few times, taking in the white Christmas ambiance.

"Any plans for Christmas?" Luther asked, breaking the silence.

Yvonne turned to look at him. "Mmm, I think maybe go to Cherise's party. She insisted I be there." Yvonne gnawed on the piece of fresh salmon sashimi, dipping it in soy sauce before engulfing it.

"Let me know if you go. I'll only go if you do." His eyes lingered on Yvonne as he spoke, paying less attention to the sushi. "But anyway, thought you might be curious—Endy is not happy." He stabbed a piece of wasabi before scooping the nigiri. "If you're still in contact with Hyouko, I wouldn't recommend it. Things'll get messy." Luther didn't elaborate after that.

Yvonne stayed quiet, munching on the tamago while she thought.

"Thank you for worrying. I can handle myself."

Luther put his hand on hers.

"I know." He smiled half heartedly.

"I never thought you would want to speak to me privately." Hyouko walked closer to Luther, hands in his pockets while he checked his sides. Luther waited for him at the old, neglected building off the corner of the common streets. It was extremely dark out, only relying on the white banks of snow and lamp posts to illuminate anything. Luther wasn't pleased to see Hyouko, but knew it had to be done.

"Well, you've forced my hand." Luther's eyes were moody, disgruntled. He kicked a bit of snow up into the air with his leather boots and watched it fall back to the ground.

Hyouko watched quietly, examining Luther's defensive demeanour. He scoffed lightly and brushed his fringe to the side, showing more of his face.

"What? You want to hit me or something?" Hyouko jeered, hoping to get to the point of the meeting.

Luther laughed curtly.

"Looks like you've already been beaten. No, I wanted to talk about Yvonne."

Immediately, Hyouko's expression changed to something more aggressive and stand-offish. His lips curled into a smirk as he ran his tongue against his canines. He was irritated but gave Luther a chance to speak.

"What about Yvonne?"

Luther's fists bunched up but he stood his ground.

"I think it's time you stopped playing games. Let go and leave. You're just going to hurt Yvonne."

Hyouko rubbed the back of his neck before responding.

"Who are you to say anything about our relationship?" Hyouko raised his eyebrow as he studied Luther, who was still stern and bundled in a ball of angst.

"I know I can treat her better than you ever could. I can provide her with a life she wants, needs, and deserves. Not some crook like you."

Hyouko gave a warning look. It was filled with a desolate void, but it sent a message to him.

"Watch it," he warned. "You and I can't say what Yvonne wants and needs. That's for her to decide. Besides, don't act like you're unstained. We both know you're not as good as you say."

# Chapter 19

He knew he was being selfish, he did. It was scary what love could do to someone. Hyouko would catch Yvonne out and about, from a distance of course, and watch her intently before going back to his task. It was a blessing to be able to see her coincidentally in areas he would've never thought he'd see her in. She looked stunning; beautiful, as usual. He envied the people around her. He wanted to hold her hand, smile, laugh, and stare into her beautiful eyes. It was a cursed thing, love.

Haruka snapped her fingers in front of Hyouko's face.

"Yvonne, again?" She was disgruntled and started showing it too. "Endy asked us to do this. It's time sensitive, you know." They had to wrap up all the loose ends of the ruse and it was putting a strain on the three of them. Daniel was outside doing something else that was assigned to him, while Haruka and Hyouko started shutting down the cyber parts of it. It wasn't as easy as it sounded, especially when a whole corporation started pulling out their front lines to catch them. Haruka was *actually* versed in cyber hacking and did the majority of the hacking itself, as well as connections and communications. That's how she was set into the role of 'Mackie.' All she did was whatever Endymion ordered her to do. It was illusive and insanely complex, her work and coding. It was notorious in the underground market. Hyouko was an investigator for cyber spaces, more so a spy, people would say, as he was critical, logical, and calm.

Daniel was like the Jack of all trades. It was daunting what the guy would do if one asked. He was rogue and had little to no reserve; it really freaked Hyouko out but he tried to pretend it didn't. Haruka and Hyouko didn't know the full extent of Daniel's capabilities, and quite honestly, didn't want to. Hyouko looked at the corner of the room where Brandy stood, watching over them.

"Can you lay off? We aren't going anywhere," Hyouko called, irritated by the fact they were being eagle-eyed like prey. Brandy grinned and shook his head.

"Endy told me to stick to you guys and watch. Especially you." Brandy thought it was entertaining to round them up like sheep and keep them in. Brandy was the executor of their team and had the same typical demeanour a law enforcer did. He stroked his peppered hair as he chuckled at them.

"Chop chop, you two." He tapped at the watch on his right hand, indicating the pressing matter. Hyouko found it difficult to slip away from his watchful eyes, but managed to do so every so often. He wanted to execute the plan he had in mind, but couldn't find the right source and materials. He so badly wanted to see Yvonne.

The plan was perfect in theory; he'd escape Endymion's gripping claws, make a new identity, and be with Yvonne. Free from everything, he would be able to be himself, and they would live happily and be a normal couple. It wasn't his intention to get her involved, truly. It wasn't hard getting a new identity with all the connections he had over the course of his endeavours with Endymion and the underground market. Shameful as it was, it was the only way out for him. He was told to meet in a small shack underneath a bridge, hidden by shrubs and rubbish. Not very secure and very evidently ignored by authorities, Hyouko abided and approached the destination confidently. There were some curious stares as Hyouko made his way through, mainly from vagrants and smokers. It was important to showcase a rough and stoic exterior in order to be respected by crooks and affiliations from the dark web and market.

"Long time no see. Going on vacation?" He was greeted by a familiar voice. "Nice to see you again finally; you stood us up last time, Sanaka."

"I apologise, Mark," Hyouko responded, extending a hand out for a handshake. "I'll make it up to you."

Mark smirked and accepted the gesture, shaking his hand playfully yet firmly. "Come on, we don't do that here. Get in here, San." Mark brought Hyouko into a squeeze, patting his back roughly. Mark was a little bit taller than Hyouko was, and had a brutish physique and beard. Mark certainly didn't look like the stereotypical lanky hacker boy and definitely intimidated people that met him after corresponding online. Hyouko gave a clumsy laugh, trying to ignore the sting that remained on his back after the series of pats.

"I'm sorry to have asked you for this," Hyouko said, diverting them to the main point. "But yes, somewhat of a vacation."

Mark cocked a brow. Mark had known Hyouko and Endymion's crew for years.

"Why the sneaking though? You asked me not to tell anyone that we met up. I think I ought to know in case I need to have a shanking object under my pillow."

Hyouko wasn't keen on letting Mark know his plans and couldn't jeopardise anything. He shook his head.

"Don't be dramatic, of course I'm going on vacation, but I don't want anyone tailing me… I want some freedom and fresh air. You know how it is."

Mark wasn't convinced but decided not to ask. Endymion was a strict dictator, so he could imagine what it was like, to an extent.

"Looks like you got some new battle scars. Home life not so good, huh?" Mark gestured to the bruising and cuts on Hyouko's face. He tsked at the sight of them and rummaged into his deep jacket pockets. "Here, take this and memorise it well. You know the drill."

Mark handed Hyouko his requested package, sealed in a manila envelope. Hyouko firmly accepted the package and exchanged it with his own envelope. Mark didn't need to count how much was in there; he knew Hyouko wouldn't swindle him like that, especially since he was under Endymion's claws.

"Pleasure doing business with you."

# Chapter 20

Expectedly, Blake was in shambles. Yvonne visited Blake's cafe the next day and every day after, finding Blake in a sea of woes. Kersa couldn't be reached in any sort of communications. Blake found themselves lost about where Kersa was. There was no closure; Kersa disappeared without a peep. It was heartbreaking to watch Blake's sorrowful eyes, confusion, and hurt. Yvonne tried to console Blake as best as she could, giving hugs and space when needed.

"I think you need a break," Yvonne said, petting Blake's back gently. She noticed their dark under eyes and lacklustre complexion. It was obvious they hadn't slept at all over the past few days. Blake shook their head, furrowing their brows.

"No, I can't stop working. The more time I have to myself, the more time I have to cry about Kersa. I'm just so confused. Why would she just leave? Did I do something? Is she okay? Maybe she's coming back, or something happened to her." Blake was spiralling and constantly asked those questions, leaving Yvonne with gritted teeth. It pained her more than anyone could imagine, withholding information, especially when Yvonne was getting a front row seat to Blake's distress. Blake was a popular person, as it turned out. There had been a flood of concerned friends coming in to visit Blake. Yvonne felt a sense of relief knowing that Blake had adequate support, and that Yvonne didn't have to pretend that she had no clue where and what happened to Kersa. In a way, she didn't, but she certainly knew more than anyone else. Yvonne found herself cursing out Kersa in her mind whenever she saw Blake's soulless expression. How heartless could she be?

"Are you sure you don't want to take a vacation? You barely eat, barely sleep, and seem less and less like yourself each day." Yvonne helped brew some espresso behind the bar. More time with Blake allowed her to gain a new skill, especially when it came from expertise. Yvonne poured a shot of espresso and pushed it towards Blake. They sighed and only glanced at the small shot of espresso. Blake's gusto for blending and brewing had dramatically decreased, which was the last thing Yvonne wanted to see. Worst of all, the closer Christmas was, the busier Blake's cafe became. Blake got up from their seat and started sorting bags of beans.

"It's alright. Thanks for seeing me so often. It's like you're my shadow." Blake still had the wherewithal to joke around, but only half-heartedly. "Don't you have to head to work? Take this." Blake handed Yvonne a hot to-go cup filled with a caramel oat latte. Yvonne made a heartfelt expression and accepted the drink.

"You shouldn't have," Yvonne whispered, taking in the rich, sweet scent. "Thank you. I'll see you later."

Blake waved Yvonne goodbye with a pained smile.

It was strange going back to work as if nothing had happened, as if she'd wrapped up a regular case. Yvonne still checked her phone often, just in case Hyouko ever texted or called. Like others, Yvonne dreaded leaving her warm bed to succumb to the frosty air outside. She bundled up warmly with a long wool coat, cashmere sweater, and scarf before heading out. There were masses of dreary faces, still waking up from their slumber while withstanding the relentless cold. Coffee was the run of the mill, permanently staining the walls with its scent. Luther came over with cups of coffee in hand, looking shocked when he saw Yvonne was already holding one.

404

"I was too late, was I?" Luther sat the cup down at her desk anyway, sipping on his own. "I added salted caramel in it, just how you like it."

Yvonne looked up at him and grinned. "Thank you, but I'll have you know that I don't need you to get me a coffee so often. I've been seeing Blake before work more often than not, and they usually send me off with a cup of coffee."

"I'd rather not take the chance you don't have one," Luther responded with warmth. "Anyway, have you heard the Christmas market is opening up? I've got two tickets. Would you like to attend with me?" He held up two slips of paper and waved them in the air. Yvonne gave a small smile, thinking about roasted chestnuts and other various holiday venues. Yvonne felt a buzz in her pocket, distracting her from Luther's question. Luther peered over in curiosity, garnering Yvonne to cover her screen. He shrugged and looked away, sipping his coffee.

*Hyouko: 9:34 a.m. Hey, I'll call you at 12.*

Yvonne's heart skipped a beat. She'd waited so long to hear from him and was worried sick.

*Yvonne: 9:35 a.m. Ok, I'll wait for your call.*

She had to keep in mind the last incident and allowed herself to calm down and not get too excited by his text. Afterall, it might *not* be him on the other end.

"Someone's happy," Luther pointed out, giving a slight nudge. He had pretty much accepted that his aggressive pursuit for Yvonne wasn't working, so he'd switched methods. He hoped that with gentle nurturing, she'd fall for him. "Christmas market? I'll text you the time and date?" he reminded Yvonne, hoping to get an answer.

Yvonne nodded and agreed.

"It sounds great. I'm really looking forward to chestnuts that have been roasted over a fire."

"Me too." Luther gave a longing look before retreating to his desk.

*"It's nice to hear your voice again."* Hyouko sounded breathless on the other end. Yvonne held the phone close to her ear, wanting to hear more.

"Same with yours," Yvonne responded. She didn't want the conversation to end. "How have you been?"

Hyouko chuckled. *"Worried about me? You're always so kind… Don't worry. I'm well. I'm more worried about you."*

"I'm alright, I promise." She was lying, but didn't want to drag down the mood.

*"Good, that's good."* There was a slight pause, giving a small space for their breathing to be heard. *"Remember the last time we spoke, I promised you that things would be alright. I've been tying some ends here and I think it's safe to say that everything is settled."*

Yvonne's breathing was almost nonexistent. She was waiting to hear more.

"You mean…?"

*"Yes, let's be together. You and me. If you'll still have me."* Despite the static sound from the other end, Yvonne heard Hyouko's voice waver, as if there were any doubts about where her heart stayed.

"Yes! Yes, please." Yvonne's voice raised in excitement and relief. Her hands trembled slightly; her nerves were still bunched and bundled. "Is that even a question?" She almost laughed in the delirium of emotions she was caught in.

Hyouko's trembling laughter could be heard before he spoke. *"I don't know, what if your heart had a change of mind? I'm overjoyed to still be in your heart and mind. I'll meet you at your place after work. What time do you get off?"*

"I'll be home at 5:30!" Yvonne responded immediately. She checked the clock, only stroking ten after twelve. She groaned. Oh how she wished time would go faster.

*"Then I'll see you at 5:30, your place, my beautiful."*

As soon as it was permissible to leave work, Yvonne darted out of the building and hailed a taxi to get to her place. She couldn't wait another minute and wanted to see Hyouko as soon as possible. She anxiously bit her lip, watching the trees fly by as the taximan drove.

"First date?" the taxi driver asked, taking notice of Yvonne's anxious patterns.

"You could say that," Yvonne said, nervously laughing, hoping he wouldn't ask anything else.

"Nothing like young love," he said, chuckling to himself. He was an older fellow with white hair and laugh lines. Crow's feet decorated the corners of his eyes and face, indicating a fulfilling life. Yvonne wanted to compliment his well lived life, but they arrived just at that moment.

"Thank you, you've made my day." Yvonne smiled as she exited the taxi. She rummaged through her purse and handed him the cash. The taximan waved her goodbye as he drove away. Yvonne saw Hyouko sitting on a wooden bench, waiting patiently for her. Panicked, she checked the time. It was only 5:23 p.m. She tucked her hair behind her ear and flattened out her coat before approaching him.

"Were you waiting long?" Yvonne's eyes met his. He had a loving glint in his eye and a soft look sprawled across his face. Despite the healing bruises and cuts, Yvonne could only focus on his beauty and charismatic features.

"No, not at all," Hyouko responded, getting up from the bench and holding her hand tightly. He raised her hand to his lips and planted a tender kiss. She missed that. Hyouko smiled against her hand before meeting her eyes once more. "I've missed you."

"I've missed you, too." Yvonne returned his longing words and refused to let go of his hand. "Endy...?"

Hyouko grimaced slightly before petting her hair with his other hand.

"Shhh," he whispered. "Don't think about it anymore. Everything is okay. It's just me and you now." Yvonne knew better than to think it was that easy, but she allowed herself to be naive and went along with it. She had to trust Hyouko's words, and did so without much hesitation.

"Let's head in, shall we?" Hyouko nodded toward the building. Holding hands, they walked inside, feelings of deja vu circulating them.

"Remember that first night?" Yvonne laughed. It gave her a warm, funny feeling.

"You mean when we got drunk? And when you fell in love with me Mr. Gray?" Hyouko teased, pushing her slightly with his body weight. They swayed off trail a little when he did that, introducing a more playful mood.

"Hey!" she exclaimed, pushing back. She missed his humour and mischievousness. It felt good to be back home, but it felt even better to be back with Hyouko.

"What do you feel like eating?" Hyouko asked as he helped remove Yvonne's coat off her shoulders. He carefully hung it on the coat rack, along with his.

"Hmmm," Yvonne pondered on the question, taking off her scarf and brushing her hair to one side, exposing the nape of her neck. Hyouko's eyes wandered to her bare neck, driving him to kiss it gently. Yvonne was startled by this change of affection as the hairs on her body stood up from the feel. She blushed aggressively as her eyes met his.

"Sorry," Hyouko said, realising what he had done. "Was that too much?"

Yvonne shook her head. She loved the lingering feeling of his lips on her skin.

"No, I just didn't expect it." She planted a kiss on his cheek, going on her tip-toes to meet his height. "How does another challenge sound?"

Hyouko smiled from her gesture of affection. "What challenge?"

Yvonne grinned playfully, brewing a pot of tea for the two of them.

"A spicy challenge. It's cold out, so I thought it would be beneficial and warm us up. Old time's sake?" They both knew what she was referring to. Hyouko loved the idea and excitedly agreed.

"I'm going to win again, and then what? What are we betting this time?" Hyouko was confident he was going to reign victorious after seeing Yvonne's limit from last time.

"Winner gets an IOU?" Yvonne suggested, knowing that it was a broad yet enticing prize.

Hyouko smirked. "Sounds like game!" He took out his phone and began scrolling through delivery apps.

"I'm going to pick the spiciest dishes I can find. You just sit and relax." Hyouko led Yvonne to the couch and plopped her onto it before sitting next to her. He encouraged Yvonne to lay across the couch, using his lap as either a pillow or a foot rest. Yvonne sheepishly chose to use Hyouko's lap as a footrest, allowing her to admire his face from afar. Hyouko browsed intensely, furrowing his brow as if he was making a life or death decision.

"I've ordered it now, so we just wait." His face relaxed and his attention was now all on Yvonne. Yvonne hummed a sign of approval and twiddled her feet. Without even skipping a beat, Hyouko began to massage her feet.

"Ah!" she exclaimed with embarrassment. "My feet are dirty…"

Hyouko fought her off with his fingers. "No, they're perfect," he said, continuing to massage them earnestly. Yvonne reluctantly laid back down to enjoy the massage. Hyouko's technique was skillful and precise. She had never felt such pleasurable massaging before.

"I'm glad you like it," Hyouko said, kissing her ankle gently. It tickled Yvonne, eliciting a giggle.

"Thank you," she said, feeling much more relaxed. Wearing heels and footwear of sorts was not exactly comfortable. "What did you order?" She knew it was pointless to ask, but she wanted to hear more of his tender voice.

"It's a surprise." Hyouko winked, now rubbing her ankles and calves. "Did you want me to start the fire?" Hyouko gestured towards the fireplace with its charcoal and soot.

"I can do it." Yvonne began to get up before Hyouko rejected her advance.

"No, you relax. Let me help you, let me spoil you." Hyouko stretched as he got off the couch and headed to the fireplace with wood. "Besides, I'm the best fire starter around." Yvonne watched him with awe, admiring his strong shoulders and back as he moved about. His long locks were something Yvonne really loved, besides his eyes of course, especially when it drooped or strayed out of his usual bun.

"I didn't know having a gentleman to stoke a fire was called being *spoiled*," Yvonne teased, kicking him in the butt with her extended foot. Hyouko chuckled and pretended to be maimed by her assault.

"Hey, you tell me; has anyone ever bragged about a handsome man doing this?" He took pleasure doing any little thing for Yvonne, but also enjoyed poking fun at her. Yvonne rolled her eyes and huffed.

"So now you're saying you're handsome; someone's got the jive for themselves."

Hyouko gave a sly look at Yvonne after tossing a log into the inlet.

"You tell me, am I handsome?" He came closer to Yvonne, bent on one knee while grappling her soft calf. Of course, this made Yvonne blush profusely and she couldn't deny the obvious; Hyouko was stunningly handsome.

"Shut up," she said, burrowing her face in her hands. He hummed in approval and kissed the top of her foot before getting up to wash his hands in the kitchen.

"Oh, that reminds me!" Yvonne exclaimed, jumping off the couch in excitement. Her feet slapped against the floor as she retreated to her bedroom. Hyouko didn't dare follow her in but peered around the corner curiously. Yvonne burst out of the room, holding an object behind her back.

"Whatcha' got there?" Hyouko was curious and tried to get a peek, causing Yvonne to dodge his puzzling looks.

"I got this for you a little bit ago. I couldn't help myself, it reminded me of you." She pulled out a stuffed bunny from her behind her back, displaying it with the most enthusiastic expression. It struck Hyouko's heartstrings like an old fiddler. He gently picked it up and held it carefully, touching the bunny's face and button nose. "Do you like it?" Yvonne asked eagerly. "I hope it's not too childish for you. Something just came over me when I saw it."

"No," Hyouko breathed. "I love it. Thank you." He held it with such tenderness, it made Yvonne's heart melt. She hugged him and the bunny with a wholesome warmth before smiling up at Hyouko.

"I'm so glad." The extent of loving nostalgia Hyouko felt in the grasps of Yvonne's arms, and the beaming of her smile, made him overwhelmed with emotion. Hyouko cleared his throat and kissed her cheek.

"I hope you're hungry!" he said, breaking the tender moment. "I think the food's here."

Yvonne watched as he made his way out to retrieve the food, placing the bunny on the table as it longingly watched as well. Yvonne took a moment to appreciate everything she was feeling, the love, the carefree spirit, and the beautiful snowy scenery outside. Although it was dark out, she could see melancholy depictions displayed through the night light, lamp post, and moon light. She leaned out of her balcony to watch Hyouko receive the order at the front entrance. It was nothing out of the ordinary, but she noticed he watched longer into the distance before heading back in.

"Was there something out there?" Yvonne asked, coming to the door to help him put the bags on the table.

"Huh? Oh, no, sorry. I was just admiring the snowfall," Hyouko responded while taking his shoes off and placing them carefully to the side. He made a glance out the window before joining Yvonne at the table. Yvonne was excitedly unpacking the food, opening the steaming hot, spicy food. Immediately, she felt the burn of the spice dancing on her eyes.

"Oh jeez," she said, blinking rapidly to protect her eyes.

"You okay?" Hyouko asked, brushing the tiny tears coming out of her eyes. "Hahaha maybe I've already won before we've even started," he said mischievously. Yvonne gave him a pouty look.

"No! I can do this. My eyes were just sensitive." She grabbed a fork and dug into a fiery red chicken and shoved it into her mouth. It burned every sensor, nerve, and factitious surface it touched. She made a gawky face but quickly tried to cover her true pain.

"Looks spicy..." Hyouko mumbled, poking at a piece with a fork. "You alright there?" he asked, noticing Yvonne's tomato face. She nodded aggressively, chewing with vigour as if that would lessen the torture. Yvonne cursed herself, cursed the chef that made this hell in a bite, and cursed Hyouko for subjecting her to the hellish experience. Hyouko gave a supportive pat on her back, hoping to help her experience become less torturous. He took a confident bite of the chicken and was shell shocked as well due to the immense heat radiating from his mouth. They both looked at each other with an ominous, unspoken agreement that the chicken was by far the worst pain they'd felt in their mouths. It was silent for the most part, as they were tethered to the pain of the spice. Hyouko took another piece of chicken and munched on it, disregarding his runny nose and blushed complexion.

"Are you crazy?" Yvonne breathed, gulping mouthfuls of air to help alleviate the pain. "I don't know if I can handle this..."

Hyouko smirked, red sauce smeared on his lips. "I know," he breathed, gulping the bite down. "That's why I got you something else." He brought out the other container and popped it open for her. Inside was a pleasant aroma of honey and garlic lathered over ribs and spread over a bed of rice and veggies.

"Oh my gosh." Yvonne was pleasantly surprised and gave a yearning expression. "Thank you…"

"Of course," Hyouko said with a smile. "I know what my beautiful girlfriend wants." Yvonne blushed at those words. *His* girlfriend.

"You shouldn't force yourself to eat that chicken." Yvonne offered the ribs to Hyouko. "We can share this. I don't think I could finish it all anyway." Hyouko shook his head and pushed it closer to Yvonne.

"No, I actually enjoyed the chicken once I got used to the spice. It's all for you, and if you don't finish, you can have it for tomorrow!"

"Alright." Yvonne couldn't refuse that logic. "Thank you again, it means a lot to me."

"You know what that means, right?" Hyouko's face lit up with zeal. "I've won myself an IOU."

Yvonne laughed. "Sounds like you've won yourself an IOU."

# Chapter 21

Nova was sitting quietly at a table, waiting for Luther. Her fur lined boots tapped at the table's leg as she surveyed the area, getting wandering looks from on goers. Maybe it was her rather provocative outfit, or maybe it was her stunning facial features, nonetheless, it was abstract to her personality. Luckily, her shades covered her detestable looks, as it would leave a sour taste in peoples' mouths.

"You might be scaring off a potential future husband." Luther pulled a chair out across from Nova.

"Pfft." Nova grinned, crossing her legs and arms while leaning back in the chair. "Unless a walking money bag comes by, I'm not interested."

"Did you order anything yet?" Luther asked, perusing the menu with a carefree attitude. This piqued Nova's interest.

"What's with your new attitude?" She leaned closer to Luther, examining his face. Luther's eyes were softened but still riddled with newfound energy. His hair was trimmed, assuming that he went to the salon, which added to his mood.

"I mean, I don't mind, but I'll bite." Nova said, hoping to get a response.

"Hmm?" Luther's eyes flicked up at Nova then back to the menu. His face was still plastered with a cheeky grin. "Just caught up with an old friend."

"Old friend? As in?" Nova wasn't dumb. She knew Luther's riddles and personality after all these years. Luther struck a cunning look.

"Just some good ol' catching up." Luther waived the waiter over. "I always forget how fruitful it is, visiting friends." Nova was peeved at the fact he was beating around the bush about the information he was withholding, but went along with it.

"I'll get the fruit parfait, please." Nova pointed at the picture on the menu.

"Excellent choice. We've just gotten our delivery of fresh fruit so you've ordered it at the perfect time." The waiter was genuinely happy to announce that. "And for you sir?"

"I'll get an americano and honey glazed croissant. Thanks!" He passed the menu to the waiter before returning his attention to Nova. She sat expectantly, tapping her foot rapidly against the flooring. "Dylan knows more about the underground than I thought." Luther bunched his fist before continuing. "Endymion is planning to execute another scheme somewhere else once the dust settles. Are you still wanting to tail them?"

Nova thought about it, scrunching her nose a little. Her eyes wandered over to another table where an older gentleman sat with a lady. He looked well off, prim and proper.

"Maybe. Depends where and if I get any other information from my own informant. Tell me what you know."

"Hah, demanding as ever. I never really asked why you're so keen on following Endymion's trail of fire but I couldn't care less."

Nova rolled her eyes. "Get to the point. What do you want?"

"I just want a law-abiding fellowship. I know you've got people, and I've got a project."

Nova's eyebrow raised in curiosity, sensing a malicious energy from Luther. It wasn't often he'd get like this, but when he did, even Nova didn't like it.

Cherise was constantly on her phone, texting, calling, and researching. Her party was coming up and she didn't want to host something half-assed. Extravagance was her goal, as well as being the talk of the town. Her roommate didn't seem favourable towards the idea but couldn't stop Cherise's pursuit, so told her to host it elsewhere since the apartment had little to no room.

"Yes, be there or be square!" Cherise chimed, blush nipping at her cheeks from the amount of smiling she'd been doing. Yvonne couldn't help but overhear her excitement and smiled at the sound of Cherise's peppy voice.

"You *are* coming, right? You have to, you have to!" Cherise was practically jumping at this point. How could Yvonne say no?

"Alright, alright, I'm coming."

"You can bring your boyfriend too! I haven't seen him in a while. It's going to be a party!!!"

Yvonne got shivers just thinking about a cesspool of drunk people at a Christmas party, but felt a bit excited about asking Hyouko to join.

"Promise me you won't drink as much as you did last time…" Yvonne groaned as she remembered Halloween night and all the other stories she'd heard about Cherise getting blasted. Cherise gave a smug look and a ditsy face.

"Christmas is an exception, right?"

Yvonne wasn't used to being surprised by Hyouko waiting for her after work. He hung around the company building in his trench coat and scarf with frost bitten cheeks. Hyouko garnered attention from women bypassers, checking him out and whispering between themselves. That was something she had to get used to. Yvonne wasn't necessarily the jealous type but she had to admit it gave her the green goblin knowing how handsome he was, and how often women took in his beauty. Hyouko gave a glowing smile as soon as he set eyes on Yvonne. He did a light jog her way and embraced her, then proceeded to spin her around in his arms. Yvonne giggled and smiled so hard, her cheeks began to get sore.

"Someone's in a happy mood." Yvonne poked Hyouko's nose, causing him to scrunch it playfully.

"I'm happy because I get to see you," he responded, giving a quick peck on her lips before setting her down. "It's almost Christmas, was there anything you wanted or wanted to do?"

Yvonne shook her head while interlacing her fingers with his.

"No, I'm just happy to spend it with you. Speaking of which, Cherise invited us to a Christmas party on the twenty-third. I hope you'll join." Yvonne didn't want to suggest the possibility of him *not* going, and hoped that he'd agree to go with her. Hyouko brought their interlaced hands up to his face and gave a tender kiss on hers.

"I would love to join."

Hyouko was such a gentleman, it made Yvonne melt like whipped butter over toast.

"Oh, that means we should get her a gift, no?"

Yvonne looked out into the distance, knowing there was a strip mall. She thought it would be convenient to go. The area was inviting, decorated with various holiday lights, hollies, ornaments, and outdoor kiosks. Santa was stationed at the corner of the street, giving his bellowing ho's while swinging his bell.

"Yes, but I think we should just get her a gift for Christmas and bring wine for the party." Yvonne had already planned on getting something for Cherise but hadn't found anything. She hoped this shopping trip would be more fruitful.

"Hahaha, wine," Hyouko snickered. "Is she really a wine person?"

"I dunno, but I feel like it's a Christmas thing to do. Something tells me Cherise would like any type of alcoholic beverage." Yvonne passed a vinyl store, a throbbing ache emerged from her chest and throat.

"Oh…" Yvonne began. "How's Haruka?"

Hyouko's expression darkened immediately. Yvonne knew it would be a touchy subject, but had already withheld all of her curiosities until now.

404

"Well, last I saw, she's good."

"You don't talk to her anymore?" Guilt simmered in her stomach.

"No," Hyouko sighed. "It's difficult."

Yvonne knew he didn't want to expand on that yet, so she let it be. She gave a reassuring look while petting his hand encouragingly.

"I'm sorry. If you ever want to talk about it, let me know. If there's anything I can do, just say it and it'll be done!" It wasn't a secret that Yvonne was the catalyst to disrupting their family bond. It was too early to have qualms and strong opinions about family at this stage, so all she could do was apologise and be supportive.

"I just want to be with you." Hyouko smiled, bringing her in closer by the small of her waist. "You make me feel human." Whatever that meant, Yvonne could feel the ache in his heart and soul.

"Eggnog? Try out our new homemade eggnog! Family recipe for over fifty years, you won't regret it!" A sales associate interrupted their moment, holding a tray of small eggnog cups. Hyouko gave an awkward laugh and picked up two cups. He thanked the associate before handing one to Yvonne.

"I guess we'll try this eggnog now." Hyouko raised his cup to hers before drinking it. It was extremely thick, rich, and spiced with cinnamon, cardamom, and a hint of nutmeg. Yvonne enjoyed it, but couldn't see herself guzzling a whole cup of it.

"Wow, I felt like a calf drinking a mother cow's teat," Hyouko commented, giving a bewildering look at the eggnog. Yvonne burst out laughing, causing people to give judging looks. Hyouko grinned at her reaction. Knowing he made her laugh that hard from a simple joke made him feel overjoyed. Her smile was enchanting and her laugh was bubbly. He wished he could see that laugh everyday, all to himself.

"You're so beautiful." Hyouko kissed Yvonne's cheek as he spoke. Yvonne immediately reddened and became shy.

"Sorry, I didn't mean to laugh that loud." It was out of the ordinary for her to be so expressive. She felt vulnerable but also surprised at the fact she could be that comfortable with Hyouko. She didn't even think about the embarrassment it came with.

"Please don't say sorry. I love seeing that out of you. Please do it more." Hyouko beamed with joy and pinched her cheek.

"Hey!" she said, giggling at how childish this all was. "I'm going to die from embarrassment." It was all really quite cushy, two love birds gawking over each other; a typical holiday scene. Yvonne winced at the sudden scent of tobacco. Hyouko helped cover her nose with his scarf, hoping it would mask the smell.

"Let's keep moving, shall we?" Hyouko suggested, placing his hand behind her back while guiding her through the narrow walkway. Yvonne agreed and surveyed the area, trying to locate the source of the smoke. Her eyes widened when she saw where it came from.

"What's wrong?" Hyouko asked, gathering that the look on Yvonne's face wasn't good. He looked in the direction of her gaze. "Do you know them?"

Of course Yvonne knew them. There Blake was, hacking away at a cigarette. Yvonne was furious but was stunned at the whole situation, leaving her speechless.

"I-I need a second." Yvonne excused herself from Hyouko and jogged over to Blake, who had been oblivious to Yvonne's presence.

"What are you doing?!" Yvonne nearly shrieked, placing a hand on Blake's shoulder. Blake whipped around with wide glossy eyes and coughed before speaking.

"Yvonne?"

"Are you really smoking now?" Yvonne furrowed her brows so deeply, Blake worried she'd get wrinkles.

"I miss her," Blake said weakly. Their lips were sorely chapped with skin peeling off, uncovering a bloody patch. Their eye bags sunk so far into their skull, Yvonne could see the outline of their bones. Their hair was unkempt and knotted in an inconspicuous nest. Yvonne's heart sank seeing the state of Blake's physical, emotional, and mental health.

404

"I'm sorry, I know." Yvonne rubbed Blake's shoulder comfortingly while staying strong for Blake. "Smoking isn't the way to go. Harming your health isn't the way to go." Yvonne carefully took the cigarette from Blake's grasp and dropped it into a nearby cigar tray. She suppressed the urge to gag at the smell, nevermind the fact that it had now tainted her fingers.

"I miss her…I want to feel her, even if it's through something like this." Blake's eyes were watery as they stared down at the muddy snow that had been run over by dozens of people. "Heck, I even miss the smell of her cigarettes."

Yvonne felt culpable knowing Blake was in such agony while Yvonne and Hyouko were having the time of their lives. It was hard for Yvonne to lie through her teeth to Blake, but she knew it had to be done.

"Hey, you never know, maybe she just had to disappear for a few days or so to handle something. I'm sure she'll come back. She wouldn't just leave you like that."

Blake glanced up at Yvonne with a little light in their eyes. It was faint, but it was there.

"You think?" They sniffled lightly against the cold. "I hope so. It was just so sudden. I just don't understand. What do I do now?"

There really wasn't an answer for that. Blake could move on, but that was easier said than done. Besides, Yvonne had a kindling hope that Kersa would reappear out of the blue after things were resolved. It wasn't fair to Blake at all, any of this, but it was for their own safety. Yvonne looked back at Hyouko, who was observing them from a distance. He had a worried look on his face but stayed put, knowing it wasn't his place to be.

"Let's get you back to your shop, shall we?" Yvonne suggested, looking around the street to see if a taxi was nearby.

"No, I can't. It hurts too much. Everything reminds me of them." Blake's face was now flooded with tears. Yvonne quickly got a napkin out of her bag and wiped Blake's tears away vigilantly.

"Okay, that's okay, you're okay," Yvonne reassured. She waved Hyouko over towards them, who immediately came over at the signal. He gave a small smile at Blake as they recollected themselves.

"Hey, I can't remember your name. My name's Blake." Blake stuck a hand out for Hyouko to shake.

"Hi Blake, it's Hyouko. Nice to see you again." Hyouko had a warm tone about him and it really suited the situation. He was good at navigating peoples' emotions and acute situations, which only made Yvonne swoon over him more. Blake laughed a little bit between their sniffles.

"Hahaha, nice to see me crying like this? God, it's embarrassing." Blake shook it off and gave a thumbs up. "It's all good," they said, acting as though their life wasn't literally falling apart.

Hyouko gave a knowing look to Yvonne and patted her on the back. He knew all the right things to do as he rubbed her shoulder.

"Why don't you join us on our little shopping adventure? I'm sure you've got a Christmas list to blow through." Hyouko gestured towards the various stores ahead of them, nudging Yvonne to also pitch into the conversation.

"Yeah! Plus my friend Cherise has a Christmas party coming up. She'd love to have you there. It's on the twenty-third!" Yvonne remembered Cherise saying something along the lines of *the more the merrier* so it only made sense to invite Blake. Blake thought for a moment before speaking.

"It sounds great and all, but I don't think I'm really in the mood right now for shopping. I'll think about the party."

It was understandable for Blake to deter themselves from the festivities. Hyouko and Yvonne didn't press Blake anymore and gave an understanding look.

"Well, if you do decide to join, just give me a call." Yvonne pulled her phone out to exchange numbers, something they should've done long ago. "Did you need help getting to wherever you're going?"

404

Blake shook their head. "No, I'll be fine. I need to get some fresh air anyway. I'll see you later Yvonne, and it was nice seeing you again Hyouko. You take care of her, 'kay?"

Hyouko nodded and saluted. "You got it captain."

Blake chuckled and waved goodbye before departing from the two. Yvonne sighed and leaned against Hyouko, who comforted her by holding her firmly against him and rubbing her shoulder.

"Are you okay?" His voice was soft and tender as he planted a kiss on the top of her head. Yvonne allowed herself to enjoy the warmth of his body and the pattern of his breathing as she briefly closed her eyes.

"Yeah, I'm just worried about Blake."

"I didn't want to ask earlier, but what's going on with them?" Hyouko sounded concerned but mostly because of how it affected Yvonne.

"Oh, right." Yvonne forgot that Hyouko had no clue about a few pertinent things that had happened. "Blake's partner disappeared from them not too long ago. No closure or explanation."

"Sounds horrible," Hyouko said worriedly. "Did they report it to the police yet?"

Yvonne hadn't thought of that but hoped Blake hadn't either.

"No, I don't think so."

"Why not? What if they were kidnapped or something? Unless they were on bad terms and they ghosted them to get out of their lives?"

Yvonne wasn't expecting the onslaught of questions, leaving her lost for words.

"Er, I dunno… I'll talk to them tomorrow about it. Thank you for caring so much." Yvonne nervously laughed to try to distract him from the whole situation. "Let's continue our shopping. The shops are gonna close soon."

Hyouko got the hint and smiled.

"Alright my love, let's go shopping."

Yvonne wasn't a beggar, but she couldn't bear to part from Hyouko. Yvonne stared out into the night sky, admiring the falling snowflakes that coated everything they touched. She watched as each landmark they passed only meant the less time they had together before the night ended. Hyouko drove her home and helped her out of the car as he usually did before waiting expectantly for her to enter her building. Except this time, Yvonne just shyly stood in front of him, fidgeting with the bags in her hands.

"Oh, sorry, did you need help bringing those up?" Hyouko asked, feeling bad about not offering initially. He reached for the bags.

"No!" Yvonne startled Hyouko, who immediately retracted his gesture. "I mean, no, that's not it."

More fidgeting.

"I don't mean to be too straight forward, but if you'd like, I mean… I'd really like it if you would stay the night," she continued.

Yvonne's face flushed, resembling that of a cherry tomato. Hyouko's heart stifled at the sight of her vulnerable state, causing him to blush, too.

"I'm sorry, I'm being too needy…"

"No." Hyouko grappled her into his arms, disregarding the jumbling bags between them. "No, you're not being too needy. I thought I was. I wanted to ask the same, but was afraid of making you think of me poorly." His heart was beating out of his chest, making it known to Yvonne how flustered and nervous he was. Yvonne giggled into his chest, feeling a sense of relief.

"I'm so glad I asked then." She looked into his sparkling eyes; they were soft and sultry. "I just don't want to be away from you."

Absolute world shaker. Hyouko squeezed her tighter in his muscular and firm arms. It was his first time feeling like an innocent, naive lover. Even through his mature and cunning looks, it was now apparent how undone Yvonne made him.

"That's pretty gross."

404

Yvonne and Hyouko darted their eyes towards a woman, who had now made themselves known, emerging out of the dark. She was of average height, sporting a long wool coat decorated with leopard fur lining. She wore animal print knee-high boots with a shiny shackle at the top. Her lips were painted with a bright red lipstick, contrasting her green eyes. The woman flipped her long, wavy blonde locks into the air as she approached them.

"Oh, silly me. My name is Lucy. No introductions needed from the two of you, I know who you guys are." Lucy looked Hyouko up and down, biting her lip casually. Yvonne got shivers at the sight of her. "Especially you, Mr. Sanaka."

"Do we know you?" Hyouko spoke with a deep and strong voice, startling Yvonne.

Lucy laughed callously before straightening herself out with a sly demeanour.

"You'll get to know me very well." She looked towards Yvonne, who was being shrouded by Hyouko's immense presence. Lucy then averted her gaze back to Hyouko. "We can do this with her here, or without her. I recommend the latter."

Hyouko's brows furrowed, narrowing his eyes onto Lucy. Lucy seemed so nonchalant, checking her long nails and blowing on them as she waited.

"Who sent you?" Hyouko asked, putting Yvonne further from Lucy's view. Yvonne gripped onto Hyouko's coat, afraid of causing a disruption.

"Doesn't matter who sent me. What matters is what you've done." Lucy pulled out a badge from the inside of her coat. "Come with me, you're under arrest for unlawful practice and conduct."

Hyouko's expression remained stern and firm. Yvonne was now shaking in fear with her face white as the snow. She tugged on Hyouko's coat with a distressed expression. His eyes softened for a moment upon eye contact but quickly resumed his position.

"I don't recognize your style. How do you know me?" Hyouko's voice reverberated through the air, almost shaking Yvonne's skull. "What do you want?"

Lucy smirked with those red lips which had now begun to look more vicious and domineering.

"I've heard you've estranged. Hard to believe, but it doesn't matter." Lucy went almost nose to nose with Hyouko. "Without Endymion backing you, how are you gonna get out of this?"

Hyouko had a deadpan expression across his face.

"What do you want?" He repeated.

Lucy shrugged and looked at her watch that sparkled in the light. Swarovski crystals embellished the wristwatch, blinging up the surface.

"Here's your options. One, you come with me and we go through the law. You'll be stuck in the system behind bars for god knows how long with your repertoire, or two, you disappear and leave with your tail between your legs. My contractor finds you a nuisance to have around. Not my business to ask why, but those are your options. God it would be a hassle to have you in the system." Lucy rubbed her temples and made a disdained face. Yvonne could see the tension on Hyouko's face, even barring a vein on the side of his forehead, and the clenching of his jaw. It gave a bad taste in Yvonne's mouth knowing there were so many dirty cops and law enforcers, but in this case she knew Hyouko *was* associated with the underground markets, and did the duties he was told. Admittedly, she felt a sense of disgust and nausea knowing Hyouko wasn't technically a pious person. It was difficult for her to make sense of it all.

"Not now." Hyouko looked over at Yvonne, who had a perplexed look on her face. The whole situation was bizarre, allowing her to forget about the frigid climate around them. "We can discuss this later, Lucy."

Lucy shrugged and heaved a sigh.

"Alright, time's a tickin'."

Neither one of them wanted to start the conversation inside, but Yvonne got fed up with the silence.

"What was that? What is happening?" Yvonne's voice quivered in her stride, but she knew she had to get answers. Hyouko helped remove Yvonne's coat and hung it up before he did so for himself. She looked so cute in her worrisome state, it was hard for Hyouko to go into something so hard.

"I'll deal with it, don't worry. Please don't stress your mind."

"I *need* to know." Yvonne was desperate to know something, anything that's going on with Hyouko. The oblivion she had hoped would stay, could not go on any longer. She feared being stranded, lost, and confused just like Blake. Hyouko hesitated and pinched his glabella before speaking.

"I'm trying to figure everything out and close all ties so I can be with you, Yvonne. You've made me realise that I don't want to live the life I had before. I had no reason to leave that life until now. I want us to live a happy life and I dunno, maybe grow old together. Lucy is an executor, like the one you had in your case; someone that is in law enforcement, usually meant to litigate and intervene when necessary. We had one whenever we took on a case with Endymion, but usually the executor is to make sure that nothing ties back to us. It's shitty, I know, but that's the point of it."

Yvonne remembered Vos being someone she hadn't heard from or seen ever, so she assumed that was their role. If only Kersa was around to answer these questions.

"So what does that mean for you? For us?" She heard Lucy loud and clear. It didn't sound like there was an option where they could be together freely.

Hyouko stared at the floor, unable to meet her eyes.

"I don't know. I was unaware that any executor was coming after me. I thought I tied all the loose ends but maybe Endymion or someone from that circle is bitter."

It hit Yvonne at that moment; how could Hyouko just up and go like that without causing mayhem in Endymion's little family?

"I don't get it. How did you leave unscathed? I doubt Endymion would let you go that easily… same with Haruka and Daniel."

Hyouko pursed his lips and tension coursed through his body. Yvonne knew whatever he was about to say would not be good.

"I didn't want to discuss this yet because I know everything is still fresh," Hyouko met Yvonne's gaze with insecurity. He took a moment to just delve into Yvonne's wide, anxiety ridden eyes. "I have to leave for some time. I got us tickets to get out of the country for a while…"

Yvonne's stomach dropped at the thought of leaving everything she knew to be with him.

"No…" She breathed. Yvonne felt faint, her mind in a whirlwind. Her mouth became dry and tingly and she searched for words. "I can't…"

Hyouko knew that it was unlikely that she'd drop everything to be with him, but there was still that small hopeful spark he had. He clenched his jaw, holding back the dam of emotions from overflowing.

"I have to go for a while. I can't come back until things are settled."

"How long?" Yvonne's voice cracked as she spoke.

"I don't know yet."

"When are you leaving?"

"Four days from now."

Christmas.

Yvonne let go of a gutting sound as her knees buckled at that exact moment. Hyouko lurched forward to help catch her, and quickly guided her down to the sofa for her body to relax.

"Are you… bad?"

Hyouko took a brief moment to respond.

"What do you mean by bad?"

Yvonne gulped at the thought of it.

"Have you… killed anyone? Harmed anyone?"

Her eyes tried to trace the expression Hyouko had on his face, but it was hard to distinguish what he was thinking and feeling at that moment.

"In retrospect, not that I'm aware of. Haruka, Daniel and I just do Endymion's bidding without much question. I can't say for sure that no one was harmed, since what we do is nefarious… It wouldn't be a surprise if the things that we have done caused harm or lead to the endangerment of someone. If I had the choice not to have that life…"

Yvonne knew that would be the case. It hurt to hear those words actually be said from Hyouko. It made her stomach churn at the idea of someone's welfare being jeopardised due to the actions of him. She knew deep down Hyouko was good, but it was conflicting to say the least. She bunched her fists up before saying more.

"You had this all planned?" A stream of tears began trickling down her cheeks and dripping off her chin.

"I'm sorry." Hyouko pleaded, holding her delicate hands between his before smothering his face into them. She could feel his tears against the back of her hand but couldn't see them as he kept his face against her hands. It was evident that their love could not continue the way they had hoped. It shattered Yvonne thinking about everything she'd been through and everything Hyouko meant to her, all gone in a blink of an eye.

"When you leave, will I hear from you?" The thought of Blake flashed into her mind. Here she was, in tears, wanting an answer, a closure, when Blake had none.

"I'll try my best." Hyouko composed himself before staring into Yvonne's weeping expression. "I told Endymion and Haruka that I was going on a vacation. I think Haruka knows I'm lying, but she didn't do more to stop me."

"You won't regret leaving?"

Hyouko shook his head with a smile.

"No, I want to be free, *need* to be free."

Hyouko was still somewhat of a stranger to Yvonne. She could barely scrape the surface of him and now he'd be leaving. There was always a lingering darkness around Hyouko but he always put a brave face on and acted like everything was ok.

"So for us?" It didn't need to be asked. It was obvious.

"I have to let you go then, if you don't choose to follow. I'm too much of a burden on you. If I'm not next to you to protect you, they'll be in a constant pursuit to find me through you." Hyouko squeezed her hand tightly.

"You're not a burden to me…" She mumbled, "I just want you by my side."

"Maybe one day." He spoke softly, whether or not those words were true or not, it didn't matter.

"Is this goodbye then?"

Hyouko kissed her hand feverishly, each individual digit, each crevice, her wrists, palms, and arms. His glossy eyes gazed into hers before he kissed her collarbone, neck, and face before whispering into her ear.

"I love you."

# Chapter 22

Holidays always brought out her mother's need for connection. Yvonne never really spent much time with her mom after high school and only reconnected during the holidays and occasionally under sporadic circumstances.

*"If you're not coming for Christmas, at least visit your ol' mother before that."*

Yvonne sighed against the pounding headache that now resided in her head for what seemed like an eternity.

"Yes, sorry mom. I'll come by maybe today or tomorrow. I just have to see what's going on today."

*"It's the Thursday before Christmas. I doubt you have things to do."*

Her mother was quite pushy but Yvonne learned how to ignore her demands and side comments.

"I'll see you soon, Mom."

She heard a clack pretty soon after, which only infuriated Yvonne more. It was the twenty-first of December, a day where people got their last minute shopping, preparations, and whatnot done. The streets outside were bustling with commotion and laughter. Red lipstick donned many women, along with soft cape coats and leather gloves. Holly, wreaths, and lights decorated every building, tree, and those alike. It was a shame that Yvonne dreaded Christmas for the first time in her life. Her eyes were puffy and red from the night before, which only made her feel worse about it all. Hyouko left that night after a long string of tears were shared. Yvonne never hated anything more in life than the time that was stolen from her. Why did it have to be her? It was safe to assume Hyouko wasn't going to attend the party on the twenty-third, and that he'd be gone by the twenty-fifth. Yvonne didn't feel very festive anymore and wished she could disappear and hide in her blanket until the new year.

*Luther: 9:14 a.m. Are you coming in today? I got you a coffee.*

She had planned to call in sick until after Christmas but it seemed idiotic to do so. More time to herself meant more time to wallow in her sorrows.

*Yvonne: 9:16 a.m. Yes, coming. Walking today so I'll be a little bit later.*

Yvonne decided to walk to work to clear her mind before delving into work. She got herself dressed in a pencil skirt, white dress shirt, and a blazer. In the reflection, she couldn't help but want to cry more. Yvonne couldn't recognise herself anymore between the puffy eyes, red corneas, bloated face, and distressed soul. Habitually, she slid on her loafers as she knew stilettos wouldn't do so well on the walk over. She covered herself with her long trench coat before taking one last look at her flat and exiting. It was tirelessly cold out, allowing goosebumps and shivers to swallow Yvonne's body whole. Her stride was brisk as she regretted her choice of walking to work. It was only a thirty minute walk, give or take, but the sleet made it harder for her to navigate. The blizzard was especially horrendous that morning, so Yvonne sought out the alleyways for cover. Yvonne had always been wary about alleyways. Growing up, her mother incessantly buzzed in her ear about the dangers of the world, especially dark corridors and the male species. Her eyes surveyed all of the objects, brick lining, and people that passed by her in the constrained area. She quickend her pace, hoping to get to work faster than her estimated time.

"Yvonne, right?"

Yvonne's ears pricked at the sound of a male calling her name. She was hesitant to look at who was calling her, but she remembered it was better to face the person straight on, as it gave the person a sense of humanity. She spun around to face a bulky man in full layers. He had a broad smile on his face when she met eyes with him.

"Do I know you?" Yvonne asked with a stern tone. She knew never to sound docile or submissive when dealing with a stranger in an alleyway.

"Hey, don't worry. I don't bite," he said, getting closer to her. Yvonne stepped back every step he took forward.

"Stay still, don't come closer." She almost shouted. Yvonne wanted to curse herself for how cliche and movie-like this whole scenario seemed. Never did she think she'd ever be in this situation.

"I have a quick question for you." The man spoke with his hands in his pockets. He wore a leather jacket that accentuated his shoulders, as well as charcoal slacks with a heavy belt. He had peppered hair as well as a light scruff going on, with a single ear piercing on his left side. It was a cuff earring in gold. She couldn't see much else beyond that due to the space between them.

"So I don't know you." Yvonne figured that, as she was pretty good with faces and fashion. She began to step backwards to hopefully make a run for it. The snow crunched under her loafers, alarming the man who instantly realised what was going to happen.

"I wouldn't do that if I were you," he warned, pivoting his foot in a ready stance.

Yvonne's heart raced under her chest. Her breath became shallow as her palms perspired. Yvonne knew how to keep a poker face under pressure, but she could feel her lip quiver in fear while she thought about her choices. She almost lost focus when she heard a cracking from the distance. His boots gave away his stealth and signified the action that needed to be done.

"Fuck," he cursed under his breath as Yvonne's wide eyes stared at him.

She made a run for it.

The man bolted towards her with grappling hands, and Yvonne sprinted as fast as she could down the long alleyway. Her mouth felt like it was full of cotton balls as she struggled to form words mid-run.

"HEL—"

Yvonne's body slammed against the freezing cement as the man pinned her down with his full weight. Yvonne began crying and shrieking against his restraint and hand.

"Shut up," he hissed, covering her mouth with his calloused hand. "If you were compliant, this wouldn't have happened."

His breath smelled rancid, which only made Yvonne cry more. She couldn't believe she was in this situation.

"YVONNE!"

Yvonne recognised that voice. She never felt more relieved to hear Luther's voice. Luther ran towards them with a furious expression across his face. It wasn't Luther that pulled the man off her, no, it was someone else. Then, Luther helped Yvonne onto her feet and held her close to him.

"Are you okay? Are you hurt?" Luther's heart was racing in his chest and throat. Yvonne could hear it as she regained her composure, relying on Luther's support to hold her up.

"I'm okay," Yvonne managed to breathe out. "I'm okay."

Her eyes settled on the man, who was now in a defensive stance, blocked off by Luther and the other person. Yvonne squinted to see the person on the other side but failed to recognise them. Her heart sank, knowing it wasn't Hyouko. Part of her hoped it was Hyouko coming to her aid, but she should've known better.

"You've got nowhere to run," the person shouted, warning the pepper haired man. The man chagrined and spat at the ground, gauging his next move.

"Fuckheads."

Luther held Yvonne tightly against him, his eyes riveted to the man. Luther gave a small signal which Yvonne could only assume was a communicative sign for the other person to charge. Yvonne watched as the two struggled against each other until the pepper haired man fell to his knees, restrained against the other.

"Who's that?" Yvonne asked, finally able to collect herself. Her cheek had a small cement burn and her hair and clothing was dishevelled.

"The man on the ground, his name is Brandy. The person restraining him is Vos."

Yvonne looked at Luther, bewildered.

"Vos?" So this was the Vos that was part of the team. She couldn't believe she actually saw Vos in the flesh. Yvonne almost began to think Vos was made up just like the case.

"He's a very reliable officer. I've known him for a few years now," Luther explained, watching the two carefully. He slowly let go of Yvonne and softened his gaze.

"I'm so sorry you had to go through that." Luther gripped Yvonne's hand firmly, his face scrunched with concern.

Yvonne shook her head and heaved a sigh.

"No, thank you for saving me... How did you know where I was?"

Luther smiled awkwardly and nervously scratched his neck.

"Don't be alarmed but Vos has been tailing you for the past couple days. I got intel that Endymion was going to most likely come after you since you were the last person that saw Kersa. Luckily Vos was here, otherwise god knows what would've happened to you."

His hands shook as he held hers.

"Thank you," Yvonne whispered. Vos had Brandy apprehended and came towards them.

"You're lucky a good guy like Luther had your back," Vos spoke. Vos had a distinctly deep voice that shook Yvonne's brain. "I'm gonna take this guy into our hands now. Corruption doesn't stand a chance in our precinct." He nudged Brandy to continue walking. Brandy glared at Yvonne as he passed, but never spoke another word to her. Luther's eyes followed the two before he released the tension in his body.

"I think you should take the day off now," Luther said, rubbing his face with stress. He looked into the distance where the sun began to kiss the horizon. Yvonne obliged; there was no way she could pretend that didn't happen and continue working normally. She nodded and fumbled for her phone. *Her phone.* Yvonne patted her pockets and searched her purse before realising she had left it at home.

"I'll take you home, don't worry," Luther said and guided her towards his car.

The whole way home, Yvonne couldn't help but wonder what would've happened if Luther wasn't there. Luther placed a gentle hand on Yvonne's lap, which startled her, causing him to retract his touch.

"Sorry," he said with surprise. "We're here. I didn't mean to startle you. You were in a trance of some sort."

Yvonne shook her head and forced a laugh.

"Sorry, I didn't mean to scare you. Thanks for the ride again…" She reached for the door handle before Luther stopped her. He shook his head and gestured for her to stay put. Luther exited the car diligently and came over to open her door.

"I'm here for you," were his last words before she disappeared into her building.

Why did she come? Yvonne stared at her mother's yapping mouth as she blanked out. Her mother had a tendency to talk a lot about nothing in particular. She was an exceptionally irate woman and often complained about anything under the sun. Yvonne sipped her coffee as she watched the clock tick, making sure to avert her attention between her mother and the clock fairly.

404

"Are you even listening?" Her mother snapped her fingers in front of her face, garnering her attention.

Yvonne blinked a couple times before responding. "Sorry, today's been crazy."

Her mother waved her hand in dismissal.

"I don't care, have you heard a word I've been saying?" Her mother tsked her tongue. "That Walter, he's a bug, that guy. He asked about you recently and I can't keep giving vague answers. How *have* you been?"

Yvonne sighed. When her mom asked about how she was, that only meant '*give me one interesting topic and nothing more.*'

"I met a guy, but things are a little difficult right now."

Yvonne didn't know what came over her to express that to her mother. From the corner of her eye, she saw her mother make a mocking face.

"Oh?" her mom said. "You know what I've told you about boys. Remember your father?"

Yvonne knew this was coming.

"I know, Mother. Nevermind, pretend I didn't say anything."

"Don't be rude now. I'm one to know. Don't give your heart out so willy-nilly now. Those boys are up to no good." Her mother smacked her lips as she tasted a biscuit. She dipped it in tea as Yvonne watched the crumbs fall into the cup and onto her chest, scattering across her thigh.

"Okay, Mom," Yvonne replied in obedience. There was no winning with her mother; that was something she had learned growing up. It gave her a pinching feeling in her chest to hear those words come out of her mouth, especially when Hyouko ended up being more of a heartache than not.

"Walter, that guy, I tell you. He's a dog. I'll bet you he's just waiting for me to let him in the coop. He comes over everyday and tends to my fire, shovels my snow, and sips tea with me."

Her mother was intolerable. Yvonne didn't know what Walter saw in her. Walter was her mother's neighbour for over a decade. He was a gentle fellow with a heart of gold. Oftentimes, Yvonne would mistake him for an angel with the way he acted around her mother. Her mother would act like she paid no mind to Walter, when in reality, she relished in his attention and affection.

"What will you do for Christmas?" Yvonne changed the subject, hoping to hear less about the troubles of relationships.

"Well, believe it or not, but my *only* child isn't spending it with me, so I suppose I will sulk in my rocking chair and stare out my window like some old hag."

It irked Yvonne to hear that. Her mother had people around giving more than enough attention to her, yet it never ceased to amaze her how much more attention her mother begged for.

"I have plans, Mom. I'm sorry." Yvonne gritted her teeth and drew all her frustrations into her fists, which wrinkled the hemming of her skirt.

"After all I've done for you…" Her mother heaved out a long and heavy sigh. "Whatever."

# Chapter 23

Saudade. If it meant for Hyouko to leave Yvonne in order for her to be safe and happy, he would do it. He *was* doing it. Every hour, minute, second away from her was like a burning hell of icy fire against his skin and heart. The light in his eyes became a dark shadow amidst the wintery scenery. Although he had everything in order for him to leave, it was like ripping a piece out of him each passing hour until departure. Hyouko recounted the memories and lingering feelings he had with Yvonne as he checked all of his belongings routinely. His fingers traced the stuffed bunny as he stared at it with love, engraving each pivot, dip, and texture into his senses. In only two days, he would be gone, leaving everything behind; the life he'd had up until now and even the burning love he had for Yvonne. Haruka had tried reaching him periodically to see how his 'vacation' was. Hyouko would lie through his teeth, giving only vague answers and leaving it at that. He expected someone to tail him through the duration of his 'vacation,' however, nothing seemed out of the ordinary. Maybe he really would get away with this without any immediate repercussions. It was a funny feeling, leaving everything he knew behind, his so-called family, his routines, everything. It was giving him more grief than he'd imagined but knew it had to be done. Hyouko had wanted to break the shackles of his binds for quite some time, and now, it was finally time. Hopeless romantics was something Hyouko would scoff at up until recently. He often found himself day dreaming that maybe one day, he and Yvonne could live a normal life together. Days spent with the comfort of each others' presences, eyes interlocking with nothing but love between them, hours spent with mindless conversations just to hear her voice… He wished he could have it all. It made him spiteful thinking about Luther and his opportunity to pounce on Yvonne, but now, it didn't matter. There was nothing he could do. He was in a position with both hands behind his back and only one way to escape. No matter how much he gritted and sulked about the matter, he had to stand tall and move forward. His eyes flittered around the shops he perused as he killed time. Knick-knacks and whatnot. He stopped in front of a bouquet shop. Forget-me-nots. How cliché could he get?

"A past lover?"

Hyouko gave a huffling laugh.

"I guess you can say that."

The woman laughed and pulled a bunch out. She admired the tiny pale flowers sprung among the green stems and sighed at their beauty.

"These beauties are one to remember." She smiled at Hyouko. "They say if you pair it with baby's breath, your love will have strength." The woman made an arrangement with the two flowers and showcased it to Hyouko. "What do you think?"

Hyouko nodded and pulled out his card. "I'll take it."

*"I love you, Yvonne. I love you, I love you, I love you."*

Things were a blur for the most part for Yvonne. Without much thought throughout her days, Cherise's Christmas party came and went and soon enough, it was Christmas day. Her Christmas began with her laying in bed, facing the wall as nothing but an idle shell. It was truly a white Christmas, as the snow fall outside was immeasurable. Yvonne could hear the laughter and joyous sounds of children and families outside as they pranced around the fluffy white substance. Hyouko was nowhere to be found nor had she heard from him since that night. As heartbreaking as it was, she knew she could only rely on herself to pick up the pieces of her wounded heart. Luther was more than accommodating and worried over the past few days. He'd often check up on her and send her wishes over texts. It was honestly bothersome to Yvonne, but she appreciated his caring nature as long as he wasn't overbearing. Cherise wished her a Merry Christmas in her usual chirpy self, and Yvonne responded the same.

*Hyouko: 11:17 a.m. I'm in front of your building, do you want to come outside?*

Yvonne held her breath at the sight of the text. She threw herself against the railings of her balcony to peer out, landing her sights on Hyouko's head. Her thumbs trembled slightly as she replied.

*Yvonne: 11:18 a.m. Coming*

In that moment, Yvonne disregarded any of her appearance qualms, threw on her long coat, and bolted out the door.

"I've missed you," Hyouko breathed as he approached Yvonne. Yvonne stood a good meter away from Hyouko, racking her brain for what to say, what to do, and what to feel. Her coat was tightly wrapped around her as she reinforced it with her arms to fight to chill."These are for you," Hyouko said, holding out an exquisite bouquet. The baby's breath framed the forget-me-nots so elegantly and purposefully, Yvonne wanted to cry. It was wrapped delicately with cellophane and newspaper and bound with hemp string. Attached to it was a small note and something that resembled a charm. Yvonne carefully approached Hyouko and tenderly held the bouquet.

"Why are you here?" Yvonne whispered. She stared down at the arrangement, finding herself lost in its beauty. As much as she wanted to see Hyouko, she hated that he came to see her before he left forever. She balled her hand into a fist and pressed it against his firm chest. Despite her best efforts not to cry, tears came streaming down. Hyouko stumbled at the sight of her tears and held her tightly into his chest.

"Let's go sit down at a bench," Hyouko suggested, guiding her to a bench near her building. It gave Yvonne time to recollect herself and face Hyouko appropriately.

"Why are you here?" Yvonne repeated, gripping the bouquet in her hands. Hyouko had a gentle hand over her knee as he yearned for her attention.

"You look beautiful," Hyouko breathed, admiring her with longing. "You have no idea how hard it is to be away from you."

Yvonne wanted to lash out at Hyouko. He was making all of this harder than it needed to be.

"Are you trying to hurt me more?" Her lips trembled as she spoke. It broke Hyouko's heart to see the amount of pain Yvonne was in. His heart dropped and he retracted his touch. Why did it hurt Yvonne so? Yvonne wanted to protest but didn't know *what* she wanted.

"I know it was selfish of me, but I wanted to see you one last time before I go." Hyouko couldn't stop staring into Yvonne's eyes, tracing back down to her perfectly shaped nose, her perfectly shaped lips, those rosy cheeks, the way her hair fell over her shoulders and framed her face. He wanted to stay in that moment forever. "I'm sorry for everything you've gone through because of me."

Yvonne didn't care much about that. She cared more about the fact that all of it happened and yet still she couldn't have Hyouko.

"If there's anything to be sorry about, it's to be sorry that you're not going to be next to me anymore."

As if that was something Hyouko needed to hear. He wanted to yell at the world for how unfair it all was; he wanted to beg on his knees for her to come with him, but he didn't.

"I'll be going to Europe for some time—"

"Stop."

"Maybe visit a few landmarks—"

"I said stop."

"I'll send you letters."

Yvonne kissed Hyouko on the lips to shut him up. She'd refrained from doing so this whole time, but something came over her. It was a tearful kiss between the two. Yvonne didn't know if this was right; was it right to love someone like him? Was it right to fall so hard over such a small amount of time? She didn't care. Hyouko held her face into his as he relished in the feel of her soft and supple lips. She felt his quivering breath as he withdrew from the kiss.

"I love you, Yvonne. I love you, I love you, I love you." His grip never loosened as he said those words. She was a mess; her face, smothered in tears, her hair, deranged from everything; and her cheeks, blossoming red like the holly that decorated the posts.

"I love you, Hyouko," Yvonne reciprocated. "I think I'll always love you, and I might hate you forever for that."

Hyouko chuckled. "Please, hate me forever."

That was the last time Yvonne saw Hyouko. The baby's breath wilted away after some time, leaving only its white, shrivelled petals behind. The forget-me-nots curled into a darker shade before dying away. After some time, Yvonne's heart hurt less, and the world around her began to regain its colour. The charm hung from her purse wherever she went. A folly little thing it was, a simple bunny made out of silk cloth no more the size of her thumb. It was something she loved dearly amongst the necklace that never left her body. Yvonne began to find herself as an individual and learned to love what she remembered, felt, and experienced with Hyouko. Love changed her for the good, and no matter how much it hurt, she thanked Hyouko for it all.

Mabert Mazyck

*Dear Yvonne,*

*I love you. There's not a single passing day that I haven't thought of you. I hope you think of me too, whether it be well or not. I hope that one day you'll forgive me.*

*Yours truly.*

404

*Dearest Love,*

*I saw a bunny outside today and while I admired it with our stuffed animal, I couldn't help but wish you were with me to see it too. I've learned some new techniques in brewing and hope that one day, I'm able to share it with you.*

*Yours forever, I wish you well, beautiful.*

# Mabert Mazyck

*As the weather begins to get warmer, I can't help but wonder what it would've been like to be with you. I imagined that one day, just the two of us, we'd visit a little cottage and enjoy the scenery and anything it has to offer. Flowers have begun to bloom where I'm at, and I've taken up gardening. If I could send the whole garden of roses to you, I would do it without a thought. Maybe one day, whether that be in this lifetime or another, I'll be able to plant flowers for you to enjoy.*

*Yours truly.*

# Chapter 24

Four years had passed since the last time she had seen Hyouko. Four years, five months, and twenty-one days to be exact. Yvonne would receive letters from him from time to time, spanning over inconsistent months with no name signed off. She knew it was him of course, and read and reread each letter whenever she thought of him. There never was a return address so she could never respond, that is, until the second last letter with what seemed to be a permanent address attached to her letter. It took some time for her to get over the slump of heartache, but found herself relishing in self discovery while advancing in her career as well. Kersa came back three years after disappearing, completely shocking Blake with an unannounced arrival at the cafe. It looked like Kersa had been through a lot during her time away and spoke scarcely of what she was up to due to the confidentiality of things. All that she disclosed was that she knew someone out in Barcelona and found a safe house there. Yvonne clued in that the person might've been Sterling. Blake ended up getting the truth, the whole truth, from Kersa. It was a wonder how Blake never moved on from Kersa and stuck with the pain till then. Soul mates, maybe.

"I'm going to miss you so much!" Cherise cried, holding onto Yvonne with an ungodly amount of strength.

"Please be careful…" Yvonne squirmed out of Cherise's grip. "You have to take care of your body more carefully…you're literally pregnant."

Cherise laughed with her usual loud and cheery self.

"Don't worry, I can't wait for her to pop out and for you to meet her. It's a shame you're leaving for six months… I don't know what I'll do without you."

Yvonne patted Cherise's shoulder comfortingly. Cherise surprisingly settled down with a guy she met at a bar two years ago. What was meant to be a one-night stand ended up being a committed relationship. Yvonne was happy for her, nonetheless, especially knowing how unpredictable love was.

"I'll be back before you know it. Besides, you'll be preoccupied with the baby in a couple months. You'll forget all about me." Yvonne double checked her desk before leaving the building, making sure everything was in place, secure, and tidy. Yvonne had saved up her vacation days over the past few years and decided it was time to treat herself.

"Look at you," Luther said, coming around her desk. "I can't believe it's time."

"Indeed it is," Yvonne responded with a grin. "You'll be fine without me." Even though Luther continued to try and pursue Yvonne, Yvonne never gave in. Luther just wasn't the person she loved. Like a curse, Luther continued to be bound to her spell, unable to move on from the lingering yearning sensation he had for her.

Luther scoffed and chuckled under his breath. "Nothing's the same without you here."

Yvonne rolled her eyes and patted Luther's shoulder.

"Don't be like that. You'll probably be preoccupied with all those cases stacked up on your desk." Yvonne nudged Luther while looking over to his area. It was filled to the brim with case files, spilling oodles of papers every which way. Luther groaned at the sight of it.

"Yeah yeah, but still… I'll miss you."

Yvonne laughed before turning around, bidding him a farewell. Yvonne's stilettos clacked against the tile flooring as she descended down the halls, her body and mind feeling lighter than ever with her heartbeat quickening in anticipation.

"Safe travels!" Cherise hollered down the hallway in her penguin-like stature. Yvonne waved her goodbye before hitting the streets.

Yvonne had to say her farewells to Blake before she left, especially when she wouldn't be there for a few months.

"Knock knock," Yvonne chimed, alerting Blake of her presence. Blake whipped around and greeted Yvonne with a smile.

"I knew you didn't forget about me." Blake hugged Yvonne tightly. "I can't believe you're actually taking time off."

Yvonne set her bag down and retrieved a small sentiment.

"I know, and this is for you." It jingled as she pulled it out. A light, delicate jingle.

"Oh my god, you shouldn't have." Blake excitedly held the little bell that was strung along with a bear holding onto its shiny surface. "Babe, look what Yvonne brought us!"

Kersa emerged from behind Blake and held them tenderly.

"Wow, you've really outdone yourself, Yvonne."

Yvonne smiled and giggled a bit. Kersa was still busy with her work doing who knows what, but at least it seemed as though things had settled to a more secure position. Though her eyebags remained prominent, Yvonne could sense how much more relaxed Kersa was.

"Babe, I swear…you smoke too much." Blake coughed into their hand and furrowed their brow.

"Sorry, sorry, I promise I'll cut back." Kersa raised her hands defensively and shrugged before giving Blake a kiss on the cheek.

"You always say that…" Blake grumbled. "How long are you gone for, again?"

"Six months," Yvonne recited. "I'll be back before you know it."

"You better visit me as soon as you land!"

"I will, don't worry. Take care till then." Yvonne waved them goodbye as she exited the cafe, carrying on the scent of roasted coffee beans into the outdoors.

They say Paris is one of the world's most sought after destinations. Yvonne believed it now that she was there. It was beyond what she had imagined—the lights, the life, and the city streets, everything had character and held sentiment. Yvonne mindlessly flipped through a light read as she sipped on a caramel iced latte. She wore a sunhat to fight the glaring lights outside as it was the middle of summer. There were cobblestones everywhere in the city streets and bustling traffic throughout. Yvonne thanked herself for packing such light, flowy dresses that easily aired out the heat she tried to keep out.

"I hope you're enjoying your beverage miss." The waiter came around with a tray and a smile. "Are you expecting another?"

Yvonne smiled up at the waiter through her large sun hat. She surveyed the oncoming traffic before looking back at him. "I hope so."

The waiter nodded and tended to other tables.

"Is this seat taken?"

Yvonne twirled her head around in anticipation. There he was. Hyouko, handsome as ever, bearing a bouquet of bright red roses. His hair was in a bun, the same as she had remembered him. His eyes were gentle and more compassionate, maybe due to age, or maybe due to his freedom, but it made Yvonne's heart melt. Yvonne sprung onto Hyouko, pulling him off balance a little. He quickly held onto her firmly. She didn't let go of him for a while as she felt his warmth and heartbeat. He pet the back of her head, her neck, and the small of her waist before slowly getting her to match his gaze.

"I've missed you so much," he tenderly whispered into her ear, placing a kiss onto her cheek.

"As have I," Yvonne breathed, taking in Hyouko's face, eyes, and body. "I've waited so long."

404

Hyouko held onto Yvonne's waist as he memorised every feature of her face. Yvonne looked almost the same, only becoming more beautiful as time went on. Rose petals blew into the wind, coming loose from the stems that held them. A light fragrance of soft, baby petals engulfed the air as they gazed into each other's eyes.

"You're still as beautiful as the day I met you, if not more." He kissed her hand gently. "Thank you for coming to Paris."

Yvonne shook her head.

"Thank you for waiting for me."

The End.

# Author's Notes

There are a lot of people I have to thank in supporting me through this exhilarating journey. Besides my dedication to someone very special, I couldn't have done this without the influence of my fourth grade teacher and principal who fostered my passion for writing as a child. Though I've been supported by most of my English teachers, none had been as fired up about the art of english, writing, and poetry as her. I also wanted to give a kudos to my mother, though we have many differences, trials and tribulations, she had always supported my dreams of becoming an author. Even though we are not currently at the stage where I want to be with her, I know that she would be beyond proud if she knew. Jerah, for being there right from the first page, being happy and excited with me throughout it all. They made me feel motivated and supported through the process as they gave feedback and compliments! Carlie, the beautiful illustrator of my cover and insert(s), had the most spectacular taste and stunning work. She wasn't afraid of suggesting things that appeal more to the public eye and not just to my strange views. It is a wonder how I was so lucky to have been able to connect with her through a simple email after a lot of admiration for her past works. Kayla D, one of the most commendable people I had the pleasure of working with, gave me the most helpful advice and top-notch proofreading/copyediting. I am so grateful she reached out to me and did it all for even a smaller price than I had listed as a novice writer. I also wanted to thank my lovely coworkers at my day job who have been supportive and open-hearted despite our only recent connections. FriesenPress has also been most admirable and professional through this all. Christoph had been patient and communicative even when I was being wishy-washy, so thank you. Nife has been phenomenal as my publishing specialist and has been supportive and efficient through all the steps of publishing. I find myself grateful for many of the circumstances I am in at this stage of life. I hope to continue my passion in writing and develop as an author. Thank you for being here through my journey.

Printed in the USA
CPSIA information can be obtained
at www.ICGtesting.com
LVHW051104290524
781182LV00007B/662